Star Struck

A Pick Your Own Plot Bedventure

Meredith Michelle

LYRICAL SHINE
Kensington Publishing Corp.
www.kensingtonbooks.com

LYRICAL SHINE BOOKS are published by

Kensington Publishing Corp.
119 West 40th Street
New York, NY 10018

All Kensington titles, imprints, and distributed lines are available at special quantity discounts for bulk purchases for sales promotion, premiums, fund-raising, educational, or institutional use.

Special book excerpts or customized printings can also be created to fit specific needs. For details, write or phone the office of the Kensington Sales Manager: Kensington Publishing Corp., 119 West 40th Street, New York, NY 10018. Attn. Sales Department. Phone: 1-800-221-2647.

Lyrical Shine and Lyrical Shine logo Reg. U.S. Pat. & TM Off.

First Electronic Edition: December 2016
eISBN-13: 978-1-60183-743-1
eISBN-10: 1-60183-743-7

First Print Edition: December 2016
ISBN-13: 978-1-60183-744-8
ISBN-10: 1-60183-744-5

Printed in the United States of America

*Dedicated to my husband, Chris, who inspired
my dreams, gave me the freedom to follow
them, and whom I may one day allow to actually
read my novel!*

*WE Weekly reports: America's Sweetheart, **Anna Chambliss**, 31, and fiancé of six months, **Hampton Rhodes**, 37, seen solo at separate Hollywood hot spots this week. Reps of each actor decline to comment. Could there be trouble in paradise?*

You are Anna Chambliss. Your perfect face is splashed across the cover of every best-selling tabloid magazine, headlines proclaiming AMERICA'S SEXIEST SWEETHEART IN TEARS!

You roll the glossy *WE Weekly* into a tight tube, deposit it into the little garbage can beside your dressing table, and look up into the dimly lit mirror in front of you. The same huge, widely spaced green eyes you've looked into since you were a child gaze back. A recent quote from the popular men's magazine *Apex* comes to mind: "Pure emerald pools with floating flecks of blue and gold." A surprisingly poetic description, considering the source.

You turn your head slowly right and then left, confirming the profile your last director described as having "not one bad angle." Your hair—all yours, not a single extension—falls in glimmering, golden waves that cascade past your shoulders. You lick your "bee-stung" pink lips, let your eyes rest upon your "strong but feminine" chin. Run your hand over your "flawless, silken" skin, all smooth lines over firm muscle without so much as a freckle or blemish.

Tucking your "impossibly long," slim legs under you on the quilted silk dressing table bench, you try to focus on relaxing for the few moments you have left before you step into the inevitable media storm waiting outside the hotel lobby.

Breathe, you tell yourself.

You bring your fingers to your hairline, gently smoothing the soft tendrils that frame your forehead. Raise your chin to admire the structure of your collarbone, the gentle inlet at the base of your throat, the soft curve toward your shoulders. Dip your fingers lower, palm flat against the swell of your breast, then gently beneath the lace fringe of your silk camisole, spaghetti strap now fallen down from your shoulder to rest on the curve of your upper arm. Your fingers send bright sparks down your spine as you reach lower, your gown now perched precariously upon the perfect roundness of your breast—the breasts that Hampton, the soon-to-be-husband you thought you knew so well, professed to find "delectable."

The thought of Hampton, of course, brings you quickly back to reality. "Delectable"? Really? You should have known.

You can't believe he hasn't called in three days. Worse, even his manager isn't returning your calls. Part of you wants to run directly to the movie set, bang on the door of his trailer, and find out what exactly is going on. If only you knew what to expect when you arrived on set—would security even let you through? The last thing you need is to be photographed being turned away.

You knew you should have been a little more wary of that notoriously seductive costar of his, Nigella Langley. But you believed Hampton when he told you he could never be attracted to any other woman, and that it was over for him when he laid eyes on you. He was the one who pursued you, after all.

Shaking yourself out of your thoughts, you remember who you are: Anna Chambliss, one of the highest-paid actresses on the big screen. Incredibly lucky and unbelievably in demand. You are not about to let Hampton ruin your career or even your day. You have a packed schedule ahead of you filled with interviews, appearances, and meetings. Hampton will probably call sometime today and you'll be too busy to talk to him.

Still, you know this nonsense will be a distraction at best and fodder for the media at worst. All of your dreams are on the precipice of coming true and the last thing you need is to be pulled into a nightmare you didn't even see coming. Part of you knows you should talk to him in person and get to the bottom of whatever it is that's going on. You were so sure yours was the one celebrity relationship destined to last more than the average twelve months, but apparently you were the last one to get the memo. Hampton's been distant for weeks—not just geographically—and the press is already reporting you two are no longer an item. You know you have to take matters into your own hands, one way or the other. Should you go to the set and confront Hampton and that awful Nigella or call him and put your doomed engagement out of its misery?

To confront Hampton in person, turn to page: 151.
To call Hampton, keep reading.

Before you allow yourself a second to think about it, you muster your courage, pick up your phone, and call Hampton's number. Of course he doesn't answer. "Your call has been sent to an automated messaging system . . ." begins the robotic voice on the other end. You speak as quickly as you can after the beep. "Hampton, it's Anna, remember me? I can't seem to get ahold of you. I really didn't want to do this by voice mail but I guess it's better than text." You pause for just a second then cut to the chase. "It's over, Hampton. Don't bother calling. My schedule is very full and I certainly don't have time for your games. I hope you have a wonderful life." You push End and feel a tiny, frigid sliver slide through your heart. At the same moment, it's as if an enormous weight is lifted from your shoulders. You take a huge breath and blow it out, feeling the sting of tears you quickly wipe away as you put the phone facedown on the little table.

"Knock, knock!" The too-cheerful voice of Buffy, your stylist, sings through the door. She bounces in, all ginger curls, dimples, and huge, sparkling, blue eyes. She's a ringer for Shirley Temple as a child—just a little taller.

"Hi, Buff." You glance over at the clock and force yourself to smile. "Is it that time already?"

"Sorry—I brought you a Starbucks, though. Skinny peppermint mocha?" Buffy sets the steaming cup down on the dressing table.

"Thanks. Hopefully I'll be awake by the time the interview's over."

"Not much sleep, huh?" Buffy begins her routine of setting out the makeup bottles and brushes and heating the curlers.

"What's the point? I keep waking up a million times thinking about everything. But I did it, Buffy. I called Hampton. Had to leave him a message of course. I think this time it's really over."

Buffy runs a brush through your uncombed hair. She's been with you through every twist and turn of your crazy *Hollywood Hampton* romance. She's never been his biggest fan, but she's always been yours. "I'm so sorry, Anna. And now you have a crazy day to get through. But you'll do great. You always do."

She starts the process of sectioning your hair, wrapping each piece around a now heated roller, and pinning it into place. "Do you have an outfit?"

"Actually, I was hoping for your input on that."

Buffy grins and says around a mouthful of bobby pins, "Where would you be without me?"

You smile at her in the mirror. "I don't even want to think about it."

* * *

An hour later, you're ready for your close-up. Dressed casually but impeccably in an ice-blue sheath, your hair flowing freely in loose waves around your shoulders, you don your sunglasses to face the world.

A gush of hot, dry air sucks into the revolving door as you leave the hotel.

LA is always too bright, the morning light reflected from the skin-deep glimmer of the city. You step out into the day, dreaming of escape. If only you could play hooky for a couple of days, take a vacation, recharge a little. But you are at the height of your success, and who knows what tomorrow will bring? As your manager always reminds you, you have to strike while the iron's hot, make the most of your fifteen minutes. So, you never say no—you take the endless bookings, meet the press, go from film to film, feeding the fame machine in hope that one day you'll be able to jump off the hamster wheel and just rest.

From page 155 (and continued from above)...

You slide into your waiting car and meet the sunglasses-covered gaze of your driver, Bodhi, in the rearview mirror. His lopsided grin relaxes you in an instant. Handsomely disheveled, Bodhi always looks like he's ready to catch the next wave.

Not for the first time, you assess him from behind—the broad shoulders tapering to tanned and muscled arms, signature linen shirt billowing just slightly in the draft from the air conditioning. You know without looking he's wearing the requisite leather Birkenstocks. His white-blond hair is finger-combed into a goofily sexy, spiky mop. He might be fun—if only you hadn't just sworn off men for the rest of your existence.

"You okay, Anna?" he asks as you ease down onto the warm, black leather seat with a huge exhale.

"I really don't even know," you say, flopping back against the headrest. Bodhi's become more of a friend than a driver. Your little chats with him in the car between shoots and interviews are just the respite you've needed lately, and he's been a wonderful support through all of your relationship drama, helping you see things from a man's point of view but somehow always seeming to be on your side.

"Anna, you really need to give yourself a break," Bodhi sighs. "I mean, you've got to take time out. Enjoy your life a little. I'll tell you what would really help: transcendental meditation."

You look at his earnest reflection in the rearview mirror over the rim of your sunglasses and can't suppress a giggle.

"Seriously, it's the best. There's a great class at the Karma Citrus, that little place over in Malibu? But I like to do it on the beach, looking out at the waves. I focus on the horizon. Sometimes I really start to feel one with the world, you know? It's beautiful. It'll totally help you forget about . . . what's his name?"

You roll your eyes but give an appreciative laugh.

"No, I'm serious. It is amazing. Better then sex."

"Well, I won't be having sex anytime soon, so maybe I should try it."

"Anna, come on . . ."

"I'm serious! I'm done with men," you say as offhandedly as you can manage.

Bodhi spins in his seat to face you, his spiky hair and one raised eyebrow lending a comical look to his tanned face. He lowers his sunglasses revealing warm brown eyes, and waggles his sun-bleached eyebrows suggestively. "Your problem is you just haven't found the right man."

"Eyes on the road, mister," you say, half-smiling at the back of his head.

"Seriously though, Anna, you would like meditation. I tell you what, after you're done today I'll take you over to the spot I like, and I'll show you some moves. It's just what you need."

You have to admit, Bodhi has a refreshing way of lightening the mood. "You'll show me some moves, huh?" you tease.

"I'm not kidding," he says earnestly. "This is good stuff!"

You breathe a long sigh because it does sound good, but you know how crazy the day you have ahead of you will be. You can barely think past your first appointment and you don't even want to think about that—an hour long interview with Janine Perillo, the infamously brash *WE Weekly* magazine reporter. She's earned her nickname, "Mean Janine," through her vicious reputation for ruthlessly reporting the worst news in Hollywood. You just hope your publicist remembered to make the call to Perillo instructing her to avoid any and all questions about Hampton.

"Bodhi, I've got meetings until all hours. It'll be really late by the time I'm done. And tomorrow I'm due on location. Thanks, though."

Bodhi is undeterred. "You know what? It's even better at night. I swear, I've reached an unsurpassed clarity in the quiet of the night on the beach. It'll be the best." He pauses, awaiting an answer. "So?"

"Let me see how my day goes . . ."

"All right!"

"I'm not saying yes."

Although now the idyllic scene is playing in your mind: the warm sand, waves rolling lazily in the dark, a man you can actually trust, and a moment to relax. You wish you could just blow off this crazy day and go right now. But you quickly dismiss the thought.

You put on your best all-business voice but smile into the rearview mirror, knowing Bodhi doesn't buy it for a minute. "Just mind your driving."

"Yes'm." Bodhi replies, pulling the sleek black car around a palm-tree lined curve and heading downtown.

As you approach the Tarento Restaurant on Sunset, you're relieved to see the usual spectators aren't milling about. In fact, the street is pretty clear. Bodhi pulls to the curb just outside the entrance and stops the car.

"See you in a few," you say, thrusting a heel onto the sparkling cement below.

No sooner have you planted your Manolo Blahnik firmly on the pavement than the glass door to Tarento flies open. Suddenly, a tall man dressed in a dark suit is upon you.

You duck your head and push your sunglasses more firmly onto your face, readying yourself to shove past the accosting fan or paparazzo. As you sidestep, he steps in the same direction, causing you to collide with his remarkably sturdy chest. You gasp for breath and catch a whiff of a subtle cologne that smells like *man* and unexpectedly makes your legs feel a little warm and shaky.

You look up, way up—this guy is tall—and find yourself gazing into the clearest grey eyes you've ever seen. Contrasted with the jet-black hair and ruggedly handsome face, those eyes are even more striking. He looks down at you for a moment, seemingly as stunned as you are, then, in the most musical accent says, "I'm sorry, I didn't mean to startle you—I just . . ."

He pauses for a long moment, holding your gaze, and you think you see the unlikely trace of a blush on his handsome face.

The moment seems to last forever and, at the same time, end much too soon. He drops his gaze and clears his throat.

"Let me start over. I'm Colm Reilly"—he pronounces it "column"—"I'm with *WE*." His extended hand is large and warm, his grip strong and firm. His low voice drops to a quiet reverence. "You're even more beautiful than I'd been expecting."

He steps back a pace and you can see him composing himself despite the red flush now clearly rising from his neck to his already ruddy cheeks.

"Sorry, I must sound like a starstruck lad."

You have no idea what to make of this man. His blush rises just above the shadow you have a feeling a good shave never really erases, making him look like a tantalizing mix of schoolboy and full-grown man.

He drops his eyes to the pavement and clears his throat again. "Here's my card." He thrusts a glossy *WE* business card into your hand.

"Thanks," you tell him, though it sounds more like a question.

"Well, then. Shall we go in and get started?"

"Okay . . ." you reply hesitantly. "What happened to Janine?" you ask as you walk through the door Colm holds open for you.

"She landed a job at *Expose*. My lucky break."

Sounds right up her alley, you think. This might turn out to be a lucky break for you, too.

You glance over at the still-waiting Bodhi in the car and give him a smile and a nod. He rolls up the window and glides away.

Colm leads you through the lobby and into a private room in the back of the restaurant. A petite waitress wearing a brightly colored kimono, her hair slicked back into a glossy bun secured by enameled chopsticks, glides into the room and slides the bamboo and paper door shut behind her. "What can I get you?" she asks.

"Chai tea, please," you answer.

"Chai it is," she says.

"Nothing to eat?" Colm asks. "My treat—well, *WE*'s treat, if I'm honest."

You smile at that. "No thanks. The tea is perfect. I have to do a talk show in couple of hours. Nervous tummy."

"Then we already have something in common," he says with a wink, then orders a strong breakfast tea.

You notice the fabric of his suit strains across his strong shoulders as he leans slightly forward to hand his menu to the waitress. You also notice her sideways glance at Colm, then the fully adoring gaze as she registers his accent.

What are you thinking? He's a reporter, for God's sake. Not the type you should be considering at all. Not that you should be considering anyone, considering . . .

"All right, then." He pulls a notebook and pencil from his jacket pocket and looks into your eyes. "How has your morning been?"

Already a departure from the questions you usually hear. You wonder how long this guy has been in the journalism business.

"Oh, fine," you respond, amused. If he only knew. "You?"

"Well, I'm meeting an international movie star for the first time on one of my first big interviews. So, to be honest, I'm nervous as hell"—his laugh is completely charming—"but enough about me."

"Actually, it's kind of nice to talk about something other than myself for a change. But I guess you're here for the goods on me."

He grins as he writes something in his notebook. How adorable is he? *Dashing* would be the perfect word. His white teeth flash as he smiles. He'd make a great James Bond, you can't help but think.

"That I am." He gazes at you for a long moment then taps his pencil twice on the table and clears his throat. "So, Anna. What attracted you to your upcoming role in *Tropical Tango*?"

After an hour of something more than the usual line of questioning, the interview begins to wind down. Usually at this point in an interview, you're edgy and fidgety, anxious to be released. But, this time is different. You feel as if you could listen to that mellifluous accent and gaze into those cool, grey eyes all day. You lift your teacup and realize you've barely made a dent in your drink.

Colm leafs back through his pages of notes. "I think I've got some good stuff here. Plenty for the article."

"Great," you say, sipping your lukewarm tea.

Years of experience with the likes of Janine Perillo force you to add your usual interview wrap-up. "All I ask is that you keep it factual. Present me as I am. And"—you add with a smile—"if you want to say anything nice, that would be good too."

Colm laughs appreciatively. "You must have had some pretty poor interview experiences to feel the need to say that."

"Don't get me started. I have some war stories," you tell him, leaning in, "the worst of which involved your predecessor."

"Oh." He looks into your eyes and again holds your gaze for what feels like minutes. "I see."

"But"—you decide to let him off the hook—"I'm sure you're nothing like she was."

"Nothing at all." He smiles warmly. "Don't fret about what I'll be writing. It will be to your liking. I'm quite impressed, Miss Anna Chambliss."

Is this guy for real? For a moment, you are speechless.

"Thanks," you manage.

"Well," you both say simultaneously, then laugh.

"It's been lovely," says Colm, again extending that roughly calloused hand.

"Yes. Thanks," you say, taking his hand in yours. Is it your imagination or are those sparks you feel flying up your arm? You pull away a little too quickly.

Before he can see the blush rise to your cheeks, you're out the door and back into the car, where your coachman, Bodhi, awaits.

"So, how did that go?" Bodhi asks casually, pulling out into the busy city street.

"Oh, fine." You leave it at that and sink back into your seat, enjoying the warmth radiating from the dark leather and from the memory of the sparks you can still feel, left by Colm's touch.

You're still tingling as you walk the cold, linoleum-tiled hall toward the studio dressing room. Rounding the corner, you see Buffy approach, waiting to provide the requisite trowels of makeup necessary for a television appearance.

"You're looking chipper," says Buffy, gesturing with a makeup brush. "Dressing room's right here."

You enter a stark white room with lighted mirrors lining the bare walls. The smell is slightly antiseptic, not unlike a doctor's office. You feel the beginnings of a knot in your stomach. These live TV appearances always have the same effect on you. You've learned not to eat before the shows—keeps the nausea at bay. You've tried a thousand times to talk yourself through the jitters, but at this point you've learned to live with them, and they've never lessened no matter how many live shows you do.

"So," asks Buffy, "how was the *WE* thing?"

"You know," you tell her, "it wasn't so bad. For one thing, Janine is gone. Went to work at *Expose*."

"Perfect," nods Buffy, knowingly. "So who did the interview?"

"A new guy. Colm ... something ..."

"Oh my, Colm, huh? Sounds—"

"Scottish, I think? Or Irish? Very tall, dark, kind of a James Bond type, and he had the most amazing grey eyes."

"Sexy accent?" asks Buffy, smiling as she sets her makeup bag on the counter and begins to unload its contents, clicking each bottle, tube, and brush methodically onto the counter.

"This might have been the only interview I've ever been on that I didn't want to end. But he's a reporter." You shake your head to clear it. "What am I even thinking?"

"You know what they say about reporters," jokes Buffy. "They give good press!"

You laugh at her bad pun. "I guess I could use someone in the media in my corner. He's way above *WE* standards, though. He won't be there long." You sigh dramatically. "I'll probably never see him again."

"Oh well," says Buffy. "There's always Bodhi."

"Yeah right," you tell her. *Seriously, is Buffy reading your mind?* You do spend more time together than most sisters, but still ... "Besides, I could never be with Bodhi. That monster iguana he calls a pet scares me to death. Did you know he lets the thing sleep in his bed?"

Buffy laughs as she tucks a paper bib into your collar and begins to sponge the suffocatingly thick foundation across the bridge of your nose. "You know what they say about a man with a five-foot iguana ..."

"Stop!" You laugh. "You're going to make me mess up my foundation."

"Ha."—Buffy laughs—"it would take an earthquake to make a dent in this."

The tingling in your tummy becomes a flock of nervous butterflies as Buffy finishes the job.

A sudden, loud knock at the door startles you both. "Yes?" Buffy asks. She turns toward the door, all business, then falls totally silent.

Standing at the door is the star of the hottest medical drama on TV, *Sirens*, and Buffy's one and only celebrity crush. Thank God he has his shirt on which, judging from the majority of his PR shots, is a rarity for this guy. Buffy might go into cardiac arrest.

"Just wanted to introduce myself. I'm—" His tanned body and white teeth seem to overwhelm the room as he takes a confident step forward.

Buffy staggers a nervous step backward in response. "I know—I mean, who doesn't know who you are? Ha-ha." Buffy laughs lamely, dropping her eyes to the floor and muttering something under her breath. She runs one hand through her copper curls, which spring obediently back into position.

"Well, hello." His slight southern drawl is a bit disarming, and his attention is exclusively on you, his eyes locked on yours. "May I?"

"Of course," you say coolly, extending your French-manicured hand. "I'm Anna. Nice to meet you." You can't help but think of how ridiculous you must look, with a paper collar sticking out of your top at odd angles and your unfinished makeup job. You're momentarily glad for the coverage, though—at least it's hiding some of the heat rising to your cheeks. No wonder Buffy finds this guy so attractive. He is one beautiful specimen of masculinity and certainly emanates an overpowering presence.

"I'm Jackson Michaels," he says, taking your hand a little too firmly in his. "I'm on a TV show—you've probably never heard of it—*Sirens*?" His renegade smile belies the fact he obviously expects you to know exactly who he is.

"Oh, I've heard of it all right," you tell him. "Buffy here is a huge fan."

Buffy shoots you a murderous look of betrayal, her enormous blue eyes even wider than usual. Her cheeks turn a wholly unnatural shade of crimson. "Yes," she finally manages, "I've been watching the show since it started. I think you're great—I mean your character . . . I mean you . . . I mean I like the show a lot."

She whirls around to the makeup box and makes a show of fumbling for a brush, her face redder than ever.

You look back at Jackson and notice the sandy hair cut into a slightly unkempt-looking, shaggy style, falling so carelessly over one prominent brow that you're sure it's set there with spray. His whisky-gold eyes are surrounded by the beginnings of laugh lines.

"Jackson," you ask, "are you up first or second?"

"I'm your warm-up act," he jokes. "Would you expect anything different?"

"Oh, come on. I'm sure the women in the audience won't scream for me like they will for you," you counter. "You certainly will warm them up, I'm sure."

"Well," Jackson says with a made-for-TV-drama smile, "I better get out there. See you in the green room?"

"Sure." You nod as he walks to the door.

The minute he exits the room, Buffy lets out a huge breath. "Oh my God!" She drops her curly head in her hands. "Could I have sounded like any more of an idiot? No wonder he didn't even give me the time of day. Of course, who would, in your presence?"

"Come on, Buff," you tell her, placing a hand on her arm. Buffy has become your closest companion over the past two and half years of your dizzying climb to success. She's your confidante, and in many ways your best friend. With equal parts laughter and tears, you and Buffy have cemented a relationship that you know will last a lifetime.

You gather Buffy into a careful hug to avoid smudging her clothes with your makeup. "He seems like a self-absorbed narcissist anyway. Don't you think so?"

"Hey!" jokes Buffy, giving you a light punch in the shoulder. "That's my boyfriend you're talking about." You both laugh as Buffy brushes the last layer of powder over your face to set your foundation in place. Her eyes are still slightly wounded, but at least there's a hint of a smile on her pretty face.

A skinny, androgynous intern wearing a plaid shirt and jeans and grasping a scribbled-on clipboard pokes her head in the door. "We're getting ready to start, Ms. Chambliss. Anytime you want to go to the green room would be great." She exits quickly and speeds down the hall.

Buffy pulls the paper from your collar, crumples it into a ball, and makes a basket in the corner trashcan.

"Score!" you exclaim as you head for the door.

Your heels click along the tiled floor as you follow the signs to the green room. You take a breath, toss your hair behind your shoulders, and open the door.

The green room is furnished in a typically bland style—and none of it green. Couches that are less comfortable than they look, and are most likely cast-offs from some defunct television production, sit against the two side walls. A TV monitor is mounted on the far wall and an assortment of snacks, sodas, and bottled water covers the surface of a long, folding table.

Jackson sits on the end of one sofa, his right leg casually crossed over his left. He shakes a handful of M&Ms in one half-closed palm, stopping to pour a few into his mouth. His other arm is draped along the back of the couch, his sleeve rolled up slightly to reveal an evenly tanned and muscular forearm. His posture is both inviting and oddly off-putting.

He gives you a one-sided smile as you enter the room. "Hello again," he says, patting the seat beside him. It takes you only a moment to decide to sit on the couch perpendicular to his, but you choose the end closest to him, just to be polite.

"I don't bite." He smiles again then pours a few more M&Ms into his mouth.

"Ha." You laugh uneasily. "It's not you. These shows always wreak havoc on my nerves."

"You're nervous about doing a talk show?" Jackson asks incredulously. "I would have thought that this all seems pretty mundane to you by now."

You give him points for using "mundane." Maybe he's more intelligent than he appears to be.

"After all, you've pretty much exposed all of who you are to the general public. What've you really got left?"

"Excuse me?" you ask with disbelief. Cleary he's a complete jerk as well as an egotist. And clearly he has no idea what he's talking about. You've always been careful never to accept a script with nude scenes, never even to allow the use of body-doubles. You've done just fine being extremely selective, and you've kept plenty to yourself.

He laughs casually. "I just mean, you don't get to keep many secrets in your position. Fame does have that unpleasant side effect."

"Actually"—you find yourself suddenly defensive—"there's quite a lot about me the general public does not know."

"Oh, now you've got my curiosity piqued." He leans forward and smiles. "Do tell."

"Believe me," you say, "if there are secrets I've kept from the public, I'm certainly not about to spill them to you."

Jackson lets out a hearty laugh. "Oh, is that right?"

You can feel your face getting hot under your makeup.

"Whoa, take it easy, Anna," he says. "If looks could kill! I'm just playing with you is all." His slow smile spreads to the corners of his eyes. "Besides, I love nothing better than a challenge."

"Well," you tell him, "you can bet that's about all you'll be getting from me."

You've decided to dismiss him entirely and focus on the chatty repartee of the talk show hosts you're about to meet when the flannel-wearing custodian of the sacred clipboard breezes into the room.

"Mr. Michaels? We're ready for you."

Thank goodness, you think, breathing an enormous sigh of relief.

Jackson rises with the same casual grace that seems to be his nature and heads to the door, a slight bow-legged swagger drawing your eyes to his rounded rear. As he crosses the doorway, he turns back for a moment to catch your eye.

"Your loss," he drawls. You quickly raise your gaze to eye level. "I guess you're not going to get to hear any of my secrets either."

"I am eternally regretful," you reply, with a dramatic roll of your eyes.

He straightens to his full height, gives a snorting laugh, and closes the door behind him.

Now that you're up next, your heart starts to beat triple time. You tap your foot nervously and try not to pick at your manicure. You practice deep breathing and focus on the television monitor. Although you can't really concentrate on the first part of Jackson's interview, you register the typical questions. And you can't help but notice that the actor's southern drawl has disappeared. You laugh to yourself and pay closer attention.

The perky female cohost glances at the index card in her hand and fires the next question, "So, I understand you're all set to make your big-screen debut?"

"Looks that way," answers Jackson. "I'm pretty excited."

"It sounds like a great opportunity," the cohost continues. "Beautiful location, fun movie, and a wonderful cast."

"Yes," says Jackson with a smile. "It should be a great experience."

"What are you most excited about?" asks the host.

"Well," he begins, with a shine in his eyes, "I guess that would have to be my costar."

"Aaaah . . . right," says the host, nodding knowingly. "A very glamorous and successful actress. And someone we happen to have here with us today."

Huh, you think to yourself, wondering who else is slated to appear, and what studio is willing to try out the rookie actor.

"Yes," agrees Jackson. "We've had the pleasure of meeting just before my appearance."

Surprise registers on the craggy face of the cohost's older, male counterpart. "Oh, you mean to tell me you'd never even met before today?"

Jackson shakes his head with a smile.

"Wow," says the host, "and right here on our show. So, how did it go? Do you think you'll get along okay?"

"Well," says Jackson, with just a touch of the southern drawl, "as I just finished telling her, I do love a challenge."

As the interview ends, the audience dissolves into applause and laughter. "Right after this, we'll meet Jackson's costar in the upcoming film, *Tropical Tango*, the beautiful and talented Anna Chambliss."

Your hammering heart skips a beat. Your costar? Your upcoming film? *Tropical Tango*? You shake your head to clear it. What happened to Grant Shipley, the forty-something heartthrob you'd been told was to be your character's love interest? You signed onto the project knowing Grant was already attached. Grant's an even bigger name than you and a guaranteed box-office draw for the female twenty-to-sixty market. Your head is spinning with questions and confusion, but you'll have to deal with all that later. The door opens and there stands Jackson, looking like the cat that ate the canary.

"Did you watch?" he asks, smiling innocently. "How did I do?"

You close your gaping mouth and manage a question. "Why didn't you tell me?"

He leans against the doorframe and crosses his arms before answering. "Didn't seem like much of a fair trade. Maybe if you'd told me one of your secrets, I would have told you one of mine."

You certainly have a thing or two to tell him now, not to mention some choice words for the producers of *Tropical Tango*. Before you can speak, in comes the stagehand again with your cue.

"Come with me please, Ms. Chambliss?"

"Gladly," you smile coolly and slide past Jackson, without a glance in his direction.

Your nerves begin to cool as you walk back to the car after the interview. The little swag bag the producers handed you as you exited the studio holds a silver picture frame, a box of chocolate-dipped strawberries, and tiny bottle of champagne you wish you could uncork immediately.

You have to give yourself credit, you actually handled the questions quite well, never letting on that your costar's identity was a surprise and changing the subject whenever you could. When the cohost asked whether you were looking forward to working with Jackson, you replied, "I'm always eager to work with young actors, especially those that are new to the world of cinema. I'm happy to share what I've learned with my costar." You then managed a laugh that the audience mimicked, and secretly hoped Jackson was watching and squirming in his seat.

You graciously signed autographs for fans in the audience during the commercial break and left to a roar of applause. Not bad for a day's work. And the best part was you didn't run into Jackson on your way out. That silly smirk would have driven you right over the edge.

Bodhi is waiting at the rear entrance with the driver's side window rolled down and reggae music blaring. His shaggy head bops to the beat, the sun reflecting off of his mirrored sunglasses. He jumps as you knock on his door and he immediately lowers the radio's volume and leaps out to open your door with a chivalrous flair. "Your chariot, my lady," he says with a goofy grin, as you fall into the backseat.

"What's the story?" asks Bodhi as he rolls up his window. "I thought you'd be relieved to have that behind you. You look even more stressed than when I dropped you off."

"You don't even want to know," you say.

"Spill it," instructs Bodhi.

So you do.

You finish your story. Bodhi is silent, which is highly unusual for him, then finally asks, "Are you sure you want to be this upset about it? Kinda sounds like this guy has the hots for you."

"That or he's a total jerk," you retort.

"No, seriously. It's the kid on the playground syndrome. He shows you he likes you by socking you in the gut? Same thing."

"Extremely mature," you respond wryly.

"He's a guy," says Bodhi. "What can I tell you?"

You can't help but think what a great perspective Bodhi has. He's never defensive at all, even of his own gender. He's just such a breath of fresh air, especially amidst the materialism of Hollywood.

"So, any more thoughts on tonight?"

Bodhi's question catches you by surprise. For a moment, you're not sure what he's talking about. You're silent for a minute too long.

"Tell me you forgot," he says. "You know—meditation, moonlight, waves crashing on the sand . . ."

"Oh, yeah," you say. "No, I didn't forget. I was just waiting to see what the rest of the day brings."

"The toughest part of the day is over, right?" says Bodhi. "And I think a solid peace session could do you some good."

"Actually, the toughest part of the day will probably be the chicken tonight," you joke, remembering the VIPP dinner and the standard menu for the typical charity event.

"So, who's the lucky guy?" Bodhi asks.

This, too, catches you off-guard. Lucky guy? What is he talking about?

"Let me rephrase," Bodhi offers, sensing your confusion. "Who's your date for the event?"

"Oh," you tell him, "nobody. This isn't one of those. Just come as you are."

"You sure?" Bodhi asks, pulling the invitation card from the passenger-side visor, "I'm pretty sure you paid for two seats."

"Let me see that," you tell him, grabbing the invitation. "Oh my God," you breathe. Your eyes open wide as you take in the line below the loopy script announcing the Victims of Improper Plastic Surgery Procedures Fundraising Gala. "You and a guest are cordially invited . . ." it reads.

"That'll look great. I can see the tabloids now: ANNA CHAMBLISS HEARTBROKEN AND ALONE, DATELESS ANNA'S NIGHT ON THE TOWN, WHERE IS ANNA'S MAN? This is a nightmare. I'm toast!"

"It won't be as bad as all that." Bodhi offers, "Even if it goes viral nobody's going to expect you to bring a plus-one this soon after."

"Yeah, right," you respond. "I'm going to be the object of public sympathy. Just great. Could this day get any worse?"

Your mind filters quickly through the men you might be able to invite. At such short notice, the pickings are slim, maybe nonexistent. You don't even have family on this coast. But just having someone, anyone, by your side will help you look more in control of the situation.

You pick up your cell phone to call Buffy for an idea, when Bodhi interrupts. "I could always be your escort," he offers, then laughs. "I mean, if you really can't find anyone else."

Your immediate reaction is to laugh along with him as you envision Bodhi on your arm, his khaki shorts and flowered shirt next to your formal gown. Then you realize your mistake as Bodhi's face falls in disappointment. You let the fantasy play out in your mind—actually, he might be quite breathtaking in a tux . . .

At that moment, you remember the card in your purse, handed to you by Colm. You picture those tabloid photos—not too shabby. And listening to that musical Scottish lilt all night would be lovely . . . then again, you really *could* take Bodhi—what would it hurt? You think for a moment, then say, "Why not?"

To call the number on the business card and ask Colm to escort you, turn to page 63.
To ask Bodhi to escort you to the VIPP dinner, keep reading.

"What?" asks Bodhi. "Come again?"

"I said, 'why not?'" you reply.

"You mean you'd actually take me?"

"Is that so hard to believe?" Bodhi really can be adorable sometimes.

"Well, I better get going. What time is the dinner again? What am I supposed to wear? And I have to shower and shave!"

"Okay, Bodhi, calm down a second. You sure you want to come?" You have to laugh. This is the first time you've ever witnessed Bodhi anxious about anything.

"Oh yeah," he says, blowing out a huge breath. "I'm there. Sorry, guess I need to chill a little."

"We've got plenty of time." You laugh. "Believe me, if I have time to get ready, you have time to get ready." Your evening routine begins to run through your mind: lay out your gown, remove your layers of television makeup, shower ... then the arduous reapplication of evening makeup and hair. *Thank goodness for Buffy*, you think for the tenth time today.

"What are you wearing?" asks Bodhi.

"A recycled Versace," you reply.

"Recycled? I had no idea the fashion world was environmentally aware."

"Not recycled like that." You giggle. "I mean a dress I've worn before—to the Chi Awards."

"Oh, that dress?" says Bodhi. "Very sexy."

"You actually remember it?" you ask him. You probably saw each other for a total of fifteen minutes that night. You can't believe Bodhi could possibly remember the black strapless dress.

"How could I forget it?" He looks back at you and says with utmost surfer sincerity, "You looked amazing that night, Anna."

"Wow yourself, Bodhi," you tell him. "That might be the biggest compliment you've ever given me."

"Aw, come on now." He smiles, "I know I kid you a lot, but you know how I really feel."

Do I? you wonder, as Bodhi pulls up to your hotel.

Buffy greets you in the marble foyer of your suite. You feel yourself begin to relax.

"I ran a bath for you," says Buffy. "I figured you'd need it."

You throw your arms around her and squeeze her tightly. "You are the best!" you exclaim. "I'll try not to take too long," you promise, heading for your room.

"Take your time," says Buffy. "I'll heat up the rollers."

You enter the bedroom and begin to undress, imagining the warmth of the water soothing your tired body. You perch on the little quilted bench and gratefully unstrap your intensely uncomfortable shoes. Rising, you toss your sweater onto the bed and reach behind you to unzip your dress.

You walk to the bathroom and gingerly climb the Italian-tiled step to the round sunken tub and lower yourself into the warm water. At the last minute, you grab the magazine sitting on the tile tub edge. It's a copy of *Celebrity*, a popular glossy, and just the sort of mindless diversion you need. You always find it entertaining to read up on the exploits, some completely fabricated and some the awful truth, of your costars. You also like to check in on the sometimes flattering but more often cringe-worthy items about yourself. You're even more pleased to find that this "Special Double Issue" is the annual "Men of Our Dreams" installment. And gracing the cover is none other than Grant Shipley, your AWOL former costar.

You flip through the pages and skim through blurbs about the usual suspects, actors and high-profile businessmen, sports stars, and the occasional real-life mortal thrown in for good measure. A familiar photo catches your eye and you pry open the pages, stuck together by the water from your fingers.

As you peel the pages apart, you're greeted by the cheesy and now all too familiar smirk of none other than Jackson Michaels. His PR guy must really be working overtime. Does this guy have to be everywhere? You catch a few phrases like, "The up-and-coming Hollywood heavy-hitter," and "The guy every girl wants to date, and every man wants to be," and suddenly remember you haven't told Buffy the good news.

"Hey, Buff!" you shout over the roar of the Jacuzzi tub jets. "Can you come here a second?"

You look down to be sure bubbles are sufficiently covering your assets as Buffy pops into the room.

"What's up?" she asks.

"I almost forgot to tell you. Guess what bombshell got dropped into my lap today?"

"Hmmm . . . let me think . . . they've cut that nude love scene with Grant Shipley you've been looking forward to from the *Tropical Tango* script. I bet you're crushed."

"Hilarious," you reply. "Actually, you're not going to believe this. They've cut Grant Shipley altogether. And guess who my new costar is."

"Who?" asks Buffy, hopeful anxiety evident in her big, bright eyes.

"Your boyfriend," you tell her.

"Huh?" she's clearly not getting it.

"You know, the Magical Mr. Michaels? One of this year's Men of Our Dreams?" You flip the magazine around to show her the photo.

"You're kidding me," says Buffy in disbelief. "Are you kidding me? 'Cause if you're kidding me, this is not at all funny."

"I'm totally serious," you assure her. "You'll get to see him every day for the next three months in sunny St. Thomas. Are you excited?" You decide to keep your own impression of him and the details of your not-so-pleasant green room conversation to yourself to give Buffy time to enjoy the news.

"Am I excited?! Okay, breathe!" she tells herself. "This is like my dream come true. I'll get to gaze adoringly at him in person for the next three months! Of course, I'll be gazing adoringly at him gazing adoringly at you, but whatever. I'll take what I can get."

You smile at your friend. "You never know, maybe sparks will fly on the backlot."

"Yeah right. After I made a total idiot of myself today he'll never even look in my direction except to laugh. But still, I'll enjoy the view."

Buffy is long on generosity of spirit and general joie de vivre, but she's extremely short on self-esteem. You know enough about her life before you came into it to realize that she comes by her self-doubt honestly. Her history sounds more like a soap opera than real life. Before she met you, she'd had a string of bad relationships, the last of which was with a handsome fiancé (you've seen the photos) who'd ended up cheating on her with a bridesmaid-to-be two weeks before the wedding.

She'd tried her hand at acting and had been sorely disappointed by her lack of success. To hear her tell it, Hollywood casting directors were nothing but perverse, mean-spirited, grumpy old men and women. She'd been given enough critique of her personal appearance from her too-curly hair to her too-short stature to her too-cute face to make her seriously consider going under the knife. After one particularly bad audition where the casting director told her wryly, "We're sorry. The role of Shirley Temple has been filled," Buffy decided to call it quits.

"Oh, Buff," you tell her with a smile, "you know I think you're great. I wish you'd think so too."

Buffy gives a weak smile, "Well, thanks. Now, you'd better get out of there before you get all pruney. We have work to do." She walks out of the room to prepare your ensemble.

You towel off and take a minute to examine yourself in the full-length mirror on the back of the bathroom door. Your long hair is still wet from the bath, the color a deep and elegant gold. Your neck is slender and long, your body smooth and sleek, tapering to a small waist and a perfectly taut tummy. Your hips gently curve toward your long, slim thighs and toned calves. You turn slightly and look over your shoulder. Your rounded rear is firm and high, not a trace of cellulite or a stretch mark on the flawless landscape of your limbs. You thank goodness in silence for the luck of the genetic draw and all it has brought you so far. Especially since it wasn't always this way.

Your mind flashes back to the days of your youth spent at St. Cecelia's, the all-girls Catholic academy you attended in elementary school back east. With nothing but girls around and the same uniform day in and day out, you never paid much attention to clothes or makeup, but you were constantly self-conscious about your gangly limbs and knobby knees. Up and out the door in fifteen minutes or less on weekday mornings, your face freshly scrubbed and your strawberry-blond hair pulled back into a ponytail and tied with a silk ribbon, you hurried to escape the insults of your two younger brothers, ruthless in the way only siblings can be, who took every opportunity to call you "beanpole" and "carrot stick." Then, in fifth grade, your curves began to show.

Your mother, an aspiring model who scored exactly one magazine cover during her very brief career before meeting your father and beginning the second phase of her life as a socialite, encouraged you to follow in her footsteps. She yanked you out of St. Cecelia's and began to homeschool you, hiring tutor after tutor to work with you on the parts of the curriculum for which she didn't have the time or patience. She enrolled you in ballet class to help your "deportment" and a finishing class to work on your posture, manners, and vocabulary. She was never late with a correction of slumped shoulders or a poorly worded phrase. Her personal favorite was always, "If you don't have something nice to say, don't say anything at all." And so as you grew older, you became deeply aware of the impression you made on those around you. Crossing your legs at the ankles and using the correct fork for the salad became second nature to you.

With your mom's encouragement and connections, your first ballet performance led to a modeling job, a small shoot for a local children's store catalog. Your first modeling job led to an agent, which led to a succession of agents who sent you on audition after audition until you began to land larger and larger roles.

Your father, a senior partner at a major law firm, was always too busy with work and too preoccupied with other women to notice or to object to your gradual rise to fame. And when he finally did notice, it was a done deal. Your mother, who always aspired to more than a mediocre modeling stint and role as dutiful wife/charity event chair/entertainer of your father's law partners, basked in the warm glow of your success and gladly moved to Los Angeles with you when you were seventeen. She was your chief supporter and your inspiration, and you tried to let her enjoy through you what she never could have on her own.

Your first major success in the film *Seven Days in the Desert* and, later, your fortunate pairing with Hampton Rhodes brought scripts to your door for review, and you've had plenty to choose from since. You remember your first magazine feature headline: OVERNIGHT SUCCESS! Little did they know you'd been hard at work for years.

Buffy's cry of, "Rollers are ready!" gets you moving again. Wrapped in a lush terry robe, you saunter out of the marble bathroom to sit on the silk-covered bench of your dressing table and face the mirror once again.

"How do you want your hair?" asks Buffy over the hum of the blow-dryer, brushing with large, long strokes.

You smile a little at your reflection in the mirror. "Remember how I wore it for the Chi awards? Hair and makeup—exactly like that."

"You got it," says Buffy, and gets to work.

When Buffy's work is complete, you stand to admire the finished product. Your hair is up in a gentle twist with golden curled tendrils falling perfectly to frame your face and highlight your eyes and cheekbones. Your makeup is soft but dramatic enough for evening, your eyelashes long and black. The beautifully structured bodice of your dress creates a sumptuous décolletage below your collarbone, while the skirt falls to the floor in a silken black sheath. You step into your heels, just hidden by the length of the gown. You shine like a light in the dim room, and smile at your reflection. "Thanks, Buffy." You give her a warm hug. "It's great."

"Have fun," Buffy tells you, beginning the work of putting away her makeup and hair supplies. "By the way, who's your escort?"

You laugh as you remember. "Well, it's kind of a long story. I was blissfully unaware I was supposed to be accompanied at all. So I asked Bodhi."

"And he said yes?" asks Buffy as she loads the last of the rollers into her silver mesh bag.

"Yes, he said yes," you smirk.

"It's just I didn't think this was exactly his thing," she tells you as she steps into her leather clogs.

"He actually seemed pretty excited."

"Hmmmm," is all Buffy offers.

"Hmmmm what?" you ask her.

"Nothing. Nothing at all. Have fun." With that, Buffy slides out the door.

You wonder what that was all about, but not for long. The hotel phone on the bedside table rings loudly. You pick up the handset and hear the voice of the concierge tell you your car is waiting.

Heads turn as you cross the marble foyer, but you move quickly enough that no one has time to approach for an autograph. Through the double glass doors you see the long black car waiting. An incredulous grin spreads across your face as Bodhi emerges from the driver's side. He looks almost shockingly different in a black Armani tux with an enormous bouquet of red roses in his hand. His usually unruly hair is slicked back from his face and shines almost white in the moonlight, a striking contrast to the darkness of the suit. His brown eyes glow, his face is scrubbed and shaven, and his perfect, surfer-white teeth blaze in a dazzling smile. He looks suddenly much bigger, much taller. His tie and cummerbund are classic Bodhi, though, red silk decorated with palm fronds and birds of paradise. You feel an unexpected heat rise to your face and small tightening in your lower belly. Suddenly the night ahead seems much more bearable.

"Don't you look handsome?" you purr as he hands you the roses and gives you kiss on the cheek. "That's very sweet. You shouldn't have."

"I wouldn't have done anything less." He opens your car door. "You look amazing."

"Thanks." You smile, stepping into the car and gathering the skirt of your dress behind you as Bodhi closes the door solidly and slips into the driver's seat. You call up to him, "I feel like you should be sitting back here with me."

"That might be a little dangerous," Bodhi tells you. You laugh but wonder whether his double entendre is intentional.

"Right," you agree as you smooth your gown down snugly over your legs.

The dinner is long and boring but Bodhi does exceptionally well, giving you your moment in front of the red carpet reporters and photographers and surprising you with witty conversation at the dinner table. When the main course arrives, he turns down the chicken. "I'm a vegetarian," he informs you politely, but he munches on the salad and bread.

He is funny and sociable, a fun date. As he surprises you with his knowledge of both world events and industry issues, you realize that you've totally underestimated this man. You wonder what else there is you don't know about him.

As dinner concludes you excuse yourself from your table and run into the legendary Virginia Blair entering the ladies' room. She wears red organdy and a toned-down version of the bouffant that made her famous in the sixties. She raises her eyebrows as she catches your eye.

"Who's the hunk?" she asks you. A famous cougar, Virginia has been linked to a chain of men half her age for as long as you can remember. You hope when you are her age you'll have half as much fun as she seems to be having.

"Oh, he's my driver, if you can believe it. I didn't know I was supposed to bring a date."

"You always have to bring a date, honey," says Virginia, arching a finely drawn eyebrow. "The older you get, the younger he should be."

She gives a low, throaty laugh and then looks at you sagely. "Nice last minute save. Any more to that story?"

"Nope, it's strictly a friendly relationship," you tell her.

"Gay?" she asks.

It's your turn to laugh. "No, not that either. Just a really good friend. Too good to mess up, if you know what I mean."

"Nothing's that good, honey," Virginia advises, leaving you with a swish of her feather-trimmed hem.

You scan the room for Bodhi's white-blond head and spot it easily in the midst of the crowd. Before you can get to him, though, a strong hand grabs your arm. You pull back and find yourself looking straight into the sexy grin of Jackson Michaels.

"Fancy meeting you here," he drawls. His date, a little cookie-cutter blonde, hangs onto his arm and looks around the room in an apparent state of extreme boredom. He doesn't bother to introduce her but leans in and whispers, "I need a minute. Go mingle."

She obediently releases his arm and takes off toward the center of the room. Jackson turns to watch her, his eyes following her twitching backside as she saunters away.

He gives a little whistle as he turns his attention back to you. "Sweet little thing," he says, then adds with mock-regret, "A little empty upstairs, though, if you know what I mean."

You don't bother to dignify his remark with a response, but force yourself to relax your arms, which you realize you've defensively folded across your chest. Not that you mind offending him, but your crossed arms are forcing your cleavage higher than you want it.

"Look," he tells you, "I know we got off on the wrong foot this morning. Let me make it up to you. I really want us to get along—you know, with the movie coming up and all." He pauses for a moment to survey the room, making you wait a little longer than you'd like. "What do you say we blow this joint and go for a drink?"

You feel a fresh sense of indignant rage surge through you and barely manage, "Are you serious?"

You turn to walk away again and to your utter disbelief Jackson grabs you a second time. He looks you directly in the eye, and for the first time you notice the intensity and tenderness behind the gruff exterior. "Please," he says. All sense of smug confidence erased from his face, he looks into your eyes with a sincerity you wouldn't have thought he possessed. "I'm really not a bad guy. All I'm asking for is a few minutes. I'll even make it easy for you. Let's head over to my place for a drink after this thing's over. Just give me a chance."

In spite of yourself, you feel your resistance melting. After all, Jackson probably had little or nothing to do with the last minute casting change. Plus, he's new, he's green, and he's just starting to experience stardom. Of course it's going to go to his head. And you don't want the whole shoot to be uncomfortable for both of you.

"Well, I do agree it would be a good idea to talk about the project a little. But tonight won't work. I need to get back to my date."

Jackson's smirk returns, his golden eyes sparkle, and his dimples emerge even as he has the nerve to raise one eyebrow and ask, "You mean your driver, right?"

"How do you—?" you begin, feeling the blood rush to your face.

"I do my homework, sweetheart," he answers.

You pause, not sure how to react, then tell him sharply, "We'll talk later."

As you turn to find Bodhi, you feel Jackson's eyes following you, and you rub the slightly tender spot on you right arm just below your elbow, the spot Jackson grabbed just a little too hard. You remind yourself to smile. *Why are you letting this guy ruffle your feathers?*

You spot Bodhi leaning casually against a column, looking like some kind of commercial for after-dinner mints.

"So," Bodhi says, rocking on his leather heels, "crowd's thinning out. What now?"

"I figured you'd want to get home," you say. "I'm sure you've had quite enough of me for one day. I know I have."

"Never," Bodhi says as he places his large, warm hands around your bare shoulders, looks seductively into your eyes, then teases, "I've had enough of you for one lifetime."

"Ah, that's the old Bodhi I know and love." You laugh, giving him an affectionate punch in the abs.

"Oof!" he exclaims. "Watch out, the girl's been working out again."

"Yeah, right," you say, and begin to head for the door.

Bodhi stops you with a hand on your arm. "So, are we going to the beach or what?"

"The beach?" You had completely forgotten. "Oh, Bodhi," you tell him, "I just thought after this you wouldn't even want to. And I didn't bring any other clothes."

"That's okay," Bodhi offers. "We can still go."

"Dressed like this?" you ask him.

"Sure," he tells you. "We just won't do the hard-core stuff. It'll be all about making you relax. We'll work around the dress."

"I don't know . . ." The thought just doesn't seem as appealing now—sand in your shoes, stuck to your dress, in your hair . . . and you remember your ungodly early flight the next morning. Just then, you see Jackson exiting the ballroom. You notice that his date is nowhere in sight. He spots you and makes a beeline to your side, stands a little too close, then extends a hand to Bodhi and introduces himself. "So you're the guy who gets my girl around in style?" he asks Bodhi.

You widen your eyes in disbelief.

Bodhi, ever the laid-back and never-jealous gentleman, replies, "That's me."

"Listen," Jackson addresses Bodhi, leaning in, very man-to-man, "you won't mind if I cut in? Anna and I have some business to discuss."

"That's cool," Bodhi replies, folds his arm, and leans back against the column. "I can wait."

Jackson flashes his white teeth at Bodhi. "I'm sure you can," he tells him, "but this might take a while. You know, industry stuff."

Bodhi's posture becomes tighter, and he draws himself up to his full height and pulls his shoulders back, making himself appear as broad as possible. *He would make a great bodyguard*, you can't help but think. You can see he is beginning to lose his patience.

"Look, dude," Bodhi begins, taking a step toward Jackson.

From the corner of your eyes you can see people beginning to take notice of the obvious tension. You know you need to stop this, now. Every fiber of your being wants to step in and give Jackson a piece of your mind, but you know the less conspicuous option would be to turn around and leave with Bodhi, ignoring Jackson's taunts.

You lay a hand on Bodhi's upper arm, stand on tiptoe and whisper, "Just give me a minute."

He looks none too happy but nods, straightens his jacket, and resumes his post by the column.

You walk over to Jackson, look him straight in the eye, and in the most controlled voice you can manage, say, "Mr. Michaels, I'm not sure exactly what impression you are under, but I am not 'your girl.' I barely even know you, and you have no right to me whatsoever, business or otherwise. I have to tell you that so far I am less than impressed by what I am seeing."

Jackson takes a long pause, looking too deeply and gazing for too long into your eyes, with that dimpled smirk that reminds you equally of a cherub and of an eagle ready to swoop down and lay into its prey. Then he leans in and presses the rough stubble of his chin against your cheek. In spite of yourself, the tickle of his lower lip against your ear sends chills down your back, and you can feel your nipples harden against the tight silk bodice of your gown. He takes a beat then whispers into your ear, "You ain't seen nothin' yet."

You lean back as though insulted, then return his gaze. Your instinct is to pull back and slap him hard across his grinning face. What is it about this guy that has your defenses up and your insides on fire? You can feel Bodhi's eyes over your shoulder, shooting knives. Maybe the best thing is to deal with this here and now. What should you do?

To ignore Jackson and leave with Bodhi, turn to page 38.
To deal with Jackson, keep reading.

You decide you have no choice but to deal with this here and now. With all the patience you can muster, you blink up at Jackson and say, "I'll be right back."

Bodhi seems uncharacteristically crestfallen when you tell him you're going to take a meeting with Jackson after all. "I'll drive you over and wait outside," he offers.

You love this guy, and can feel his need to protect you like a tangible weight on your shoulders. "Bodhi, it's really okay. I can take care of myself."

He closes his eyes and sighs, then responds with resignation, "Okay. I don't like it, but I'm not gonna tell you what to do. I'll keep my cell phone on. And right beside me."

"Thanks, Bodhi." You smile up at him and lean in to give him a kiss on the cheek. He blushes adorably, ducks his head, and heads out into the night.

"Okay," you tell Jackson coolly, "I'm all yours. Let's go talk."

Jackson helps you into his red Ferrari—so new Hollywood—and closes the door firmly when you are seated. You sink down into the too-deep bucket seats of the flashy sports car.

"What happened to your date?" you ask as the car purrs to life.

"Sent her home," he answers. "Three's a crowd, after all. Most of the time." You don't know whether to laugh or to cringe as Jackson puts the car in gear and speeds off into the starry California night.

Jackson's home is a modest bungalow in the hills that he's managed to design in an ultra-contemporary style. The low, sleek furniture and dim lighting lends an edgy but inviting feel to the glass-walled rooms. The lights of the city sparkle through the walls of windows.

You gratefully accept the glass of red wine Jackson offers. It's a relief to have something to do. The ride with Jackson was almost silent. For some reason you could think of almost nothing to say. Jackson motions to a glossy black leather bench. You sit and breathe a sigh of relief when he remains standing. Maybe this meeting will be brief, after all.

"So," you straighten up and ask, "what did you want to discuss?"

"You know," Jackson drawls in his low, gravelly voice, "I really just wanted to get to know you. I read something in the script about chemistry between our characters, and I thought that might be a little hard to swallow when the two of us had never even met."

"It's called acting," you tell him.

"Hey, no need to be sarcastic." Now the sincerity is back, and there's no hint of the smirk. His eyes are wide and focused on yours as he eases down into the leather chair opposite you. "This is my first big project. I want this experience to be a good one. And maybe the start of something great. I mean, I know you've got this stuff all figured out. I'm just trying to find my way."

Once again you find yourself feeling inexplicably tender toward Jackson. Something about him is so endearing when he's genuine, maybe because it's such a sharp contrast to his usual bravado.

You sigh and set your empty wine glass down on the table. You have no idea how its contents disappeared so quickly.

"Look, Jackson," you tell him, "I'm not trying to be rude, but are you aware that you can be a little overwhelming?"

Jackson laughs, making the adorable dimples reappear on each side of his face. He pulls his bowtie loose and undoes the top button of his shirt, running a finger along the inside edge of his collar. "I've heard that on a handful of occasions," he replies.

He rises to refill your glass, lifts it deftly from the table, and places it in your hand. As he approaches, that disorienting sensation returns, as though Jackson draws all of the air from the room. Your face feels suddenly hot.

You find yourself taking another sip of wine despite the heat. You're feeling more and more relaxed, but your heartbeat quickens. You don't know why Jackson is having this effect on you. You're the one in the position of power, after all.

You set your glass down with determination. "You know," you tell him, "I've worked with plenty of other rookies, Jackson, and I'm happy to help you. I know your first big break can be a lot of pressure. You're welcome to come to me on set any time. But right now

I really should get back. Tomorrow is going to be an early morning, and we'll have plenty of time to talk shop once we're on location."

Jackson's face drops and you think you see a tiny flicker of something other than disappointment, but he recovers quickly, a mischievous light glimmering behind his eyes. "Okay, then, let's not talk shop. Let's just relax."

He walks toward the bookshelf behind your chair and for a moment you're sure he's about to come around behind you and start to rub your shoulders. You ready yourself to pull away, but instead Jackson produces a small, glossy, box from the shelf. "Care to play a friendly game of cards?"

Cards? you think. *He wants to play cards?*

"Jackson," you begin, "I really need to get back to the hotel."

"Just one game," he promises. "What the matter? Afraid you'll lose?"

"Okay," you reply, your competitive side taking over. "What's your game?"

Almost an hour and two more glasses of wine later you've beaten Jackson at Gin Rummy six times in quick succession. He's taking it like a man and seems genuinely impressed, as he leans on one elbow with his undone bowtie dangling toward the floor.

This time when you win, leaving him stuck with a hand full of points, he flops facedown onto his stomach and groans, throwing his hands on top of his head, "I can't take it anymore!"

It might just be the wine, but you find you've become extremely comfortable with Jackson.

He looks up at you with an adorably dangerous smile. "I surrender!" He groans, "You are the undisputed Gin Rummy champ."

You laugh and begin to collect your cards but when you start to stand, a sense of giddy dizziness overwhelms you. You try to lower yourself back to your seat in the most graceful way possible.

Jackson stands, smooths his rumpled dress pants, and refills your wine glass—again.

"I think it's only fair," he says as he walks back to his spot on the shaggy area rug, "that we play one hand of a game I'm a little better at. I wouldn't want you to think I'm a complete loser."

A bubble of laughter escapes you.

He raises an eyebrow. "No, no, don't try to hide it. I know what you're thinking."

"I really don't think you have any idea what I'm thinking," you tell him, giggling again. In fact, you can say with almost one hundred percent certainty he has no idea what you are thinking, which is that Jackson's fly is unzipped and the tail of his starched white shirt is sticking suggestively out of the open fly. Somehow you find this irresistibly funny and cannot hold back your laughter.

"Okay, Anna, I get it. You think I'm hi-larious." Jackson begins to shuffle the cards and as you continue to try to suppress your giggles he actually begins to look a little annoyed. "Well just you wait, 'cause I'm taking you down with this game."

Though it's even funnier that he remains totally unaware of his current state of exposure, you manage to sober up for one minute. Between giggles you ask, "What are we playing?"

"Five card stud."

The serious way Jackson says this, combined with the silhouette of his protrusive shirttail as he stretches his back, sends you right back into peals of laughter. He slides to the floor and pats the spot beside him invitingly.

Why not? you think and lower yourself onto the floor, propping your back against the bench. The thick, shaggy rug feels marvelous. At this late hour, you couldn't care less if the twice-worn Versace gets completely wrinkled.

"The thing about poker," Jackson begins as he reaches across the rug to deal five cards to each of you, "is that it's all about the risk. It's not much fun without any stakes."

The cuff of his starched white shirt brushes just slightly against your silk-sheathed thigh as he completes the deal. "So I have a suggestion." He looks up from underneath his jet-black eyelashes with a purely piratical grin and names his game. "Strip poker."

You reflexively tuck your legs more tightly beneath you, cross your arms over your chest, and begin to object.

"Wait, wait, wait," he interrupts with his slow, casual drawl, "I'm not suggesting you strip—after all, you are only wearing two items of clothing, if I'm not mistaken." The way his eyes travel appraisingly over the curve of your breasts and down to your hips elicits a fresh, hot blush.

"So," he says, bringing his eyes up to meet yours. "I happily volunteer to be the one to strip. High stakes for me. The odds are firmly in your favor. What've you got to lose?"

You reach up to retrieve your wine glass. You take a sip and try to regain your composure. You're not sure what game he's really playing. "Jackson, this is a bad idea."

Still, you're not moving from your comfy spot on the rug. Somehow the idea of seeing Jackson in less than his full armor seems appealing—and a little dangerous.

"You know what Anna? I'm changing out of this penguin suit one way or another, and this way just happens to be a little more fun."

You take a deep breath and another sip of wine. "Okay," you tell him, raising your chin resolutely. "You're on."

Three hands later Jackson is lighter by his jacket, tie, and cummerbund. Either he's so skilled at poker that you can't tell he's throwing the games or you're really better than you thought. One more game and it's the shirt that has to go, and you're not sorry.

Surprise, surprise, you win again. At this point, even if this is all a ploy, you're fine with it. The wine, the flickering candles in the dimmed light, and the scent of Jackson's cologne have your head spinning. This boy is sexy, there's no doubt, and he may just be the next big thing. And from the look in his eyes, all he wants right now is you.

Jackson struggles with the top button of his shirt collar and looks at you for help. You rise to your knees and move toward him, smiling and ready to help him with the button, when he grabs you suddenly by your wrists and pushes you firmly back onto the rug. Suddenly his mouth is on your neck, hot and unrelenting, and his hands pin your wrists, pushing them painfully down into the pile of the carpet. His strong chest is pressed against yours as he crushes you to him, and you can feel the harder urgency of him below his waistline.

He moves up from your neck and looks you hungrily in your eyes, then kisses you deep and strong. The rough stubble of his chin scratches your face and his tongue plunges forcefully into your mouth. Then, just as suddenly, he pulls away.

Jackson eases back onto one elbow and casually piles up the cards. His mouth is red from the smear of your lipstick and the bulge below his belt is hugely obvious against his black tuxedo pants. He begins to shuffle the cards. "Glad we got that out of the way," he says.

You are stunned into silence, your head spinning, warm desire coursing through your body but battling with your hammering heart. You are aware of the slightly swollen, bruised feel of your mouth and the lingering soreness of your wrists where Jackson's hands were locked. You are completely confused by your desire at once to run from the house and the insane urge to grab his wrists, dig your nails into his strong arms, and return the favor.

Jackson smirks as though he has you right where he wants you and looks at your untouched cards. "What's the matter? Don't you want to finish the game?"

You're suddenly more excited by the prospect than you ever thought possible. You look him in the eye and slowly reply, "Of course."

Two more hands have Jackson down to his boxers. You are one hand away from victory and you're determined to finish what you started. The next game doesn't go as well and for the first time tonight, you lose. Jackson looks at you expectantly.

"Uh-uh," you remind him. "You said you were the one doing all the stripping."

He gazes down at the only item he has left to be lost. "Well, looks like I'm there." He smiles up at you jeeringly. "But it doesn't really seem fair—the one time I win I get nothing in exchange. Besides"—he looks down thoughtfully as if studying the fuzzy pile of the rug beneath you—"it doesn't have to be the dress."

You smile in understanding and stand slowly, trying to keep your balance as the room tilts dizzily around you. You can feel his eyes drawn like magnets to your body. You are aware of your dress clinging to every perfect curve. You turn away in mock-modesty, lift the hem of your dress, and in one smooth motion remove the tiny, lacy panties beneath it. You look over one shoulder and fling the flimsy red thong at Jackson. He catches it deftly in one hand but his eyes never leave your body. A new mischief lights his face and he tells you, "Be right back."

When Jackson emerges from the dark hallway he walks toward you with a steady determination, then pauses at the threshold to the living room and strikes a pose that would make any GQ model jealous, with one hand on his hip and the other stretched casually against the doorframe. The first thing you notice is his perfect, hairless chest. You recall the intense pressure of him pinning you down and you feel yourself melt like liquid mercury. You can't keep your eyes from traveling down the length of his taut stomach and you are stunned, there's no other word for it, to see Jackson's hugely stiffened cock emerging from the thin, frilly lace edge of *your* underwear! You don't know whether to laugh or gasp, so you do both. "What are you—?" You have no idea what to say.

"I know, I know," Jackson offers, "I'm unbelievably sexy. You don't have to try to hide it."

"You really are insane!" You laugh as Jackson walks back toward you and grabs you by your bare upper arms. You instinctively tense but you hold your ground, pulling away but smiling all the time. "You are certifiable!"

He increases the strength of his grip and moves his face toward yours, pressing his lower half against your hips. "Don't try to tell me you're not filled with desire." Jackson's large, warm hands are traveling down the length of your body to your hips and then around to grasp your behind. Jackson lets out a low, appreciative groan. "Every woman loves a man who's in touch with his feminine side."

You haven't realized how large this man really is until this moment, nor how powerful. You can feel the slight prickle of the coarse hair that coats his strong thighs through the thin fabric of your dress. He's backing you slowly toward the low sofa behind you and not taking his eyes off of yours.

Suddenly, you're on your back and Jackson is on top of you, one large hand pressing down on your shoulder and the other working its way up from the long hem of your gown. You know you should stop him, that you should put an end to this crazy, unpredictable night, but something about his desire to possess you feels so good that you just can't bring yourself to tell him to stop. Besides, you're sure he's totally harmless. He's just a boy who likes to pretend he's dangerous, and there's no way he would risk harming his career.

He has your dress up to your knees and then to your thighs, and you are all too aware that you have no second line of defense—he's wearing it. His hand brushes over the soft, slight curve of your belly and then down again between your legs, where his thick fingers find the spot that sends bright sparks up from your toes straight up the top of your spine. Now he moves his hand up to hold your one free arm, and uses the tip of his cock, the completely unprotected part protruding from the lace edge of your panties, to rub insistent circles on your most sensitive part. You try to loosen one arm to reach down between you, but Jackson makes a little "Uh-uh" noise and uses his shoulders to pin you more firmly to the sofa.

His mouth is on your chest, your neck, his sharp scruff scratching the tender inlet at the base of your throat. You try to bring one hand up to protect the skin you can feel is already beginning to redden and bruise but again Jackson seems to predict your movements and brings his hand to pin your wrist, a little painfully, against your right shoulder. You feel an instant of intense fear as you realize that his other hand is now on your neck, his thumb and forefingers splayed and pressing slightly, but steadily, against the pulse point just below your jawline.

You try to say Jackson's name, to tell him to stop, but his mouth is on your mouth, his lips locked hard against yours, his tongue blocking your ability to speak, and only a muffled noise that probably sounds more like pleasure than panic is all that escapes.

Your pulse feels stronger than usual, as though fighting Jackson's attempt to stop it. You hear blood thrumming in your ears, and you begin to see a small starburst pattern in front of your eyes. You struggle to free your hands but are utterly paralyzed by the force of this man.

With one quick movement Jackson has your gown hiked up to your waist and you can feel the urgency of his thrusting intensify as he moves aside the lace of the panties he is still wearing to release his full length. You feel him hot and bare against your thigh and with a quick flash of fear and anger you roll quickly to the side, freeing one leg, and bring your knee up hard into him.

"Owwwwww!" Jackson's groan of pain is intense as he rolls off you onto the floor, clutching his knees against his chest and curling into a fetal ball.

As quickly as you can you get to your feet and smooth your gown. You grab your tiny Versace bag and run to the door as you hear Jackson's strained yell, "Hey! Hey!" You slam the door and run down the stone-graveled drive. The night air hits you and you suddenly feel more sober than you have in your life.

You pull the cell phone from your bag and begin to scroll for a number. But who should you call? Bodhi, whose big, warm eyes and slow, soft smile seem as comforting as a feather pillow on this suddenly cold night? But what if he ends up attacking Jackson, unable to control his anger when—if—he finds out what happened? Judging from his reaction to Jackson earlier tonight, you wouldn't put it past him.

Or Buffy, whose shoulder you could really use right now, but whose eternal optimism and out-and-out adoration for Jackson would be shattered. No, you can't do that to your friend, and you know she'll read you like a book the moment she sees the state you are in.

You realize that at this late hour your only option may be to call a taxi. You envision your unsteady walk to the end of the long driveway, praying Jackson won't follow, and hoping the taxi driver won't out you to the media. A big enough tip should ensure silence, but you can only imagine how you must look. You do your best to smooth your hair and, taking your little compact from your clutch, wipe the smeared lipstick from around your mouth and dab at the mascara that's run slightly around the outer corners of your eyes. *That will have to do*, you think.

Your head is spinning but you know you have to take quick action before Jackson comes looking for you. Hiding like a thief behind a stand of small shrubs, you run your tongue slowly over your stinging lips and taste a slight, metallic tinge of blood. You lift the phone and dial.

To call a taxi to take you back to the hotel, turn to page 70.
To call Bodhi, keep reading.

The longest five minutes of your life later you hear the crunch of tires on gravel as Bodhi turns the sleek black car into the end of Jackson's driveway. He brings the car to a lurching stop and is instantly at your side.

Though it's dark, you can feel Bodhi's eyes searching yours as he guides you back to the car. Your head is spinning and you feel angry and embarrassed at the same time. You know it took Bodhi far less time than it should have to get to you and that he must have stayed close, just in case.

"Thanks for coming so quickly," you tell him, the words not even approaching how grateful you feel.

"I knew not to trust that guy," Bodhi says gruffly. You can hear the underlying protectiveness in his voice and your heart squeezes in gratitude. You're grateful, too, that Bodhi isn't asking questions.

You find you don't need many words and that you and Bodhi have an unspoken understanding.

"I'm okay," you tell him. But you're not, and you're wondering how you can go to work in the intimacy of a movie set with this person who has just stepped so far beyond the bounds of propriety that there's no way to go back. But how will you explain this to the studio, how will you deal with the scandal, and can you even get out of the contract if you try?

"I'll stay with you as long as you need me tonight," Bodhi says with a tone that leaves no room for argument before opening your door and helping you into the car.

Your gown suddenly feels constricting and hot and your heart pounds in your chest. You can't even think about tomorrow. All you want now is to escape, and Bodhi suddenly seems to be just what you need.

From page 29 (and continued from above) . . .

Back in the mercifully dim, cool car, you consider Bodhi's meditation idea. After everything you've been through today, it might actually be really good. A million stressful thoughts battle with a strong desire to surrender yourself to this trustworthy man and obliterate your hectic day.

"Bodhi, how far is that beach spot you mentioned earlier?"

You feel the car lurch slightly as Bodhi involuntarily hits the brakes. Clearly you've surprised him. "You mean the meditation spot? You really want to do that? I mean, I'll totally take you if you want to go."

Suddenly a wave of doubt washes over you, along with the harsh reality of what you've been through tonight and what you face tomorrow. You shouldn't have said anything. "Never mind. I shouldn't. Let's just go back to the hotel."

Bodhi pulls the car to the curb, turns, gazes straight into your eyes, and lowers his voice slightly. "Anna, the thing is, I don't know when we're going to get the chance to do this again." The disappointment on his face is almost too much to bear. "You fly out first thing tomorrow. This really could be our last chance."

"I don't know what I'm thinking, Bode," you tell him, shaking your head. "I'm just so exhausted right now."

"Then this is exactly what you need. And I'll make you a deal," he offers. "If we get out there and you're really too tired, just say so, and all we have to do is hop back in the car and I'll take you straight home."

The sincerity in his eyes and in his words pulls at your heart, but exhaustion and anxiety are making your head swim.

Bodhi's eyes search yours as he waits for your answer. He has the uncanny ability to infuse his features with the irresistible appeal of an adorable puppy.

"Okay," you tell him, looking him decisively in the eye. "Let's do it."

"Yes!" shouts Bodhi, then more quietly, "Let's do it. You won't be sorry."

Until that six am wake-up call, you think, but you push the thought out of your mind.

You rest your head against the back seat until you feel Bodhi pull off the highway. The lights are fewer and the stars clearer here, and you can feel a distinct change in the air as you approach the shoreline. He guides the car into a quiet inlet near the beach and turns the motor off.

"Here we are," he tells you, pulling off his bow tie and tossing it onto the passenger seat. He rounds the back of the car and stops to remove a worn leather satchel from the trunk, before coming around to your door and pulling it gently open. He holds out his hand and helps you out.

Standing before him, his warm eyes locked to yours, you experience a woozy moment when you think he may actually try to kiss you. Instead, "Ready?" is all he says, and begins to walk toward the beach.

You pause at the place where the pavement becomes sand to step out of your shoes. Bodhi slides out of his as well. "Let me," he offers, slipping your shoes into the leather satchel on his shoulder.

You marvel again at how considerate he is, and how genuinely willing he is to attend to your needs. He's always been there for you as your driver, but he was being paid for that. Tonight is strictly overtime.

You follow Bodhi down onto the beach, the residual warmth of the sand soothing your tired toes as you walk. The surge of the waves against the shoreline brings a familiar primal feeling of oneness with the earth and sea, with the night sky above. *Jeez*, you think, *I'm starting to think like Bodhi.*

"This is a good spot," Bodhi says, and tosses the soft leather satchel onto the sand. You stand with your hands on your hips, facing the dark ocean, and feel the stress of the day begin to drain away.

The moonlight turns the white crests of the waves luminescent as they break toward the shore. Beyond, the sea is a mirror of moonlight, shimmering and sparkling in the dark.

Bodhi kneels on the sand to pull a blue flannel blanket from his bag of tricks, spreading it with a flick of his wrists. "After you," he says.

You kneel on the blanket and face the sea, your legs tucked under you, your gown around your knees.

Bodhi lowers himself to sit beside you, cross-legged and barefoot in his tux, still managing to look completely in his element.

He reaches into the bag again, and this time pulls out two long-stemmed glasses and a heavy glass bottle.

"What else do you have in there?" You laugh. "A coat rack?"

"Champagne, of course," he says with a faux-French flair. "Would you expect anything less?"

"I just wasn't aware alcohol was part of the whole transcendental thing. No wonder it's so popular."

"Ha, ha," Bodhi replies. "This is just for tonight. I figured it's a special occasion, my first Save the Surgically Altered event and all that."

You roll your eyes in his direction.

"Just kidding," he appeases. "I just thought this might make it a little easier to relax, after the day you've had."

"Well, then"—you smile—"I'm all for it."

He braces the bottle between his thighs and expertly pops the cork, sending it shooting into the darkness without spilling a drop. He pours out two glasses and hands you the first, stopping momentarily for a toast.

"To learning to relax," he says.

You smile in agreement. "I'll drink to that." You clink glasses and sip.

The bubbly sweetness sizzles across your tongue and throat then descends in a flutter of warmth.

Bodhi downs his drink in a swallow and tosses the glass aside. You raise your eyebrows.

"We have work to do!" He shrugs off his black jacket and tosses it into the sand. His shining hair, bright teeth, and white shirt gleam against the backdrop of the black sky. "Now," he tells you, "assume the position." He kneels on the blanket facing the water, closes his eyes and rests his hands on his thighs, palms turned toward the sky.

You take one more sip of champagne and, suppressing a giggle, try to match Bodhi's posture. You feel warmth begin to bloom in your cheeks, whether from the champagne or something else, you're not sure. You do your best to embody Bodhi's stillness, but a giggle escapes you.

"What's so funny?" Bodhi asks with amusement in his voice.

You giggle even more in response. "Nothing."

"You lightweight," Bodhi teases. "This is very serious business."

This makes you laugh even more. You reach for your glass and down the last sip of your champagne, then try earnestly to settle into your meditation.

"Begin by quieting your thoughts," Bodhi intones, his voice calm and even. "Close your eyes and concentrate on clearing your mind. Listen only to the sound of your breath."

The minute you close your eyes you are instantly hit with a wave of dizziness that makes you fall sideways into the sand. You're glad Bodhi's eyes are closed so that he doesn't notice your wobbly attempt to regain your balance. You successfully steady yourself and resume your effort to concentrate on the sound of his voice.

"Now, take a series of breaths, and with each breath, imagine yourself blowing away negative energy and stress. With each breath in, you'll renew yourself with clean, clear, positive energy. Out with the bad, in with the good . . . out with the bad, in with the good . . ."

Following his direction, you take a few breaths, but your mind keeps wandering. Images from your stressful day appear behind your closed eyelids. You steal a peek at Bodhi. Eyes firmly shut, he's methodically breathing and achieving a look of almost silly bliss.

Maybe a little more champagne will help, you think. You reach out stealthily for the bottle and glass lying in the sand beside you. Bodhi is blissfully unaware as you pour the fizzy liquid into the glass, but as you finish the job, the clink of glass on glass betrays you.

"Hey! You're supposed to be meditating."

"I'm sorry," you apologize. "I just can't stop thinking about everything. I'm fixating, I know, but I can't help it."

"Okay," Bodhi says, releasing a sigh, "let's try something else." He moves to kneel on the blanket-covered sand behind you and puts his hands on your shoulders. "Go ahead, hold onto your glass."

You take a sheepish sip and kneel in front of him.

Bodhi takes your shoulders firmly in his strong hands and begins to massage, moving his hands along the length of your bare neck. You can't help but gasp at the pleasure of his touch. How long has it been since you've had a neck rub? You don't have much time to wonder as Bodhi's strong, sure hands move up into your hairline and then down to your back, his thumbs moving in circles with just enough pressure to work your muscles into gentle submission.

"Man, you're tight!" Bodhi says, continuing to work his magic. "That's some serious stress."

"Mmmmm . . ." You sigh. "Tell me about it," you mumble appreciatively as his fingers move expertly up your spine then back to your neck and shoulders once more. You can feel his warm breath on the back of your neck, making the soft hair there stand on end. He finishes by running his fingers gently down the center of your back.

"How's that?" he asks. "Better?"

"Bodhi," you tell him, "I think you've missed your calling."

"Just wait," he laughs.

"Okay, now turn to face me," he instructs, and you dutifully obey. He takes your hands in his and begins to gently massage small circles into your palms. Maybe it's the champagne, but the firm insistence of his touch sends an electric current up your spine. You're glad for the padding built into your bodice, without which the evidence of the chills you're experiencing would be obvious in the moonlight.

"Close your eyes," he tells you, and you do, only too anxious for whatever pleasure he has in store. But he does nothing more than continue the circles on your palms as he begins to speak again, his voice magical, deep, and even.

"Imagine yourself at one with the night. You are the stars, your thoughts disappear into the air around you, your breath is the ebb and flow of the ocean waves . . ."

Try as you might to concentrate on his words, you can't help but sneak a peek at Bodhi. At that moment, he opens his eyes and he locks his gaze with yours. You don't know whether it's the intensity of his eyes, the heady spin of the champagne in your blood, or the magic of the sand and sea at night, but you're overcome by an irresistible urge. You lean in to Bodhi, your hands still in his, close your eyes, and kiss him fully on the lips.

Bodhi returns the kiss completely. His lips lock with yours, pushing hard and urgently against your mouth. He thrusts his tongue into your open mouth, and swirls it against yours. His kiss is hungry and pulls you into his body like the undertow of the sea. He tastes of mint and moonlight, and your head feels light and dizzy. You begin to lose your balance again and lean your weight into his. Bodhi grasps you firmly, his large hands on your upper arms, your breasts against the warm firmness of his broad chest. As you lean into his body, you feel the hardened bulge below his cummerbund. Your heartbeat quickens as you lean into him more fully, relishing the feel of him against you. You're surprised by his size, not that you'd ever given it much thought, but it certainly feels . . . substantial.

You begin to reach down lower on his body, feeling the definition of his chest, running your hands against the crisp cotton tuxedo shirt to feel the taut stomach beneath, then to his lower stomach, equally firm under the slippery silk of his waistband. As you run your index finger inside the upper edge, pressing your left hand against the broadness of his chest, Bodhi's hand falls to your lower back, pulling you closer. His hand travels lower and grips the round curve of your rear while your hands explore further inside his waistband. He breathes in sharply as you reach his navel and then the very tip of something else.

You gasp in pleasure but hesitate and pull your hand away. You move your hands back to his upper arms and pull away from the depth of his kiss. For a moment, your head ceases its spinning and you close your eyes to steady yourself.

"Bodhi . . ." you begin.

"Anna," he breathes heavily, his voice deeper and huskier than you've ever heard it. He pulls you back to him and presses his full lips against yours.

You save yourself from breathlessness by pulling away, and look Bodhi squarely in the eye. "Bodhi," you say again, trying to slow your breath and your pounding heart, "maybe this isn't a good idea."

"Anna," he sighs, his eyes soft and full of moonlight, "you're my fantasy."

You feel your heart melt even as a million thoughts rush through your mind. Bodhi is your very closest male friend. You know if this goes any further it could ruin your relationship.

You tell yourself to stop and think, and make a choice.

To allow Bodhi to pull you into another kiss and back into his arms, skip to the bottom of the page.
To stop your embrace with Bodhi and return to your hotel, keep reading.

Slipping the key card into your hotel room door, weariness and guilt overwhelms you. You hate disappointing Bodhi and you're more than a little let down yourself.

Still, you're proud of your self-control. Bodhi's friendship is too valuable to ruin with a one-night stand. Plus, you do have to be up ridiculously early. You gaze longingly at the luxurious bedding neatly turned down for you as you kick your shoes aside and zip out of your dress. You leave it puddled on the floor and climb under the cool, smooth sheets, feeling the day melt away.

At the last minute, you remember your up-do and quickly pull loose all the pins you can find, setting them on your bedside table. You shake your hair until it falls free, hardly noticing the pins you've forgotten as you nestle your head into the deep, down pillows and fall into a totally enveloping and dreamless sleep.

Turn to page 70

From top of page...

The delicious lightness of the champagne, the magical moonlight, and eternal pull of the sea sweep you back into Bodhi's strong arms. You tilt your head up and glance quickly into his sparkling eyes before closing yours. His hands travel lower, lifting your long skirt and exploring the length of your thighs. He slides his fingers down the inside of your hipbones, letting his thumbs play over your navel. You consider for a moment that someone could walk up and discover you. For all you know, there could be paparazzi hiding behind the scraggly dunes. But these thoughts are as fleeting as bubbles of champagne and the risk makes you even more excited. You feel a shower of sparks ignite in the deepest part of you as Bodhi moves his fingers lower.

"Bodhi," you begin, but before you can get anything more out, Bodhi sweeps you off of your feet—literally. The butterflies rise and flutter as he pulls you up off the sands into his arms. You feel the firm bulge of his biceps against your back as he easily lowers you onto the blanket. He slips one hand into your hair, causing fresh shivers to run down the back of your neck. He works his hands through your hair, pulling the bobby pins free, then runs his fingers through your loosened mane and gently presses your shoulders back down onto the blanket. He kicks aside the empty champagne flutes and stands over you, like a lion savoring his prey. His hair is wild in the beach breeze and his eyes shine with desire.

You smile to yourself. The hesitation you felt before is as distant as the stars above you. Bodhi bares his white teeth in a smile and lowers himself to meet you. You toss you hair back as he attacks your neck hungrily, sending chills of pure pleasure from your head down to your toes. You breathe in deeply, drinking in the scent of Bodhi's musky skin mingled with the sea air, and the last bits of tension melt away.

There's something hungry about Bodhi's approach, and a fantasy begins to float through your mind. An image comes to you of lions on a dry, sandy plain. Bodhi is a big-muscled male, all sinuous flesh and full, shaggy mane. He prowls around you, the female he's pursuing, little growls escaping his massive throat as he advances. His broad, tanned body ripples as he walks toward you, huge paws sending up puffs of dust from the dry ground. When he finally reaches you, he goes straight for your neck. The line between fantasy and reality blurs as Bodhi bites lightly, and you feel totally connected to him.

He pauses for a moment to look at you, as if to remind himself that he is really here, with you, then kisses you again, moving to your chest. He traces the top of your cleavage with the tip of his tongue then glances at you to gauge your response as, in one smooth movement, he pulls the bodice of your dress down to your waist.

You fleetingly realize he must have unzipped the dress at some point, but your thought is interrupted by the realization that your breasts are exposed in the night air, your nipples hardening quickly from the light breeze. Bodhi caresses your left breast with one hand briefly then takes your other nipple into his mouth. You gasp as he runs his tongue around it then begins to suck hungrily.

You feel the heat rise to your groin and you use your hands on his hips to maneuver his body on top of yours. You feel the sand compress beneath you as his weight settles onto your body, and you feel the hardness of him pressing urgently against you. Bodhi thrusts slightly as he begins to work on your other breast, making the heat you feel rise higher. You bring your hips up to meet his, loving the passion between you.

Bodhi moves his mouth down to your stomach, pushing the bodice of your gown even lower, while using both hands to squeeze and massage your breasts. You slip the long, slender fingers of your hand back into his waistband. You feel the intense heat of him. When you can't wait any longer, you slide your hand lower and grasp his hard, thick base. Bodhi gasps as you explore the length and width of him with your fingers. You wonder whether he can be as big as he feels, and you don't want to wait to find out.

You find the buttons of his tuxedo pants then slide the zipper until it stops. You move your hands around to grip his perfectly firm buttocks. Bodhi rises to his knees to make the job easier, and you notice as you slide his pants down to his muscular calves that he's not wearing anything underneath. You laugh, look up quizzically, and Bodhi reads your thoughts. "You know I like my freedom," he explains gruffly, and you realize as he slips your dress past your toes and tosses it into the sand, so do you.

You stop for a moment to take in the magnificence of Bodhi's physique. His muscled body gleams in the moonlight. Moving your eyes down across his washboard abs, you gasp a little, taking in the sheer size of him, then glance up into his eyes and lower his head to kiss him there, using the lightest touch of your lips to caress him. His taste is clean and salty, and you hear him groan with pleasure as you explore the smooth length of him with your tongue. Finally, you take him into your mouth. Bodhi breathes in sharply but gently lifts your head and leans forward to join your lips again with his, pressing you firmly back onto the soft blanket. Before you can say a word he proceeds to use first one finger to caress you in small circles, then two to plunge in deeply, connecting with the most sensitive part of you, then his mouth and tongue to bring you to the luscious edge of desire. You moan as you massage his blond head with your hands.

"Anna," he groans, "you taste so good."

When you can take no more, you gently pull his head toward you, but he doesn't budge. His tongue continues to flicker and thrust around your ultra-sensitive flesh and you reflexively push your pelvis into him.

"Bodhi," you say, trying to tug him upward again.

"Uh-uh," he manages as he returns his concentration to you.

"Bodhi, come on, I want to feel you," you plead hoarsely.

Finally, Bodhi grins and raises his head.

He kisses his way up your belly, chest, and neck, then rejoins your mouth with his. As he does, he wraps his arms behind your back and pulls you to him. He braces himself against the sand and pulls you on top of him slowly and gently, and you feel the tip of his erection against you. You wrap your arms around his thick neck and pull yourself into his lap, lowering yourself onto his tantalizing sheathed length. As he enters you, he bites gently on your earlobe and whispers a low, steady growl.

Bodhi begins to rock under you, slowly at first, so that you gradually feel the length of him filling every part of you. You glance down in front of you, over Bodhi's smooth shoulders, and notice that your dress and his tux are covered in sand. You laugh to yourself, and let the lightness of this night lift you again as you close your eyes and lean into Bodhi's full-bodied embrace.

You rock with him as he thrusts more deeply and you feel the pressure building. Suddenly, he lets out a deep growl and thrusts so deeply it almost hurts. You feel him filling you and arch your back to push yourself deeper, and there's nothing at all in the world besides you and him.

You open your eyes to see Bodhi staring intently into yours and you find yourself lost in waves and waves of exquisite pleasure. You thrust yourself into him and moan into his neck, biting gently. You collapse back into the sandy blanket with Bodhi on top of you, and breathe deeply into the cooling night air. Bodhi kisses your neck then rests his head on your shoulder. You run your fingers through his silken hair as your breathing begins to slow. You lay like this for what feels like hours, until Bodhi gently rolls to your side.

"Anna," he tells you, "that was amazing."

Slowly and silently, stopping to kiss you tenderly every few moments, he helps you back into your gown, shakes the blanket free of sand, and wraps it snugly around you to shield you from the cooling air.

Back in the car, you sprawl yourself across the dark leather of the rear seat. Your limbs are loose and languid and an overwhelming sense of relaxation overtakes you. In your mind, you see nothing but stars and moonlight and you smile to yourself. It feels strange to be reverting to your former roles, Bodhi driving you home and you staring at the back of his rumpled hair. You begin to speak but can't think of the right thing to say. Bodhi seems to feel the same and turns the soft music of the radio up to mask the silence. You're grateful for the chance to luxuriate in the satiety of your body, and you rest your head against the seat back and close your eyes. Before you know it, you've fallen asleep.

You wake as the car comes to a stop in front of your hotel. You sleepily open your eyes and try to focus your bleary vision on the lighted doorway. The doorman stands at the ready, eyes politely diverted. Bodhi exits his door and opens yours, offering a hand to help you to your feet. You take it and feel a shimmer of the sparks you shared reignite. He follows you through the revolving glass door.

At the bank of elevators, you turn to face Bodhi. He looks at you with those big, brown eyes, raises his eyebrows, and inhales with a smile. As his shoulders lift, he looks so much like a teenager after his first kiss that you have to laugh.

"What?" Bodhi asks you.

"Nothing." You smile. "I just think you're kind of cute."

Bodhi breaks out in a grin. "Cute is all I get?"

"That's all you get for tonight," you reply, then stand on tiptoe to plant a last kiss on his lips.

"Anna," he begins.

"Shhh," you tell him, placing a finger over the spot you've just kissed, and slip into the elevator with a smile.

As the doors slide shut, your body thrums with elation and you feel like a child with a wonderful secret. You wait as the elevator operator presses the button for the penthouse suite. He looks at you out of the corner of his eye, smile lines creasing his face as he notices your mischievous grin.

"Had a good night?" he asks in a droll British accent.

"Very," you tell him, and try to retain your composure as you exit the elevator into your hotel room foyer.

Back in your room, you strip off your clothes and fall into bed without even turning on the light. The mixture of sea air, champagne and, well—other things—have worn you out. You fall into a dreamless sleep, the sound of ocean waves still echoing in your ears.

You're awakened much too soon by the sound of incessant pounding. You're momentarily disoriented by the harsh morning light streaming through the windows. You shield your eyes with the back of your hand and pull the downy comforter over your head. The pounding stops for a moment, then resumes with even more force and you realize the sound is a lot closer than you first thought. You toss the blanket away and squint to look at the clock. Six forty-five. *Six forty-five! Oh my God*, you think, as the realization of where you are and where you are supposed to be comes crashing over you. You can only hope the clock is wrong. You ordered a wake-up call for five thirty a.m., and although you'd like to believe it's earlier than that, the sunlight tells you the time on the clock is likely accurate.

The pounding starts up again, this time even louder. In a panic, you gather the bedsheet around you and stumble across the floor and out to the foyer to see who or what is about to knock your door off its hinges.

Through the little glass peephole you see Bodhi standing on the other side. Before he can knock again, you push open the lock and pull him into the room.

"For God sake, Anna." Bodhi is flushed and out of breath. "I was about to call the paramedics. I've been knocking on your door for half an hour!"

"Oh my God!" you say as you plop back down onto the bed. "My head is pounding."

"Sorry, but seriously, I waited in the car for as long as I could, then tried to call and text you fifteen times . . . I didn't know if something happened to you or what." Bodhi looks into your eyes, then covers his face with his hands and sighs up at the ceiling.

"No." You take Bodhi's hand and engage his eyes. "Nothing happened. Just freaking out that I slept so late. God! I was supposed to get a wake-up call."

"They tried," Bodhi tells you. "You didn't pick up."

"Ughhhh!" You flop back headfirst into the pillows. "Well, with any luck I'll still be able get in by early afternoon. Help me get my stuff together, will you? Can you call the pilot and tell him I'm on the way?"

Bodhi bites his lower lip before saying, "Actually, I already called him and asked him to wait. He couldn't hold the flight."

"What?" you say in disbelief.

"Well, the whole film crew was there waiting, and the plane was due for another flight out later this afternoon from St. Thomas, so they went ahead and . . . left."

"Fabulous!" you say, flopping back on to the unmade bed. "What am I going to do now?" You blow out a huge breath and realize too late you haven't even brushed your teeth.

You pop up and drag the sheet clumsily along with you as you haul yourself into the bathroom. Closing the door, you drop the sheet and replace it with your robe—not that modesty is really all that necessary. You rinse your toothbrush, load it with whitening paste and begin to scrub your teeth as you crack open the door. Bodhi sits on the edge of the bed, waiting patiently. You rifle through the stream of thoughts running through your mind and talk around a mouthful of toothpaste.

"I know—I'll call Buffy. She's probably waiting for me. She can call the studio and tell them I came down with a twenty-four hour bug and ask them to send a plane back out as soon as they can. She's great with that kind of thing."

"Buffy was on the flight. She's already gone," Bodhi tells you in a monotone.

"What? She went without me? Wasn't she worried about where I was? I can't believe she didn't wait for me!"

Bodhi looks down at his sandals. "I kind of told her I knew where you were and that I'd take care of everything and make sure you were all right. I pretty much convinced her to go."

"Bodhi!" Your eyes widen in disbelief. "She works for me! That was not your decision, or hers, to make!"

Bodhi begins to speak, then seems to think the better of it. He closes his mouth and looks at the floor.

You toss your hands in the air. "Seriously, Bodhi, now I'm just totally on my own!"

"Look, Anna, I knew you and I would figure it out. I really don't think it's that big of a deal. You'll just get there a little after everyone else. Give them time to settle in before you make your big entrance and all that. You may have to fly commercial but I'll make sure it's first class."

Despite your annoyance, you smile with relief. Bodhi is so good at making you feel like everything is taken care of and clearly he's prepared to help you figure this out.

"You're right," you decide. "What difference is a few hours going to make anyway?"

* * *

Three hours later, you're sitting on your private jet, in a leather airplane seat, waiting on the tarmac for clearance to depart. Your phone begins to buzz, and you search through your oversized travel bag to extract it. The number is not one you recognize. You hesitate before picking up.

"Hello?" you answer.

"Is Ms. Chambliss available please?" asks a deep and raspy female voice on the other end.

"This is she."

"Ms. Chambliss, this is Trudy Long, talent coordinator with PMG. Mr. Jeffries asked that I call."

Nice, you think, *the big-time director, Jeff Jeffries, couldn't even bother to call you himself?*

You run your fingernails back and forth over the edge of your seat and wait for the "talent coordinator" to continue.

"Mr. Jeffries would like to begin the script reading, Ms. Chambliss, and he is a bit concerned that his headliner isn't yet in attendance."

"Please tell Mr. Jeffries that I've been . . . unexpectedly delayed . . . and that I'm on a plane now. I should arrive in a few hours. Didn't my assistant, Buffy, tell you I was on my way?"

"I'm sorry—I don't know a . . . a . . . Buffy?" replies the raspy voice, obviously clueless and annoyed.

You sigh and shake your head. "Never mind."

"Then we'll see you shortly?" asks Trudy.

"I'll be there as soon as I can," you assure her.

"All right, then. Please do report directly to the set as soon as you arrive." You're about to hit end when Trudy's voice comes through again. "Oh, and Ms. Chambliss?"

"Yes?"

"Mr. Jeffries did ask me to add that he hopes this isn't going to become a habit. He likes to keep a tight schedule. After all, time is money."

"Right," you respond, and hit end with unnecessary force.

The heat rises to your face, flushing your cheeks, and you feel the blood rush to your head. You really can't believe this. All signs point to this being a nightmare project. And these situations usually go from bad to worse. First you find out you're working with a rookie costar of questionable character instead of A-lister Grant Shipley, then you miss your flight, and now you're chastised by a glorified secretary? It's probably not too late to pull out. You grab your phone again to dial your agent.

Voicemail immediately answers. "Hi, this is Rona. Your call is very important to me . . ."

"Darn," you whisper. You end the call, your thoughts racing. You really need to talk to someone—this is not the kind of decision you're good at making on your own. In fact, you rarely ever make any decision by yourself, whether about the length of your hair or the next movie deal. Normally, you'd call Buffy, but she's in St. Thomas, surrounded by the people you want to talk about, so that won't work. Who can you call?

Suddenly, it occurs to you—Bodhi. He'll help you think logically and probably also help calm you down about the whole thing, which is just what you need.

"Finished?" asks the flight attendant, a fussy-looking man with a receding hairline and wearing a dark blue polyester suit. "We're cleared for takeoff, Ms. Chambliss." He pronounces your name with a pointed stare at your cell phone.

"Can you wait two seconds?"

"Oh yes, let me just ask the pilot to radio the tower to let them know you need to make another phone call before we take off," he replies with an exaggerated snarkiness. "I'm sure everyone will be very patient." He makes a show of folding his arms and leans against your seat back, drumming his fingers on the headrest.

Undeterred, you dial Bodhi. He picks up on the first ring.

"Hey, Anna. I was just thinking about you."

"Oh?" a smile plays across your face then you remember the reason for your call.

"I need some quick advice."

"Shoot," says Bodhi.

You plunge right in, "So, you know the whole deal with the studio signing that new guy on as my costar and all that."

"Right," says Bodhi, waiting for you to go on.

"Well, listen to this." You glance sideways at the flight attendant and proceed to tell Bodhi about your phone call from Trudy Long and your doubts about continuing with the project.

Bodhi listens intently then pauses before saying, "You know what I think?"

"What?"

"You totally deserve better. You're probably the only reason anyone would even go to see that movie. I don't mean to sound harsh, but it's another fluffy romance with a mostly no-name cast and without you it may as well be a movie of the week."

You're stunned by Bodhi's response. "I thought you were going to tell me to take a chill pill and that I was overreacting."

"Is that what you wanted to hear?" You quietly marvel at Bodhi's insightfulness.

"No," you stammer. "I just thought that's what you'd think. So what do you think I should do?"

"Well," Bodhi begins, "I can't make the decision for you. What I know is that you've been really stressed and that the last thing you need is the tension of a bad situation to make it worse."

"I know, but if I back out it'll be a ridiculous battle about breach of contract, the tabloids will have a field day, and the next movie deal may be a lot harder to come by."

Bodhi laughs. "As if, Anna. You know you could take a year off and still be in demand. Maybe even more in demand."

"I don't know, Bodhi. I really don't."

The flight attendant clears his throat loudly, and you look up at him. He inclines his head toward the cell phone, his eyebrows raised.

"Okay." You sigh, resigning yourself to heading to St. Thomas to try to smooth things over on the set.

"Bodhi, I guess I have to go." You can't believe how reluctant you are to end your call with Bodhi. Just the sound of his voice is calming your nerves tremendously. "I'm already on the plane, so I might as well head down there and figure this out in person."

Then you remember that Bodhi will have three months to himself while you're on set in St. Thomas. Besides, you really don't want to hang up just yet. "Hey, where are you off to while I'm gone?" you ask him.

"Headed to Kauai later today to do a little surfing and a little communing with nature. Should be fun." He seems less than thrilled at the thought.

"Yeah," you say, imagining the lush, unspoiled greenery of Kauai's landscape, the gorgeous assortment of natural white, pink, and even black beaches. Not to mention the perfectly translucent turquoise water, so clear the candy-colored fish are visible even from the surface. It's been way too long since you were in Hawaii.

"Well," says Bodhi, "I'm sure I have room to smuggle you in my suitcase if you want to come with."

You laugh wistfully. "Thanks, Bodhi. And thanks for being there for me."

"That's why they pay me the big bucks," Bodhi jokes.

The flight attendant hasn't moved a muscle. He clears his throat more loudly and makes a show of checking his watch.

"We can go," you tell him.

"Why, thank you. The pilot will be so pleased." He waits a beat then asks, "You are planning to end your call? The use of electronic devices during takeoff and landing is strictly prohibited." His voice drips with sarcasm.

You reluctantly say goodbye to Bodhi. "Well, I'll see you," you say. "Have fun."

"You too," Bodhi says, then adds, "I'll miss you, Anna."

He hangs up before you can reply, and your heart squeezes painfully. You notice that the annoyed flight attendant is still standing over you.

"Okay," you tell him, turning off your phone and tossing it back into your bag. "Let's go."

Your blood pressure begins to rise at the thought of walking onto the set of mostly strangers already annoyed by you. You know you're going to have a tough time being sweet and cooperative with a director who's treated you like a second-class citizen. And you can only imagine the self-satisfied smirk on Jackson's face when he finds out he's outshone you already.

You close your eyes and lean your head back against the leather headrest as you try to picture crystal-blue water lapping at sugar-sand beaches dotted with gracefully swaying palms. You imagine digging your toes into the warm sand.

The unbidden thought of Bodhi laps away at the edges of your fantasy as you slide toward sleep. Your neck tingles as you imagine the feel of his fingers working the tension from your body, his lips on your neck, his teeth grazing your skin, the moment he pulls you to him and . . . a shiver runs through your body, ending in a deep and sudden clenching low in your belly. You take a deep breath and open your eyes.

"Wait!" you yell, jumping up from your seat. You step out into the airplane's aisle and run to the front of the plane.

In an instant, you know it's time to make your decision and take your life into your own hands. You've felt like little more than a pawn since you were seventeen years old, and you're ready to start calling the shots. You feel a sudden surge of resolve not to walk onto that set without laying down some ground rules.

You lean in to the flight attendant who walks toward you in protest. "Please, Ms. Chambliss . . .

"I'm so sorry," you tell him. "I need to make one more call."

He rolls his eyes massively and groans. "Ms. Chambliss, if we're going to go, we have to go now."

"Give me just one more minute," you plead. "It's extremely important."

"I'd say no if I thought you'd take no for an answer," he sighs sourly as you run back to your seat and grab your phone.

To call the set of *Tropical Tango* and give the director a piece of your mind, turn to page 160.
To dial Bodhi and tell him you'll join him in Kauai, keep reading.

You dial Bodhi's cell and get his voice mail. Of all times! You try again, then a third time with the same result. Should you leave a message? You decide yes. You hit Send one last time, but this time there's a ring on the other end. Bodhi answers.

"Anna?"

"Bodhi, I—"

Bodhi picks up the panicked tone in your voice. "What's wrong?"

"No—nothing's wrong." You try to sound calm. "Listen, I've made a decision. I'm coming with you. To Hawaii."

You wait for a response for what feels like minutes.

"Hello?" you ask into the silence.

"Yeah," Bodhi sputters. "I mean, I was sort of kidding when I said that about the luggage and all—but . . . are you sure?"

"As sure as I've ever been about anything," you tell him.

One hour and one extremely grumpy flight attendant later, you're back in the car with Bodhi—his car this time, a topless Jeep Wrangler, of course. Your hair flies wildly in the wind as you race to Bodhi's apartment. You've made a single call to Trudy Long to advise her not to expect you on the set. After a brief argument that ended with Trudy threatening legal action and you hanging up on her, you turn off your phone. All you want to think about are the moments ahead. You'll deal with the mess you've left behind later.

The LA air is smoggy, hot, and thick, the open car making you even more aware of the city's ugly side. The heaviest traffic is beginning to thin as the day makes its way toward late morning. You can't wait to get away from all of this.

"I'll just be a couple minutes," Bodhi tells you as he pulls into a spot at the back of a low, gated, white stucco building.

"Wait, I'll come." You jump down from the Jeep and slam the door shut. Then you remember your luggage, sitting out in the open in the back seat of the car. Bodhi follows your gaze.

"It'll be fine," he assures you and swings open the wrought-iron gate leading to his building.

It's funny to see where Bodhi lives after all this time. You feel as though you know him so intimately, but you've never even given a thought to the place he calls home. You walk to the door of Bodhi's apartment across the tiled courtyard with a lovely, trickling, Spanish-tile fountain at its center.

You're expecting a mess of flowered shirts and khakis on the floor, tapestries hung over the windows, an unmade bed and dishes in the sink. What you see when Bodhi opens the door is more surprising.

Bodhi's apartment is large and beautifully decorated, the main room a mix of deep browns and golds with an expensive-looking, dark, carved wood table at the center. The windows are covered with burnished wood blinds, which let in a filtered light that casts a warm glow about the room. The kitchen is small but spotless and well-appointed, with ceramic tile on the floor, granite counters, and sparkling, stainless steel appliances.

"Wow," you say, taking it all in. "It's really nice."

"You sound surprised," replies Bodhi, tossing his keys onto the table.

"I didn't know what to expect," you tell him, "but this doesn't look much like a bachelor pad."

"I like it." He shrugs.

Bodhi heads to a room at the back of the apartment. "Let me just get my stuff."

You wander around, looking at the framed black-and-white photos of waves, canyons, and mountains as Bodhi rustles around in his room. You're curious about what his bedroom looks like. You wander toward the back of the apartment and peek your head in the door. Bodhi's back is to you and on the bed is a huge duffel bag into which he's tossing clothing. His bedroom is gorgeous as well, the walls the same deep brown as the rest of the apartment, the bed covered in a cream-and-gold spread, the matching pillows neatly arranged at the head.

"Did you do all this?" you ask.

Bodhi jumps and turns around to face you. He laughs. "Do all what?"

"The apartment," you say. "It's beautifully decorated."

"Thanks, but no, I can't take all the credit."

He moves the bag onto the floor and puts his strong hands on his hips. "You know," he tells you, "now that you mention it, this bed is way too neat."

He grabs you by the waist with a huge smile and swings you onto the bed, kissing you and running his hands through your hair. Taken by surprise, you give into the moment, the thick, soft comforter cool and smooth beneath you.

Bodhi reaches a hand up your short skirt and releases a low growl as he begins to stroke you. You close your eyes and relax as he works his magic, teasing you with light brushes of his fingertips. He hikes your skirt up over your hips and deftly moves off of the bed and onto his knees, placing each hand on one of your thighs, kneading them firmly as he positions his head between them. He breathes over your most sensitive areas, and follows each breath with a tiny flick of his tongue. The sensation is subtle but stimulating.

He grins up at you, raises his eyebrows, and abruptly ceases, moving to your thighs, kissing and gently biting his way from your knees back to where he started. He pauses momentarily, and you savor the moment of anticipation. Instead of moving back down, he climbs back onto the bed and removes his shorts. Using the smooth, hot shaft of his cock, he pushes gently between your legs and strokes up and down, up and down. You look down between you and the sight of you joined, but not quite, together with the feel of him on your now ultra-sensitive skin, brings you quickly to the edge. You grasp him hard to you as you climax, and thrust yourself into him while burying your head in his neck as you moan with desire.

When the waves of pleasure finally begin to subside, you reach down, ready to return the favor. But Bodhi gently lifts your hand to his lips, bites your palm softly, and then covers it with a kiss. He shakes his head and lifts his shorts back up, gingerly zipping them over his arousal. You giggle at the sight, "Bodhi!"

"I'll be good in a few minutes," he says with a raspy sigh as he cuddles up behind you on the bed. "It's kind of a tantric thing, a little self-deprivation," he explains. "Just wait until I get you to Kauai!" You resist the urge to thrust backward into him, knowing that would be a hugely unfair tease.

"I can't wait," you tell him, with complete sincerity. After a few blissful minutes, Bodhi kisses you on the neck then rises and rifles through his chest of drawers, tossing a few last items into the duffle bag. You lie on the wonderfully soft bed and stare up at the ceiling, painted with an intricately patterned cream medallion surrounded by gold. You can't help but wonder again about the decorator.

"So, who's this mystery designer anyway? She must be the best-kept secret in LA."

"She," says Bodhi, as he gazes down at you and strokes a finger along your upper arm, "was someone who moved in for a while and who was really into making this place her personal domain. It's grown on me, though, so I kept it."

You can't help but wonder who that "someone" might have been.

"Everything looks so new. How long ago was this?"

"About six months," Bodhi tells you, moving across the room to zip his duffel bag. You sense a change in his tone.

Six months ago? Bodhi was dating—no, living with—a girl only six months ago and he never even mentioned it? You feel an unwelcome stab of jealousy as you pull down your skirt and stand up from the bed.

Bodhi buttons his white oxford-cloth shirt, then brushes past you as he heads to the bathroom. You stand stock-still, leaning against the doorframe.

"What's up?" Bodhi asks as he reemerges. "You're suddenly quiet."

You're not sure what to say. You've made so many assumptions about who Bodhi is that you're suddenly uncertain you know him as well as you thought.

"I just—I never even realized you lived with anybody."

"Well"—Bodhi plants a firm kiss on your lips and runs his fingers tenderly along your jawline before he swings the duffel over his shoulder, his eyes gleaming—"I guess I'm just full of surprises." He grabs your hand and leads you from the apartment.

The skies are a brilliant sapphire as your little plane finally touches down on a runway lined with swaying palms. The sultry island air embraces you as you walk the short stairway to the tarmac and then into the open-air terminal. Bodhi collects your bags and takes you by the hand. You have no idea what's in store but you're determined to let him lead you willingly into whatever comes next.

You share a string of exquisite days and incredible nights in a tiny villa with a thatched roof. The days and nights fly by in a haze of warm air, warm water, and warmer breezes. The balmy weather requires almost no shelter but for the occasional shade of a palm tree. Bodhi spends hours each day surfing the regular and perfectly curled waves that roll onto the pink sand outside your rustic home. You alternately read, sleep, and watch him surf beneath the warm sun.

At night, you admire his deepening tan and his washboard stomach, running your fingers down the hard rippled surface, and he shows you how much he admires every inch of your body. The temperature never veers below seventy-two or above eight-five degrees. This is your idea of heaven.

On the Tuesday morning of your third week in paradise, you wake from a deep and dreamless sleep to the sound of a female voice coming from outside the bedroom. You sit up and push aside the gauzy mosquito netting that hangs protectively around your bed. You listen, catching only bits of the conversation from the front of the house. The female voice floats toward you, followed by the low resonance of Bodhi's response, then the laughter of both voices intermingling. You swing your feet onto the warm, dark wood floor and pull on your robe. Before you leave your room, you take a quick glance as you walk by the mirror and stop to push the rogue strands of hair back from your face.

You peek around the thick, wood doorway to see Bodhi lounging on a low rattan sofa, his arm around a breathtakingly beautiful young girl, obviously of Hawaiian descent. Her sleek black hair swings heavily around her shoulders as she laughs and her perfect chestnut arms and legs are inclined toward Bodhi in an intimate manner. You feel an immediate surge of jealousy and stop your instinct to advance, pausing to collect yourself.

Well, you tell yourself, *Bodhi never said anything to indicate any kind of commitment.* You remind yourself of your obligations on the mainland and of the glamorous and hectic life you've left behind. Did you really think this would last forever?

"I know," says the woman in a melodious, velvety voice with just a trace of an accent, peeking sideways at Bodhi through her veil of jet-black hair. "I missed you so much." She smiles at Bodhi, and he reaches over to squeeze her knee affectionately.

"I just hate it that I never know when or for how long I'll get to see you."

"Well," replies Bodhi, and you don't think you've ever seen him look happier than when he tells her, "I'm working on making this a more permanent arrangement."

You pause at the door and look at the floor. It was inevitable that you would have to awaken from this dream at some point, and now is as good a time as any. You think about your options. You could quietly pack your bags and sneak out the door off of the bedroom, across the little wooden path, and be gone within the hour.

You glance out the window into the surrounding garden of wide, glossy-leafed palms, the early-morning sun filtering in slashes to the ground. You listen for a moment to the hypnotic sound of waves gently crashing on to the beach. This really is paradise. It's a heavenly illusion, and one you hate to surrender.

You're torn between the prospect of facing the fallout that awaits you back in LA and the prospect of facing Bodhi's mystery woman. Maybe it would be best to leave Bodhi to his own bliss. He didn't really mean to ask you to accompany him here anyway. You pretty much invited yourself, practically forced him to bring you. What was he going to do, say no to his boss?

Bodhi thinks you're still sleeping, and you know you have a decision to make.

To sneak out of the bungalow and return to LA, turn to page 159.
To meet Bodhi's mystery woman, keep reading.

You take a breath and enter the room, mustering the bravest smile you can. Approaching the seated couple, you extend your hand and introduce yourself.

"Hi there. I'm Anna."

The woman jumps to her feet and again you're stunned by her beauty and by her height. She stands at least four inches taller than you. Her body is long and slender; her hair falls perfectly to her tiny waist. She looks like a beautiful, traditional Hawaiian doll. She shakes your hand, and you notice her long, strong fingers and perfect but unpolished nails.

"Of course I know who you are," she responds enthusiastically. "Even if you weren't famous, Bodhi's told me so much about you. I'm so glad to finally get to meet you!"

Wow, you think, *what a tolerant woman.* Bodhi's been telling her all about you (while telling you nothing about her) and she's thrilled to make your acquaintance?

"You are so much prettier in person!" she says, "I mean, I always thought you were gorgeous, but seeing you now, wow! And you just rolled out of bed? I mean, this is just so neat!"

Neat? Her childlike enthusiasm is oddly disarming and strangely familiar. She seems to be totally unaware of her own physical beauty. You're starting to warm to her in spite of yourself.

"Oh my gosh." She blushes. "I haven't even introduced myself. I'm Lana."

"What a pretty name," you tell her, then cutting your eyes to meet Bodhi's, "and what a pretty girl."

Bodhi rises from the couch, stands by Lana's side, and returning your gaze, drapes his arm around her shoulders.

"Well, I knew you two would meet sooner or later," he says. "I just hope you don't mind the early hour. And I'm really hoping you two will hit it off," he adds, crossing his fingers.

He gives Lana's hand a little squeeze and clears his throat before saying, "Anna, this is my sister, Lana."

"Your sister?" Relief sweeps over you as you give her a hug full of the instant affection you feel. "You never told me you had a sister! I'm so glad to meet you! Bodhi, how come you never told me?"

"I don't know," says Bodhi. "I guess I wanted to see how things went between us before I got the family involved." He cocks an eyebrow and gives you a half-smile. "You know, Lana can be pretty pro-tective."

Lana gives her brother a sisterly punch in the shoulder. "Yeah right! Anna, let me tell you, I've been practically breaking the door down to meet the woman who's been making my big brother so happy."

You blush and smile at her words, and at the thought that his sis-ter approves of the two of you being together.

Bodhi steps to your side and hugs you to him, kissing you ten-derly on the top of your head. "See, Lana, I told you she was great."

You sit down to orange juice and fresh fruit as the warm sun kisses your little group through the open-air porch. You have that ex-cited, Christmas Eve tingle in the base of your stomach as you learn more about Bodhi's family.

Bodhi's sister—well, half-sister—is the proud mother to an adorable and mischievous young boy named Nick. Bodhi's mother met Lana's father on a trip to Hawaii a year after Bodhi's dad passed away, when Bodhi was just nine. It was a trip the mature-beyond-his years Bodhi had insisted his mom take, and one he paid for with his childhood acting career savings. He wanted nothing more than to help his mom to recover from her grief.

Little did he know her trip would change his life as well as hers. His mother first befriended and then fell in love with a dashing and jovial Hawaiian that Bodhi soon would affectionately call "Pops." Within a year they moved to his successful island coffee bean farm and Lana came soon after. Bodhi, who had never had a sibling, loved his new little sister. They grew up with just enough distance in age to become best friends.

You too find a wonderful friend in Lana. She lets you in on all the secrets of the island and takes you to her favorite spots from markets, to beaches, to mountains. You laugh together as you happen upon a stack of *WE Weekly* magazines, and the headline, *WE EXCLUSIVE! ANNA CHAMBLISS'S HOT DATE NIGHT WITH DRIVER OF MANY YEARS, FORMER CHILD ACTOR, BODHI BANNER. IS ROMANCE IN THE AIR FOR THE HOT STAR AND HER SEXY CHAUFFEUR?* You couldn't feel more distant from the glossy world obsessed with celebrity gossip but you smile at the knowledge that only you and Bodhi know the truth behind the head-line.

Lana's energetic little Nick becomes a "nephew" and refers to you as Aunt Annie. Your days are spent shopping, island hopping, and sunning on the beach. Your figure rounds out a bit, but you don't mind since you no longer have to worry about maintaining the unnatural thinness required for an on-screen career. Besides, Bodhi loves your fuller figure and pays special attention to your new curves.

Bodhi surfs most mornings and works on the coffee farm most days, learning from Pops as he runs and oversees the business. On any given day, Bodhi might be repairing machinery, hiring laborers, hauling huge sacks of beans, or analyzing accounts. He seems to enjoy the work and he returns to you sweaty and spent, hair scraggly and muscles bulging. The two of you make a ritual of an evening shower together, followed by sweet and effortless hours in bed, and then unwind on the tiny beachfront porch to watch the sun set in a dazzling display of oranges, purples, and pinks. You've never felt so relaxed and carefree in your life.

Two months later, you find yourself feeling a little funny, and a trip to the doctor confirms what you already suspect. You are pregnant with Bodhi's child. You and Bodhi plan a sunset wedding ceremony on the beach, with Lana as your maid of honor and little Nick serving as ring bearer. Your mom and brothers fly in for the wedding, as does Buffy. No one else from Hollywood attends, and that suits you just fine. Your wedding makes the tabloids back on the mainland, but the only ripples you feel here on the island are of pure happiness.

As you and Bodhi walk hand-in-hand down the sandy aisle, your guests applaud and smile. The sun sets behind you and you're warmed by the thought of the new life growing inside of you, and the knowledge that you've finally found your paradise.

THE END
**To take Anna on a new Bedventure, go back and choose
a new path.**

From page 18...
"Why not take a chance?" you mutter under your breath. Your heartbeat quickens at the thought of Colm on your arm as you walk the red carpet that evening.

"What did you say?" asks Bodhi.

"Nothing," you tell him distractedly. "I think I actually have someone I should take."

The reflection in the rearview mirror shows Bodhi's face drop, making your heart clench.

"It's just a PR thing, Bode. You'd hate it. Believe me."

"It's cool." Bodhi's mouth hardens into a thin line as the car glides gracefully back to the hotel.

Buffy greets you, curling iron in hand, as you enter the suite.

"Let's do it," she says, gesturing toward the dressing table.

"Wait, wait," you respond. "I have something I have to do first." You pause for a moment and think. "Would you mind going out in the hall for a minute?"

"What? Why? Are you okay? It's not like I haven't seen—"

"No—I just—" You hold your breath and decide to spill. "Okay, I'll tell you, but promise you won't laugh."

Buffy leans back against the doorframe, crosses her arms, smiles, and waits.

"Promise?"

"Seriously?" She moves to the vanity table and sets the curling iron down with a *thunk*. "What's the big deal?"

"I have to make a phone call."

"You need me to leave the room so you can make a phone call?"

"I had no idea I had to take an escort to this thing tonight. Luckily Bodhi told me."

Buffy leaps from the doorway and hops up in the air, curls bobbing. "Ohhhh . . . I get it. You're asking Mr. Irish Eyes to go with you!" She hops forward and gives you a patented Buffy hug, long and strong. "I think it's great!"

You roll your eyes as she releases you from her grasp. "Scottish, Buff. And I'm glad you approve, but I feel kind of funny calling him with someone else in the room, so . . ."

"Okay, how 'bout if I go into the bathroom and try to figure out the proper lingerie for you? Those grandma pants you have on definitely won't do."

"Oh, stop." You smile. "You know I'm not that kind of girl."

"That's too bad," Buffy teases. "Sounds like you might be in for a fun night."

"We don't have to do *that* to have fun," you retort.

"I guess." Buffy shrugs as she heads for the bathroom, "But if he happens to find the keys to your chastity belt, at least you'll be ready."

You laugh as she skates off to the bathroom and shuts the door firmly behind her.

Colm's business card is safely tucked into the bottom of your clutch. You pick up the bedside phone and dial for an outside line. Pacing as far as the phone cord will allow, you start to rehearse what you're about to say. Before you have a chance to come up with anything, a thickly accented voice answers.

"Colm?" you ask.

"It is," he replies. The rich sound of his voice sends shivers up your spine.

You hesitate for a moment then go for it. "Um, this is Anna . . . Chambliss . . . from this morning? We met at the interview?"

Ugh, you think. *Could you sound any lamer?*

"Uh, no, actually. Anna who?"

Your heart drops as you realize you've made so little an impression that he doesn't even remember you from a few hours before. What do you do now? A sickening silence fills the air between you.

"Anna?" asks the voice on the other end of the line.

"I'm here," you tell him in a slightly strangled voice.

Colm breaks into a deep-throated laugh. "Anna, I'm having you on. Of course I remember you. How could I forget?"

You breathe an enormous sigh of relief and smile. "I completely thought you were serious."

"I could tell," Colm says, still laughing. "Sorry, I couldn't resist."

You laugh, too, and your heartbeat starts to slow a little.

"So . . . are you calling to retract everything you told me this morning?"

"No, no. Not at all. In fact, I can't wait to see how the piece turns out. I really enjoyed the interview with you. You did a great job."

"Mmmmm," purrs Colm, his accent suddenly stronger. "Flattery will get you at least five more lines."

This gets you laughing again. You feel like a teenager, unable to control your giggles.

"Actually, I am calling for a reason." You pause again to regain your composure. How do you do this, anyway? You've never really asked a guy out before, and certainly not one you've just met that morning. This is totally unfamiliar ground and not comfortable in the least.

But Colm makes it easy. "Let me test my telepathy skills," he says. "You're calling to tell me what an incredibly sexy specimen of masculinity I am, and that you simply cannot do without me another minute of your life."

A blush heats your cheeks as he hits the mark much more closely than he knows.

"Uh, that's close." You laugh. "I actually called to ask you an enormous favor. And please feel free to say no." You stop pacing and force yourself to place the business card you've been nervously massacring with your fingernails onto the cold, marble countertop. You clear your throat to continue.

"I have this thing tonight—it's one of those boring benefits where they drone on and on about the latest cause, and this one's a doozy . . . Anyway, the dinner is most likely going to be barely palatable, and the drinks watered down, but . . . turns out I need to bring a date—I mean an escort—I mean . . . Well, I mean, I was wondering if you might be available to join me."

After a long silence, Colm responds with a low laugh. "Well, you've made the evening sound absolutely scintillating. How could I possibly resist?"

"You can, I mean, really, if you have something else to do . . ."

"Anna, not only do I have nothing else planned, but I wouldn't pass up a chance to share an evening with you for the world. Plus, it will certainly help to flesh out my article."

Laughter bubbles up again inside as you realize you have, for the first time, asked a man on a date—and you succeeded! "Okay, then! Great! I'll have my driver come get you at . . . seven?"

Colm laughs yet again, "I think it would be more proper if I come pick up you. Where are you staying?"

"Who said chivalry is dead?" you ask, and direct Colm to your hotel.

Much to your surprise, the VIPP dinner seems to fly by. After the headliner, famously botched rock legend, Maxx Swagger, finishes his speech, you barely listen to the endless donation appeals that follow, intent instead on your conversation with Colm. There hasn't been a single lull or dull or awkward moment. For the sake of intimacy in this fairly public setting, you scoot closer and closer to Colm, until your legs just touch beneath the table. You're all too aware of the heat generated between the two of you, and you wonder whether Colm has noticed it, too.

Colm speaks like a born storyteller. "So, my childhood was kind of a fairy tale, if I'm honest. Not that it was perfect, but my memories are warm ones. Lots of cousins around all the time, games of hide-and-seek in foggy fields of heather, that kind of thing. Da inherited some property, so we never really had to want for much, and he did love his woodworking. Learned the craft from his father before him, my Grandda, and toiled away for hours in his workshop. Drove my Ma almost to drink it did, with us wee ones running around and him coming in late with his hands full of splinters and smelling of varnish. But the beautiful items he made always made Ma smile, and she was proud of her beautiful home, and happy that he was happy."

You smile as he laces his fingers with yours under the table, tracing the outline of your palm with his slightly rough thumb as he continues. "I was always dyin' to know how Da took those rough-hewn lengths of walnut and cherry and transformed them into something altogether different, the hard edges softened and glowing, the joints of each piece fitting together just so. When I was finally grown enough he let me watch him work, still not trusting me around the lathe and saws, but soon he was letting me help and teaching me his craft. I had a knack, he saw, and I loved learning." He breaks off and gazes out into the middle distance, then gathers himself up, as if returning to reality. "But, as Da always said, you can't make a living in a workshop, not the kind of living he wanted for me, anyway, and I always did love to write. Took top honors in school for it, then came to the States for a degree with some meat to it. So here I am, just a touch disillusioned that *WE*'s been my only offer so far, but I'm just getting started. Didn't quite know it would be so dog-eat-dog out here, you ken?"

Gazing into his eyes, you feel you've known Colm far longer than the brief time you have, and you're suddenly sad that the evening has to end. As the last speech comes to a close and the applause dies down, Colm leans back in his chair to stretch his muscular arms. You can't help but feast your eyes on the play of the crisp white cotton of his shirt against the firm flesh beneath. Neither of you has made much of a dent in the now cold mushroom-smothered chicken on your plates. Colm reaches his large, warm arm over your chilly shoulders and inclines his head to whisper, "So, would you fancy getting some real dinner?"

You smile. "Sounds perfect," you say.

Colm takes you to his favorite Italian restaurant and orders a bottle of wine. You can't get over how much you're enjoying his company and hope that the feeling is mutual. You order a sinful lobster-filled ravioli and savor every bite. Colm wolfs down his thick slab of beef lasagna in what seems like three bites. You find yourself leaning over the table to bridge the distance between you, unconsciously twirling a lock of hair around your finger as you and Colm trade childhood stories. You feel you could listen to his voice forever.

Sometime during the dinner, he's taken your hand across the table and gently massages your fingers as you talk. Could you really be feeling this strongly after knowing Colm for only one full day? You know you'll be awake tonight analyzing and replaying every perfect moment.

At midnight, Colm suggests he take you back to the hotel, remembering your early flight the next morning. He pulls the car slowly into the circle in front of the hotel and comes to a stop, lingering for a moment before putting the car into Park. Is it your imagination or is he as hesitant as you are to let this night end?

"Well, Anna," he begins, "I can't thank you enough for a lovely evening. I truly can't remember the last time I enjoyed myself so much."

You feel another blush rise to your cheeks. "Me too. I can't think of anyone I would have rather spent the night with—I mean the evening with. I mean . . ."

What is wrong with you? You've never been this tongue-tied and awkward around a man. You shake your head in embarrassment and look down at your hands.

Colm takes your left hand in his and gently lifts it to his lips. The soft brush of his kiss sends a tremble all the way to your toes. You look up to his eyes and he returns your gaze, your hand still in his. His right hand reaches up to the back of your neck and he gently but firmly takes the small of your neck in his large, warm hand and pulls you close, looking deeply into your eyes. You catch your breath as he pulls you into him, and your lips meet in the most effortlessly amazing embrace you've ever experienced. You feel as though you're spinning as he kisses you deeply, and you see fireworks burst behind your closed eyelids. You never really believed that actually happened! You reach out to run your fingers through the thick, soft hair at the nape of his strong neck and are overwhelmed by the heat rushing through your body.

You kiss and kiss again, feeling like a girl on her first date, when kisses meant everything.

Much too soon, Colm pulls gently away. You breathe in his fragrance, masculine and musky. You feel safe and warm, and like nothing else matters but the two of you in this moment. The feel of his broad, firm chest under the cool, smooth fabric of his shirt against your skin is almost too much to bear.

He moves to look again into your eyes, rests his forehead against yours, and, smiling, gives you the smallest kiss on the tip of your nose. You return his smile and brush your cheek against the roughness of his face, and feel completely at home. Your heart beats fast and you realize you're feeling something entirely new: a need to be with this man that overpowers every other need you've ever known.

You have the overwhelming urge to tell him that you love him, but how silly would that be? You silently chide yourself. Is there such a thing as love at first sight? You've never believed it, but maybe . . .

"Well," says Colm, still smiling in the most adorably handsome way possible.

You look at him and smile in return, then take what feels like the first breath of your life.

"You've an early plane to catch," he says, "and I've kept you late enough already."

"I'll be fine," you tell him. "I can always sleep on the plane."

"Well, in any case"—Colm smiles—"I need my beauty sleep. I've an early date with a cubicle."

"You're welcome to come up . . . for coffee . . . if you'd like," you offer.

"Anna, I would love to—you've no idea—but honestly, this night has been so perfect . . . we should sleep on it, don't ye think?"

You manage a smile around the profound disappointment you feel. "Okay. You're right. It's just, I hate the fact that I'll be leaving in the morning for so long, and this time with you has been so wonderful, and we've had so little of it."

You realize you sound close to desperate, but you just can't stop yourself from trying for a few more moments with this incredible man.

Colm looks at you tenderly and takes both of your hands in his, then presses his slightly callused palms against yours.

"Anna, I have loved this, every single moment. And it has been too short. But I'm a believer in fate, and I know that if it's meant to be, it will be. Even if it is in a few months' time."

Although you can't stand the thought of being apart for even a second, you know in your heart that he's right. You take his face in your hands, kiss him deeply one last time and thank him for a magical evening. As you pass through the door to the hotel and walk toward the elevator, you wonder if you look as transformed as you feel.

From page 37, from page 44 (and continued from above) . . .

Back in your hotel room, you fall into a dreamless sleep until the phone rings loudly, jolting you awake in what must be the middle of the night. You brush your hair off of your face and squint at the bedside clock. *Five a.m.* Could it possibly be morning already? Thoughts of the day ahead immediately assail your sleepy mind. You push back the warm blankets, swing your legs over the edge of the bed, and rub your eyes. All at once, the memory of the night before catapults into your consciousness and you freeze on the edge of your bed in that twilight state where dreams and reality intermingle. You shiver at the confusing jumble of memories.

You stumble out to the foyer and quickly scan the flimsy industry newspaper, *The Dailies,* slid under your door in the wee hours of the night. You don't have to look far for the headline about you: IT HASN'T EVEN BEEN A HOLLYWOOD MINUTE SINCE HER BREAKUP WITH **HAMPTON**, BUT IS ANNA ALREADY ONTO A NEW ROMANCE?

Really, this so-called news source has become just as bad as the tabloids. You don't bother to read the rest of the article but toss the paper onto the bedside table and gather your messy hair into a ponytail. Suddenly the day ahead doesn't look so bad.

Arriving at the airport, you offer Bodhi a quick goodbye and wish him a happy vacation.

You luxuriate in the sunlight streaming through the little window of your private jet and listen to the familiar sounds of pre-flight preparations. You're completely lost in thoughts of the night before when Buffy comes bouncing up the aisle and lands in the seat next to yours, making you jump.

"Did I scare you?" she laughs. "You almost leapt out of your seat! What are you dreaming about anyway? Your upcoming quality time with J-Mike?"

"J-Mike? Oh Lord"—you laugh nervously—"you've already given him a nickname?"

"He is smokin' hot, don't try to deny it! How can I help myself?"

"Cool your jets, Buffy," you say, not even trying to stifle a yawn. "Believe me. He's not all that."

"Bah humbug! Someone woke up on the wrong side of the bed!" Buffy says, kicking off her clogs and stretching her legs out in front of her. "Ahhh, this is the life!"

You stare out the window in silence, hoping Buffy will actually notice you have something else on your mind.

Finally, it clicks.

Buffy turns to you slowly, narrowing her eyes. "So, what is up with you? What happened last night anyway?"

"Last night? Nothing!" You can't help feel a twinge of panic at how close to home she's hit.

Buffy laughs, reaching up to adjust the fan above her seat, then stops when she notices your expression.

"What is that look?" she asks you.

You see the opportunity and take it. "I don't know," you tell her. "I was just thinking about Colm. The guy is pretty great."

"Great like you're writing your first name with his last name in your notebook great?"

"Come on, you know what I mean," you say with a chuckle. "He's just seems like a real person—you know—totally grounded."

Buffy, never afraid to ask the hard questions, asks a doozy. "You sure he's not gay?"

"Buffy!" you scream, laughing and embarrassed at the same time. She certainly knows how to cut to the chase. "Not gay. Definitely not gay. But that's not what I meant."

"I know. I'm just kidding," Buffy assures you. "But take it slow. You just met the guy."

"Just worry about yourself, missy. And 'J-Mike,' of course," you tell her, successfully diverting the conversation back to Buffy's favorite subject.

As the little plane circles the tiny white islands below and begins its descent toward the brilliant, turquoise sea, you replay the memory of your evening over and over in your head. The thought makes a hot blush rise from your neck despite the chill of the stale, re-circulated cabin air.

You distract yourself from the nervous pit in your stomach with thoughts of Colm. What would it be like to have him by your side, helping you off the plane, carrying your luggage, settling into the production trailer you would be sharing? At least it's a fantasy you can hold close as you navigate the uncomfortable, early days on set with an unfamiliar cast and crew.

From page 163 (and continued from above) . . .

The flight seemed to have passed in an instant, and before you know it you are taxiing along a runway lined with swaying palm trees. You emerge from the plane into a sultry tropical breeze. A rickety taxi with no air conditioning takes you directly to the set where folding tables are set up on the beach for your first script meeting and table read. Buffy busies herself inside your trailer, parked in an unglamorous paved back lot on the other side of the low, rocky dunes separating the beach from the main island. Bulky scripts sit squarely at each place along the table. A flowery tropical drink in a coconut shell, complete with a colorful umbrella plus a skewered tower of pineapple wedges and cherries, stands beside each script. *I could get used to this*, you think as you head to the table. A sea-scented breeze gently lifts the hair from the back of your neck.

You find your spot. MS. CHAMBLISS is written in bold script across the front of your book. You look to your left and right and are glad to see that Jackson's spot isn't right next to yours.

Jeff Jeffries, the little balding director, greets you with a sweaty palm. "Well, Ms. Chambliss, so glad you could make it." He looks out of his element in this climate. Sweat beads his head and his linen shirt flaps limply in the island breeze. He compulsively wipes his glasses, steamy from the humidity and heat. "Please summon the rest

of the cast!" he yells over your shoulder at one of the on-set assistants then grins and gestures to his appearance. "What we don't do
for our art," he says with a grimace as he takes his place at the head
of the table.

You can't help but laugh to yourself. What would be many people's idea of paradise is almost insufferable to Jeff Jeffries. He'd be
more at home on the streets of New York in winter, but he's the best,
so he's here.

"Jeff," you begin, "I really need to speak with you for just a few
moments before we begin. It's about Jackson—" Before you can finish, the remainder of the cast arrives to take their seats. The crew
finds spots on the low chairs scattered about in the sand, and you see
Jackson swagger onto the set. You have to admit, he's strikingly
handsome with his slightly too-long hair blowing in the breeze and
his tanned skin glistening in the heat. The backdrop of white rock
creates an appealing contrast.

Jeffries places a sweaty palm on your shoulder, "We have plenty
of time to talk, Anna, plenty of time. But we need to get this show on
the road. Time is money, and today all I've been doing is watching it
slip through my fingers." He scoops up a handful of sand and lets it
slide from his hand in illustration. "Can it wait?"

"Uh, I don't really—" You are interrupted again as Jackson
makes his way to your side.

"Well, if it isn't Ms. Anna Chambliss! Fancy meeting you here,"
he drawls in mock amazement.

Jackson pulls out the chair nearest his script but, before he can settle in, Jeffries stops him. "No, no, no," he sighs in exasperation. He
waves his hand impatiently at Jackson, gesturing to the chair beside
yours. "You two need to sit next to each other. Here, honey," he says
to the older woman currently occupying the seat beside yours. She's
a well-known character actress you've met at many parties but you
can't remember her name at the moment. "You two switch."

She obediently rises and gracefully moves to the other side of the
table, while Jackson plops unceremoniously into her now-empty
seat, spreading his legs wide and leaning back in his chair, script in
hand. He doesn't say a word, but reaches for his coconut, takes a sip,
and winks, smirking in your direction. You roll your eyes dramatically and wait for the table read to begin.

Midway through the reading you find your mind drifting. The sun on your back, the tiny bit of the drink you've sipped, and your lack of sleep combine to make you feel like you're about to fall into coma. Images of Colm keep popping into your head like bits of a dream—the fabric of his jacket straining against his broad shoulders, the rough stubble beginning to show along his jawline, his warm and spicy scent . . .

Suddenly a balled-up object flies at you.

"You awake, there, Sweetheart?"

The launcher is none other than Jackson, and you awaken to find everyone staring impatiently in your direction.

You smile lamely, picking up the napkin and using it to blot your glistening forehead before tossing it back in Jackson's direction. "Sorry, I'm just a little overheated."

"I'll say," remarks Jackson. "Your line, darlin.'" He turns his attention back to the script.

Late that night, as you are finally putting your feet up in your trailer after a long day of readings, costume fittings, and meetings, Buffy settles down next to you with a glass of red wine. You feel oddly uneasy but you can't really pinpoint why. Maybe you just need to catch up on sleep, but suddenly you're not a bit tired.

"What's going on in that head?" Buffy asks.

"Nothing really," you tell her. "I just need to get settled in I guess. It's so weird—I can't stop thinking about Colm." What you don't say is that Jackson keeps popping into your head too, and the look in his eyes as he jolted you from your trance at the table read. You really do need to have a talk with Jeffries. But still, Jackson was relatively inoffensive on set today. Maybe the stress of the new shoot and the sudden change in costar is getting to you. Could it be possible you are overreacting?

"Well," says Buffy, "I say we take your mind off your troubles and play some rummy. What do you say?"

Buffy grabs a deck of cards from the tiny kitchenette and shuffles them expertly. She deals and takes the first turn. Little does she know the card game does anything but provide the intended distraction. Finally you decide to share.

"It's just grating on me already. All day Jackson seems to be everywhere I am. He even showed up during one of my fittings. He just has such nerve. I mean, what is he thinking? I keep feeling like he could come crashing through the door any minute, wherever I am. It's like having the paparazzi here on set. I have to keep avoiding him but I can't. I guess he just doesn't get it. I know he's new at this, but seriously."

"Well it's probably only going to get worse. You should see your wardrobe for the beach scenes. Pretty skimpy," Buffy teases.

"Ha, ha." You know she's trying to lighten the mood, but this whole day has given you a cold feeling in the pit in your stomach. "Seriously, do you think he's anything to be concerned about?"

"Are you serious, Anna? I think the sun is getting to you. He's totally harmless. There are tons of people around. Besides, I'm still planning to put myself between him and you at some point."

A line of concern appears between Buffy's ginger-colored brows. "Anna, why would you even feel like that about him?"

You're not sure how much to tell her about why you feel how you feel, and now you've begun to doubt yourself. Maybe you need to give Jackson a second chance. "Buffy, he—" you begin, but something stops you from elaborating. "I don't really know, Buff. I just get a weird vibe from him, I guess," you tell her, completely understating the truth. You fan your cards out, draw, and quickly discard. "You know how they always say you should listen to your gut?"

"Well," says Buffy, an impish grin on her face, triumphantly grabbing the card you've just thrown down, "my gut is telling me he is one fine-looking specimen just waiting for the right woman to set him straight."

"Maybe you're right," you tell her, though the sense of uneasiness still grips you. "You're probably right."

Day one of shooting is decidedly less pleasant than you were hoping. Between the grit of the sand, the sticky saltwater clinging to every exposed inch of makeup-covered skin on your body—and there are lots of exposed inches—and the bikini bottom that keeps riding up every time you walk more than two steps, you are more than ready for the sunset, which will shut down production for the day.

Between shots, Jackson finds himself a lounge chair and plops down, one hairy leg hanging over, and assesses you with amusement as costume and makeup flurry in to blot your face, adjust your bikini, and de-frizz your hair. *It's so much easier for guys*, you think. *So not fair.*

At last, the sun reaches the critical angle and Jeffries calls cut for the final time. You cannot wait to strip off the cloying bikini, the heavy fake eyelashes, and the pasty makeup you can feel running in sweaty rivulets down your neck and chest.

When the water in your tiny trailer shower finally runs clear, you blot dry with the soft towel Buffy brought you from home. She's gone off to find something refreshing and hopefully alcoholic for you to sip. You crank up the air conditioner and lounge on the trailer sofa, cooling off after the long day. Buffy returns in a flurry, hoisting a tall, frosted glass filled with something purple and delicious-looking into your hands. She begins talking before you can get a word in.

"Oh my gosh, Anna, I am so excited. Guess what? The whole cast and crew is going into town tonight to check out the local scene. Jeffries rented like a whole bar and there's going to be a reggae band and open bar, and island food, and probably dancing. He wanted to surprise everybody after the first day of shooting, so . . . and guess what? Everyone's going. Like everyone. Even Jackson, I mean. But of course I have nothing to wear. All I brought are shorts and bathing suits. I didn't really think I'd be doing anything but working. But now, I mean I guess I can wear some shorts, but I'd really like to look a little cuter. Maybe I just shouldn't go." She plops down despondently beside you. "Yeah, I'll just stay here."

You feel your instant affection for this girl who has become your best friend and who always makes you smile.

"Buffy," you tell her, "of course you're going. We're going. Come on, I brought way too many clothes."

You rifle through your luggage and play dress-up until you find something that fits Buffy perfectly, a stretchy little sundress that falls lower on her legs than it does on yours but clings beautifully, accentuating her tiny waist. The airy fabric sways as she walks, making the most of her adorable curves. She looks in the mirror and glows, running her hands down her sides and then executing a joyous little twirl. "Thank you so much!" she gushes. "You're sure this is okay?"

You feel a thrill at how happy she is. "Of course it's okay. But I'm not finished yet. Sit down."

She perches on one of the tiny kitchenette stools and you duck into the bathroom for your makeup bag.

The immediate look of alarm on Buffy's face is almost comical.

"Um, Anna, thanks but I can do that—it's kind of what I do, you know."

"No you're not. It's my turn tonight." You search through your bag for the big, fluffy makeup brush and jar of loose powder, "Don't worry, I've learned a thing or two watching you. Besides, I have a vision."

Fifteen minutes later you run the brush over her forehead and cheeks once more for good measure and tell her to open her eyes. Not too bad, if you do say so yourself.

You spin Buffy to face the mirror and are gratified by the look in her eyes. She turns her head slowly to admire both profiles and bats her long lashes. "Well, Mr. Demille," she purrs, "I do believe I'm ready for my close-up."

The bar is loud and smoky when you arrive. Dreadlocked Rastas on a little wooden platform in the corner croon unintelligible lyrics to a steel drum beat. Buffy leads you by the hand to a table in the center of the room, clearly enjoying the eyes that turn to watch you as you walk by. You're wearing a thin cotton sundress, too, still trying to cool down from the heat of the day. You've pulled your hair into a simple twist off your neck and the slight breeze from the ceiling fans overhead feels delicious.

You sit and tap your foot absentmindedly to the rhythm and look around the room. The bar is crowded with crew members tossing back neon-colored shots. A few members of the cast have taken to the dance floor. You and Buffy spot Jackson at the same moment. He's chatting with Jeffries, facing away from you and rocking back at a precarious angle in his teak chair.

"BRB," Buffy says, and sashays over to the bar, making sure to cross in front of Jackson's sightline. To her credit, she does a good job of appearing to make a beeline for the bar while attracting more than a few glances from the men, Jackson included. His gaze flickers down the braided fabric at her back, lands on her backside, and affixes itself there for a few noticeable seconds before breaking free to return to the director.

She comes back with two frosty-looking tropical drinks and sets them on the table. "Thanks." You lean in and whisper, "Guess who was checking you out just now."

Buffy's eyes widen. "Seriously?"

"No joke. Along with like every other guy in this place. But Jackson definitely noticed."

"Yes!" she squeals. "Maybe I do have a chance with him after all?"

"I still don't see what you see in him," you tell her, "but he'd be lucky to have you."

A few glasses of liquid courage later, as the band launches into a well-known Marley song, Buffy giddily grabs your wrist. "Come on! Let's dance!"

You head out into the haze of smoke and sweat on the little dance floor at the front of the room. Before you know it, you feel a hand on your waist pulling you slightly off-balance. You turn to find Jackson at your side as the music slows. He leans in and whispers low into your ear, "May I cut in?"

After a moment of confusion you see his gaze focused solidly on Buffy and realize it's Buffy he wants. "Oh! Sure!" you answer awkwardly and shuffle from the dance floor as couples fall into one another.

You find your table and slowly sip your quickly thawing drink. *God*, you think, *I've probably gained ten pounds here already*. You'll have to hit the gym hard after this. You twirl your straw around in the slushy contents of your glass and look longingly at the dance floor, as Jackson pulls Buffy close and they move to the music. You feel an odd twinge as you watch and can't help but picture yourself in her place. It would be nice, to feel like that again. But you're not really picturing yourself with Jackson. Maybe if it were Colm? Your thoughts are too blurred by the heat and the smoke and the alcohol to know what you're feeling.

The song ends and Buffy leads Jackson by the hand back to your table. The gleam in her eyes is unmistakable. You know this is a dream come true for her, and you're happy she's happy.

"Mind if I join you?" Jackson asks with a smile. You really are trying to keep an open mind but the mix of attraction and aversion you feel whenever he's near is almost overwhelming.

You scoot your chair as far away from his as is politely possible. "Sure. Have a seat."

Buffy and Jackson drink and flirt for the better part of the night. You sip glass after glass of iced water and make small talk with people who approach your table every so often. You have no clue what time it is when Jeffries climbs clumsily onto the bar and raises a toast to the cast and crew, then orders everyone to go home and get some rest, ending with a buzz-killing reminder that tomorrow's shoot schedule begins at seven.

Jackson gets to his feet and stretches like a big cat, a low purr in his throat. "Guess that's our cue."

Feeling like a clumsy third wheel, you push your chair into the table and begin to follow everyone else out the door.

Buffy has hung onto Jackson's every word all night, eyes following his every movement in unabashed adoration. Clearly, she is in heaven. Still, you have a nagging sense that you don't want to leave Buffy alone with this guy.

You linger between the crowd and the two of them, trying to decide what to say or do. Finally, you put your hand over your mouth and yawn hugely, trying to get their attention. "I'm beat," you tell them. "I'm headed back to the trailer. You coming, Buff?"

She begins to detach herself from Jackson's hand but he stops her before she is able. "I've got her," he drawls with a little grin. "Don't worry, mom, I'll have her home by midnight."

You feel an instant sense of alarm and lean in, grabbing Jackson's upper arm, and with a ferocity you aren't expecting, hiss into his ear, "You'd better not hurt her!"

He's taken aback for a moment and reels as though slapped, but he quickly recovers. He wraps his arm snugly around Buffy's waist and pulls her close, scooting deftly around you, and exiting the bar with Buffy in tow. She glances back once and gives you a look of pure, heartbreaking joy.

You sleep fitfully as you wait impatiently for Buffy to return. You turn to glance at the clock every half hour before you finally hear the door open and shut gently. Grateful that she's back safely, you pull the covers tightly around you and fall back to sleep.

The temperature cools a bit and the following days pass almost blissfully on set. Although you're exhausted after long hours of filming, you savor the small moments you get to curl up on a hammock, swinging peacefully between the towering palms gently swaying in the island breeze, the kiss of filtered sunshine on your face. During these quiet moments, you find that memories of your evening with Colm replay over and over in your mind.

Even Jackson manages to be inoffensive and Buffy is mysteriously absent for longer and longer stretches. She hasn't shared the details, but you imagine she and Jackson are probably spending every free moment together and you are happy for her, though you feel a tiny sting of worry each night as you sleep alone in your trailer.

Late one night, you're roused from a deep sleep by the door shutting more loudly than usual. You turn over restlessly and are almost back to sleep when you hear what sounds like sniffling coming from outside your door. You listen quietly until you're sure, then sit up drowsily and reach toward the foot of the bed to retrieve your robe, wrapping it snugly around you. You find Buffy sitting on the little sofa, legs pulled up to her chest. She's sobbing gently into her fists, keys still clutched in one hand.

"Oh, Buff," you walk toward her and wrap your arms protectively around your friend. You feel an instant and instinctive pang of fear. You know Jackson is the cause of this and you can only imagine what he's done.

Buffy sniffles twice and reaches for a napkin from the pile on the table, blows her nose, and looks up to the ceiling, "I'm okay," she says, without meeting my eyes.

You try to be as gentle as you can when you ask, "Buffy, what did he do to you?" Everything in you wants to say, "See, I told you he was horrible," but you know that's not what Buffy needs to hear right now.

"He didn't do anything, Anna!" she replies fiercely. "It's my fault and I should have known I wouldn't be good enough for him. I'm being obsessed and clingy as usual. What is wrong with me?" She bangs her fist hard into the table, shaking loose the neat pile of napkins, and as she does, you notice a red mark on her wrist—no, four red marks, in the unmistakable shape of fingers.

Your eyes widen at the sight. "Buffy! What is this?" You grab her hand and stretch out her arm, getting a better look. "What did he do to you?"

Buffy drops her eyes and wrenches her hand out of yours. "It's nothing, Anna. It wasn't even his fault."

"What do you mean it wasn't his fault? You did this to yourself? I will kill that bastard—I told you, Buff!"

Buffy jumps from the sofa and throws her napkin to the ground. Tears streaming again from her red-rimmed, puffy eyes, she screams, "Anna, you don't know everything!" before marching to her room and slamming the door behind her.

You want to break down her door and demand the details or go hunt Jackson down, but you know it's best to just leave Buffy alone at the moment. You lean back, cross your arms, and wait. A million emotions run through you as you stare at the ceiling and breathe slowly to calm your frazzled nerves.

You awaken to the sun streaming harshly into your eyes through the slatted window above the little sink. The angle of the sofa edge has left an awful stiffness in your neck, and your right hand is tingling with sleep. You wipe the bleariness from your eyes and listen for sounds of life from Buffy's room. Hearing none, you stumble to the shower and turn it on hot, letting the water run over your neck and back as you attempt to wake up.

As you open the door to the bathroom to let the steam escape, you spot Buffy quickly exiting the front door. "Hey!" you yell. "Buffy!"

She turns her head for only a moment and shouts "See you on set" too casually before pulling the door shut.

The days that follow seem interminable and the filming schedule is brutal. Buffy's made it clear she will not talk with you about Jackson, and you try to keep from thinking about what is going on between them. You try several times to broach the subject, only to have Buffy none-too-subtly change it. Even the marks on Buffy's wrist disappeared too quickly—a result of makeup magic, no doubt.

While she's doing your makeup each morning you peek for signs of other bruises or marks, but you can see none. You miss the closeness you shared and feel more alone than ever. Worse, you're starting to feel angry that Buffy has so easily chosen Jackson's affections over your friendship.

Most days you find yourself so exhausted after shooting that you simply come back to the trailer and crash. You're too tired even to feel lonely. You fall asleep each night with thoughts of Colm floating through your mind. You try to conjure his scent, the warmth of his touch, hoping the memory will transform itself into a dream that will comfort you in the night. Sometimes you are aware of Buffy coming into the trailer long after you've fallen asleep, sometimes not.

You're finally granted a day off as filming begins to wrap. You cannot wait for a day of true relaxation, and plan to do absolutely nothing but park yourself on a towel on an unoccupied part of the beach far away from the set.

Your day off dawns with the sky a perfect blue, just a few shades different from the slightly greener and perfectly translucent water below. You stuff your book, your sunglasses, your sunblock, and two bottles of water into your tote, slip your cover-up over your head, and grab a towel.

As you are about to reach for the handle, the trailer door unexpectedly opens. You're momentarily blinded and can scarcely believe your eyes as Buffy hops through the door. It's the first time you've seen her outside of your morning makeup sessions. She catches you so much by surprise that you react instinctively and pull her into a big hug.

She too seems taken off guard and genuinely pleased that you are so happy to see her. For a moment you almost believe everything will be okay.

"So," she begins slowly, "day off, huh? Have any plans?"

"Going to the beach," you tell her. "I cannot wait to just sit. What about you?"

"Just kind of having a low-key day." You notice her eyes don't meet yours as she answers. "Jackson is renting a little skiff from this boat-rental place on the beach. Supposedly there are some gorgeous, untouched, tiny little islands just off the coast. He wants to check it out."

You smile as she looks up at you. "Sounds fun," you say.

Buffy finally manages to look you fully in the eyes. "You know what I was thinking?" Her eyes brighten and widen to their usual starry state. "You should come with us!"

It's the last thing you expect to hear.

"No, Buffy, but thanks. The two of you go. That's the plan. I don't want to be a third wheel."

"You wouldn't, not at all. We would love it if you come. You could get to know Jackson better. He's way different when he's not working. It'll be so much fun!"

Buffy's tone is bordering on frantic as she begins to gather her beach gear into a straw tote. Is there a note of pleading in her voice, or are you imagining things? You never thought you would so much as run into Buffy today, much less be invited along on a boat trip with her boyfriend.

Buffy emerges from the tiny bathroom after a quick change into her swimsuit. She takes a breath and pauses to look up at you. "So?"

"Does Jackson even know you're inviting me?"

"As a matter of fact, it was his idea."

This is more surprising than the invitation itself and now you truly do not know what to think. Buffy's nervous, frantic tone, the pleading note, the whole thing has you thoroughly thrown off, and more than a little worried. You pretend to sort through your beach tote for a minute trying to process it all. Finally you decide to just ask.

"Buffy, what exactly is going on here?"

She laughs and looks away. "Nothing. What do you mean? I'm— we're just asking you to come with us. If you don't feel like it, I get it. It's fine." She takes a breath and finally looks you square in the eyes. "Please come," she says in a tone that melts your heart. "I miss you."

"Buffy, I—" you begin to answer but decide to think it through first. Why would she want you to come along so badly? Why would Jackson even suggest it, if in fact that's how it happened? And why is Buffy suddenly interested in you getting to know Jackson better? Is she asking for help, or does she genuinely miss your friendship?

You think back to the lazy day you have planned and feel pulled in two directions, although you realize one of them is completely selfish. Plus, if you stay, you are going to worry about her all day, and probably not be able to relax. On the other hand, if you do go with them, isn't it going to be weird and awkward? But maybe it's totally innocent and it actually could be fun... and you do miss spending time with Buffy. Suddenly you picture the two of you laughing about everything that's happened these past few weeks, re-connecting as you lie side-by-side on the beach while Jackson snorkels off in the distance.

You so need the rest, but you also need your friend. What should you do?

To say no to Buffy and decide to rest by yourself on the beach, turn to page 94.
To accompany Buffy and Jackson, keep reading.

"Okay," you tell Buffy decidedly, "I'm in."

A look of mixed joy and relief washes over Buffy's glowing face. She claps her hands like a delighted child. "Thank you! I'm so glad you're coming! We'll have so much fun!"

After Jackson finishes the paperwork at the beach-front boat rental stand, he turns and grins playfully as he takes the two of you in. "Well, isn't this a sight for sore eyes. Look at the two of you! I couldn't ask for better company. Ready?"

The scenery along the shoreline is breathtaking. Tall palms sprouting from low, scraggy dunes give way to the stunning contrast of pure white sand against the liquid perfection of the incandescent turquoise water. It's an image you wish you could burn into your memory for any time you need a mental vacation.

A small, red-bordered sign posted on a beach catches your attention. "Let's go check it out," says Jackson, turning the boat sharply toward the shore.

As you approach the deserted shoreline, you squint to try to make out the sign, surely some kind of warning. "It looks like a pretty place to relax. But it's totally deserted," Buffy says.

When you're a few yards from shore, a single, diminutive, and very wrinkled man comes jauntily jogging from a path you couldn't have seen before, two little Jack Russell terriers bouncing along at his feet, as the sign finally becomes legible.

The three of you make the pronouncement at once, "CAUTION, NUDE BEACH!" You laugh hysterically as the fully naked man flops and flaps along the shore in all his glory.

Jackson revs the little motor and cuts away from the beach. "Sorry girls, can't compete with that."

"We wouldn't want you to try!" Buffy tells him, still in hysterics.

You begin to catch your breath, but giggles keep bubbling to the surface as you replay the hilarious scene. You feel yourself finally beginning to relax. Maybe this day will be just what you need after all.

As Jackson steers the boat out into the open water, you look over the side. The view straight to the bottom through the glass-clear water is dizzying. "What's all that?" you ask as Jackson slows the motor over what looks like a line of mossy rocks beneath the surface.

"It's the reef. Pretty, isn't it?" Jackson asks.

You can see the tiny figures of fish darting in and out among the rocks and coral. You feel a swooping sense of vertigo as you realize how deep the water is.

"You know," drawls Jackson, unzipping a sturdy black tote and pulling out a set of masks, snorkels, and fins, "I do believe I'm in the mood for a little sightseeing. Anyone care to join me?"

"We'll pass," Buffy answers for both of you. "Have fun!"

"See ya on the surface, ladies," Jackson says, before pulling on his swim fins and executing a headfirst backflip into the water. He surfaces once, blowing water from his snorkel, then disappears below, leaving you and Buffy bobbing on the gentle current.

You smile at Buffy and lean back against the side of the boat, adjusting the brim of your hat. The strong sun, the warm air, and the gentle rocking has you feeling relaxed.

"How do we know we won't drift away from him?" you ask Buffy.

"He'll stay close," she answers. "Believe me."

You pause for a moment and close your eyes, then take the opportunity to finally ask what's been on your mind.

"Buffy, what is going on with you guys? I've hardly seen you, you don't tell me anything, and now you suddenly invite me to come with you today? Are you two serious? I mean, I can see you like him, and he certainly seems to be into you, but what is the deal?"

Buffy's expression is suddenly dead serious. She peers at you over her huge sunglasses, then says in a whisper, "Okay. I'm going to tell you why I wanted you to come today."

Okay . . . you think as she pauses dramatically.

"I want you to help me find out how serious he really is about me. I want you to test him."

You shake your head and blink at her. "What? What, what, *what?*"

"Listen, it's not a big deal, it's just . . . Okay, so he says he really likes me and that I'm the only one he's seeing, but he's such a flirt and it's hard to tell, so . . . The thing is, I really like him, Anna, I mean, like I *really* like him. I think he feels the same about me, I mean he gets jealous anytime another guy even glances at me. I think this could be the real deal. But then, at the same time, I think maybe he just sees me as an on-set fling. The point is we're about to wrap, and I don't really want to get my heart set on something that's not going to go anywhere after we leave. So, will you help me?"

Buffy ceases her rapid-fire talking, and a million thoughts run through your head. You don't know which one to express first, but you try to dive right in.

"First of all, jealousy does not equate to love. You do know that? And second, why don't you just ask him? Have you even had this conversation?"

"We have, but we don't get a lot of time to talk and when we're together he wants to unwind and have fun. He says he's serious about me and he can be so sweet, always giving me compliments, and he's super attentive when we're together." She bites her lower lip wistfully. "I just so hope this is real, Anna."

You hope for her sake it's real, too, but the more Buffy says the more certain you are he is quite the opposite of serious and probably not anywhere near where Buffy is emotionally. Part of you wants to play along, just so Buffy will be forced to face the facts. But you don't want to hurt your friend, and you know this can only end painfully.

You scan the water's surface for any sign of Jackson before you say more. Water spurts from the tip of his snorkel a few yards away, then the tips of his fins disappear as he dives below the surface.

"Buffy," you begin as gently as you can, "I don't want you to get your heart broken either. I really don't. But why not just let it develop and see what happens? Why not let it take its course?"

Buffy takes off her sunglasses and lays them on a lifejacket sitting on the bottom of the boat. She places her hand gently on her belly and it all becomes much too clear. "There's a reason."

You are stunned into silence and have no idea what to say or do. Should you really "test" this man—who you know will fail miserably—for the sake of your friend's future? Given the bombshell she's just dropped, do you really have any choice? Suddenly this day has taken a turn that makes you wish you had stayed back at the beach, blissfully ignorant. You are at a total loss.

"Where is he?" you ask, as you realize you haven't seen Jackson reemerge. "He can't stay down that long, can he?"

You both begin to get a little panicked. "I hope we didn't drift," says Buffy as she looks over the side of the boat.

You peer over your side and both of you scan the water in silence as you search for Jackson. Each moment that passes with no sign of him makes you more and more anxious. You reach for a set of fins and a mask, when a huge splash of water sloshes over the boat from the stern as Jackson leaps in over the side in one fluid motion.

You and Buffy both jump in fright. "Gotcha!" Jackson yells, amused.

Buffy throws a snorkel at him. "You scared the crap out of me!"

You wonder how much he's heard—and where he has been all this time. If he overheard anything he gives nothing away, confidently pulling the cord on the boat's little engine and steering you toward a tiny dot of land in the distance.

Jackson wades through the water to pull the boat close to the pure-white strand of deserted beach on the tiny out island, this one with no posted warning signs. You hop from the boat and wade through the bath-warm water beside Buffy, as Jackson hauls the anchor up onto the beach. He tosses the snorkel gear, your towels, and various beach bags up onto the beach. Buffy shakes loose a blanket and spreads it gracefully over the sand. Somehow she manages to look entirely relaxed. Meanwhile, you are a bundle of nervous energy.

Jackson plops his glistening body down onto the edge of the towel, unzips his bag, and pulls out a glistening bottle of Jack Daniels along with three clear, plastic cups and another little bottle of an unlabeled liquid. He pours generous servings of both liquids into each cup and passes them around. He downs his like a shot and promptly jogs for the shoreline, dives in, then turns onto his back and swims toward the open water in a graceful backstroke.

Buffy wrinkles her nose at her drink and pours it into the sand, then wades through the gentle surf to join Jackson. You watch as he swims back to meet her and as they embrace, Jackson lifts her squealing into the air and tosses her, laughing, into the water with a splash.

Maybe they are okay, you think as you slowly sip your drink and settle back onto your towel, letting the heat radiating from the sand below and the sun above envelope you.

Before you know it, you're waking up from a dreamless sleep. You're completely disoriented and scramble to push up onto your elbows. The sun is low on the horizon and the sky has taken on an unearthly shade of magenta. You roll onto your stomach and scan the beach for Jackson and Buffy. How long have you been asleep? You must have been more exhausted than you thought. Everything seems strangely blurred in the pinkish twilight. You impatiently push your sunglasses up onto your head, but it doesn't help.

You shake your head hard to bring things into focus, and you spot something lying unmoving a few yards from where you've been sleeping. For a moment your heart catches in your chest and you can't breathe. You peer closely at the still figure of Buffy, then jump up from your spot on the sand to go to her.

Suddenly you hear a splash from the water and a cold wet hand grabs your waist.

"Boo!" Jackson yells, swinging you around, his sopping hair splashing around his sun-bronzed face.

"Jeez, Jackson, that's the second time today!" You feel both silly and incredibly uncomfortable. Maybe you overreacted. Obviously Jackson wouldn't be joking with you if something were wrong.

"Sorry, Sunshine," he drawls with a mischievous grin. "You walked right into that one."

"I can't believe I slept so long. I was just checking on Buffy. Is she okay?"

"Don't worry, Mother Hen, she's safe and sound. Just a little too much sun. She's pretty red but I've dutifully slathered her with fresh sunblock and made sure she's in a shady spot. Note the trees?"

Sure enough, Buffy's blanket is positioned carefully beneath the filtered shade of swaying palms. Still, you're worried about her. She seems to be out cold and something just doesn't feel right. Just then, Buffy startles in her sleep, snorts, and turns onto her side.

"See?" Jackson assures you. "She's just fine."

"What time is it?" The shadows lengthen by the moment. At this latitude, sundown comes early and suddenly.

"No worries, mon," Jackson says in his best Rasta accent. "We in de islands. Jus' hang loose."

"You don't think we should get back? It's getting kind of dark."

"It's all good. It's probably only a twenty minute run back. Remember, we took a few detours getting here. We have plenty of time. Just relax and enjoy it while you can."

You realize he's probably right. Tomorrow will be a day of solid shooting, and this is the only time you'll have to enjoy this beautiful paradise. You gaze over at Buffy again, wishing she were awake to keep you company.

Jackson slides back into the water, floating on his back and splashing around like a little kid. "Man, this is the life. I could do this all day."

"You have been."

"What, don't you swim?"

"Of course I swim. It's great exercise."

"I mean for fun. You know what they say about all work and no play . . ." Jackson trails off in a lazy crawl then turns sharply to send a huge splash of water in your direction. You jump out of the way but not in time to avoid the deluge, and your cover-up is sopping wet.

"Hey!" you shout, marching toward the water. "No fair!"

Jackson splashes you again, this time sending droplets of water all over your sunglasses and hat. "I never said I was playing fair!"

"You asked for it," you mutter, strip your cover-up over your head, and toss your sunglasses and hat onto the blanket. You execute a perfect shallow dive into the crystal water and streamline toward Jackson, surfacing directly in front of him and splashing him squarely in his smug face.

"Ugh!" he sputters, clearing the water from his eyes. You flash a satisfied smile and float away, Jackson-style, letting the salty buoyancy carry you.

The moment you begin to float, memories of childhood summertime fun come flooding back to you.

Jackson floats up beside you and for a moment there is peace between you. When he speaks it is with a quiet reverence. "Beautiful, isn't it?"

You smile up into the spectacular sky, slashed with gold, purple, pink, and indigo. "It is."

Of course Jackson can't let the stillness last for long. You feel a pinch on your upper leg and jump. You didn't even see his hand move toward you.

"Ouch! Jackson, that hurt."

"What are you talking about?" he asks with an impish grin. "Must've been a crab."

"A crab called Jackson!" you shout and leap toward him in the water, trying to pinch anything you can grab.

Suddenly, you are in a full-on water-wrestling match, laughing and splashing like two little kids. You are exhilarated and energized, and having more fun than you've had in a long time. It feels so good to let go and just play.

The sun moves lower on the horizon, and you feel its warm kiss even through the water. The white sand beneath your toes is like silk, and the slight breeze moving through the air feels like a benediction.

Maybe you've done something right after all, taking the time to get to know Jackson and giving him another chance. Maybe you've totally misjudged him. Is it possible your suspicions about him were all in your head, that you reacted too strongly? Or perhaps his time with Buffy has changed him. You go in for one last grab just as Jackson ducks, sending you face-first into the water. He lifts you up and tosses you playfully backward as though you weigh nothing at all.

"Okay," he says. "I surrender."

"You give up way too easily!" you say and giggle.

Jackson advances on you slowly, all gleaming muscle as he threads through the glimmering water. "Oh really?"

Before you know it, he is upon you, firmly holding you by your upper arms. His strong hands send an unexpected wave of pleasure through you. His face is inches from yours, and for a moment you cannot breathe.

You have only a moment to think *I was right* before you decide what to do. Do you give into this moment and let what will happen just happen, let Buffy see the truth and decide what she will, or do you pull away and stay true to your friend, even if she hasn't been completely true to you?

To put an end to it, turn to page 163.
To give in to the moment with Jackson, keep reading.

The spell of the sun, the sand, the salty water, and the undeniable chemistry is too much to deny. Besides, Buffy wanted to know, did know, really. Now she'll know for sure. He pulls you close, one arm slipping to your waist as the other finds the back of your neck. A single kiss, warm and deep, sends you into spirals of dizziness.

All too quickly, Jackson pulls away. Before he leaves you, he leans close and whispers gruffly into your ear, "I told you I never give up." Then he dives under the darkening water, now a mirror for the low-hanging sun, leaving you confused and flustered, fumbling your way back to the beach. You glance guiltily at Buffy's sleeping form. She doesn't appear to have moved an inch.

The next day on set is busy and hot, and you are in every scene without a moment to rest. You're relieved that everything with Buffy seems perfectly normal but wonder how to break the news to her that what she suspected is completely correct.

Jackson doesn't let on that anything happened between the two of you. In fact, he barely acknowledges you unless you are in a scene together, and he's off to his trailer right after every wrap. It's an infuriating game.

*   *   *

One morning in makeup, as Buffy administers a final dusting of powder, she asks off-handedly, "So, what happened between you two?"

You are so surprised by her question you can't answer for a moment, which you know makes you look guilty. Stupidly, you ask, "What are you talking about?"

"Seriously, Anna, I'm not a complete idiot. He's barely said a word to me since we got back."

You take a deep breath and shore up your courage to tell your friend what you know she doesn't want to hear.

"Buffy, I'm really sorry. You asked me to test him and I did. And you were right. He's a complete jerk. He doesn't deserve you."

Buffy looks down at the brush in her hand and breathes deeply. Your heart squeezes in pain for your friend. You hate to see her hurt and disappointed.

She sucks in another breath and looks up again, the essence of the strong, ebullient woman. "You're right. He doesn't. But"—she places her hand on her belly and a small smile lights her eyes—"this one deserves more than an absentee dad. I'm not going to let that happen."

You close your eyes. Although you understand how she feels, you simply can't let your friend make what could be the biggest mistake of her life.

You decide to give it another try. "Buffy, this might sound crazy, but please listen to me. You don't need him. I get the attraction, I really do. He's got this weird magnetism. But you have got to pull yourself away before it's too late." You gesture toward her still-flat middle. "This does not mean you have to be stuck with him."

For a brief moment, you think the message resonates, but then Buffy slaps the makeup brush down on the counter. "What do you mean you 'get the attraction'? I thought you found him utterly repulsive."

"Buffy, I didn't mean—" You break off as Buffy hastily tosses her brushes and compacts into her makeup case and slams it shut. She looks at you with tears in her eyes.

"You know what? You will never, ever know how it feels to live in the shadow every minute, every day, of someone you will never outshine. Do you ever stop to think that everything I've ever wished for, you get? Huh? Do you see that at all? I'm not going to let it happen this time, Anna. I'm just not. Believe it or not, at some point he will see that I can be every bit as desirable as you."

Buffy's words bring tears to your eyes, and you make one last attempt to salvage your friendship. "Buffy, just tell me what you want me to do. I will do anything for you, you know that."

"You know what you can do? Just stay away from us." With that, Buffy bursts through the door, leaving you alone in your chair, ready for your close-up.

That night, there's a light tap on your trailer door. You're instantly hopeful and leap to open it. Your mood immediately darkens as you see not Buffy, but Jackson, standing in the dim moonlight. He leans casually against the doorframe, a bottle of champagne and two glasses in his hands.

He doesn't wait for an invitation before promptly pushing you back into the trailer with a deep, long kiss that makes your head swim. You can taste the alcohol on his breath. You have enough presence of mind to shut the door quickly before anyone sees. You bolt it behind you, stumbling back from Jackson and wiping your mouth with the back of your hand.

Jackson noticeably recoils from your withering look. "Hey," he says indignantly, "that wasn't the greeting I had in mind."

"Jackson," you ask in an unnecessary whisper, "what do you think you are doing?"

He fixes you with a brown-eyed stare and a crooked smile, "Why, I'm celebrating, darlin'." He pops the champagne and begins to pour out two tall, fizzy glasses.

"Don't bother," you tell him. "I'm not drinking tonight."

"Well, that makes one of us," Jackson says with a laugh and downs his glass in one swallow.

You move to the window, push the curtain aside, and peer out. Thank goodness there's no one in sight. You've got to get Jackson out of your trailer.

"What're you looking for, sweetheart?"

Your heart is racing as you try to figure out a way to get him to leave quickly, "Nothing." You think for a minute. "Hey, have you seen Buffy today?"

"Had lunch with her this afternoon. Sweet little thing." He pauses, savoring some memory, "But she's not you, Anna. She's not you."

Clearly Buffy hasn't told him anything. She's probably afraid to scare him away. Or maybe she just wants to handle things on her own, on her own schedule. But the more time that goes by, the harder that might be.

Before you can say another word, Jackson is on you again, kissing you so hard his stubble burns your skin. Why is it that you can't even think when he is kissing you? You allow him to continue a moment longer before pushing him forcibly away.

"What is it, Anna?" Now he's pressing against you, and you can feel the hard insistence of his erection as he moves. His hand lifts the hem of your halter top and his fingers slide roughly below your waistline. "Tell me you don't like this."

His breath is coming hard and fast and yours is too. Why is it that every touch from this brazen man feels like an electric spark against your skin? You feel your head getting light again and want so much to give in to the moment. Now he's kissing you again and you can't even think. His tongue slides wet and strong against yours, and you cannot stop yourself from returning his kisses.

He begins to work on your neck, his mouth sucking greedily and sending waves of pleasure through your body. You finally open your eyes and bring yourself back to the present moment.

"Jackson, stop."

Jackson speaks through his ragged breath, "You like this, Anna, and I do, too. Just stop talking and let me take care of you."

He begins to unbutton your jeans, falls to his knees, and uses his teeth to lower the zipper. Now his mouth is on your stomach, and moving lower. He bites at the top of your lacy thong and as his spiky chin brushes the top of your pelvis, a groan of pleasure escapes your throat.

You shake your head again, willing it to clear. "Jackson. Jackson, please."

Jackson laughs hoarsely. "You don't have to beg, baby. I'll give you anything you want."

"Jackson, enough." He continues to caress you, brushing the tip of his tongue just below your navel. You grab his head and force him to raise his chin. "Jackson, I said enough!"

Finally he seems to hear you and looks up, laughing as he rocks back on his knees. "Now, Anna," he drawls with a smile, "you know that's not enough."

You take a step back and re-zip and button your jeans, smoothing your shirt over your stomach. You look him in the eyes and say quietly, "Jackson, that's enough. Don't make me tell you again."

"Okay, okay, jeez, Anna. Don't get your panties in a bunch. I get the message."

Jackson rises unsteadily to his feet and brings his face inches from yours. "You, my dear, need to learn to have some fun."

You gaze at him icily, finally fully in control.

"You," you tell him, "need to learn to take no for an answer. And you need to have a serious talk with Buffy."

Jackson has the nerve to smile, shrug, and shake his head. He opens the door of the trailer and turns to you before jumping down the little stairway.

He shoots you a look of pure mischief. "To be continued. Enjoy the champagne."

He tips an imaginary hat and then heads out into the night.

You pour the champagne down the sink and stuff the glasses into the bottom of the trash can, then sit down heavily and wonder what to do next. That night, sleep takes a long time to come.

The next day on set seems endless. You're a sweaty mess by the time shooting is over. You can't wait to have a moment to yourself. You need a quiet spot and a little time to think.

You decide to grab a towel and head for the beach. One advantage of the closed set is that there's no danger of unwanted photos of your melted makeup and humidity-soaked hair. You pile it up into a sloppy bun and close your eyes against the sun, now dipping hastily toward the horizon.

From page 83 (and continued from above)...

You sleep in solitude on the soft sand for what feels like hours, blissful dreams of Colm playing behind your closed eyelids. You awaken slowly to the feeling that someone is watching you. *Probably my imagination* you think, and try to drift back into dreams of Colm again. After a few minutes you still can't shake the feeling you're being watched, and you think you hear some kind of shifting beside you.

Cautiously, you peel your eyes open and slowly turn your head.

Sitting beside you is a true sight for sore eyes, though you're not entirely sure what you're seeing isn't an illusion, some strange extension of the dream. Then Colm sneezes and you can't conceal your delight.

"Colm!" you scream, catching the attention of some of the crew still lingering on the shoreline. "Oh my gosh! You're really here!"

Colm laughs and blushes handsomely. "In the flesh," he says in that liquid accent that makes you melt. "Good morning, Sleeping Beauty. I didn't think you'd ever wake."

You rise to sit and look at him. He's more gorgeous than you even remembered. The setting sun sends sparks of gold dancing across his beautiful grey eyes. "What are you doing here?"

"Working," he says with a smile. "I am officially on assignment." He clears his throat and puffs out his formidable chest. "My mission: to capture the actress at work and bring back the genuine article. BEHIND THE SCENES OF *TROPICAL TANGO*."

He leans in to whisper gruffly, "Between you and me, the PR machine on this is enormous. They even gave me my own photographer." He cocks his head toward a geeky-looking guy in cut-offs leaning against a nearby palm. Three cameras hang around his neck and he's busily cleaning his lenses when he notices you looking his way. He squints in your direction and gives you a thumbs-up. "Don't worry," Colm confides, "he won't get in the way."

You laugh, taken aback and at the same time thrilled that he seems to be picking up where the two of you left off. You tingle with pleasure at Colm's implied promise.

Colm jumps to his feet and brushes the powdery sand from his knees. "Right," he says, "off to the trenches." Before leaving, he squats down, making the muscles in his calves and thighs bulge beautifully. "Have a lovely rest. I will catch up with you a bit later."

You admire the view from the rear as he begins to walk away. You almost stay silent but know you can't let him just leave. "Hey, Colm?"

He stops mid-stride and turns back in your direction. You give him a sleepy smile. "I'm glad you're here."

He pauses, returning your smile, before he says, "Not nearly as glad as I am."

You lower your head back onto the soft pillow of sand under your towel and gaze happily at the beautiful sunset.

Later that evening, there's a knock on your trailer door. You open it to find Colm standing with one foot on the little stairway. He extends a hand to you, the gesture somehow regal yet unpresuming. "Fancy a walk on the beach?"

There's no one else in sight on the little back lot. You slip on a pair of flip-flops and take Colm's warm hand. Again you feel the rough calluses and again a shower of sparks flies up your arm, leaving goosebumps.

The sand and the water sparkle magically in the moonlight. Colm's voice is low, soft, and melodic. "I think when my editor told me I may have actually blushed. All I could think about was seeing you again."

For a moment you say nothing, then bravely decide to drop your guard. Colm's presence beside you makes you feel secure. "I've been thinking about you a lot, too."

The warm waves lap gently at the shoreline and the silken sand feels sensuous beneath your feet. The suddenly romantic evening has taken on a magical quality. You reach down to pick up a delicate spiral shell that's floated up to your toes.

"Ouch!" you say, reaching to rub your neck.

"What's happened?" Colm asks with genuine concern.

You laugh it off. "It's nothing," you tell him. "Just a cramp in my neck. All those long hours lying on the beach. Occupational hazard," you say sarcastically.

"Indeed," says Colm. "Let me just take a look." He lifts your hair, sending chills up and down your spine. "Ah, I see. Nothing a little massage won't cure." He surprises you by sweeping his hand under your legs, lifting you off of your feet, and holding you there for a moment. He gazes so deeply into your eyes you feel you might melt, then lowers you gently into the sand.

He works his large fingers into your hairline and begins to massage your neck, gently at first, then with more and more pressure until you feel your muscles loosen, and the stress you've been carrying melt away. He finishes gently running his fingers through your hair, lifts it one last time, and then plants a single, delicate kiss at the base of your neck. You feel tiny explosions throughout your body.

"How's that?" he asks.

"Colm, that felt amazing," you tell him. Once again, you're looking deeply into his eyes and you find yourself waiting—and hoping—for him to kiss you.

Instead, he grasps your hand and pulls you to your feet, gently brushing the sand from your backside.

Walking back to the set you find yourself a little confused and wishing once again this time with Colm didn't have to end. "How long are you here?" you ask him.

"For the week. They fly us out on Friday. Lots to do between now and then."

Why is it that the thought of him leaving makes you feel completely desperate?

"Well, then," you tell him, "we'll have to make the most of our time together."

"We will," agrees Colm. "I only wish this were a true holiday and not a working one." He turns to face you and takes both of your hands, entwining his fingers with yours. "But that time will come, fair Annie, if you'll wait for me." At last, he pulls you close and kisses you deeply, playing his tongue around yours and sending you into an absolute meltdown.

It takes you a moment to come back to yourself, and when you do, you realize you're already back to your trailer. You smile at Colm. "Can you come in?"

"Anna, I can't tell you how much I would like to," Colm says with a frown, "but I cannot. I have to e-mail two hundred words to my editor tonight. But I so wanted to see you."

You can't conceal the disappointment you feel as your eyes drop to the ground.

Colm places a finger beneath your chin and brings your eyes up to meet his. You think he will kiss you again, but instead he takes his index finger and touches it to the tip of your nose. "Anna," he says, "you are truly delightful." He places a single kiss on your forehead and turns to leave.

Your eyes follow him as he walks away, and as he does, you catch a glimpse of someone walking between trailers farther out on the lot. You can't tell in the dim light, but the cocky stride looks suspiciously like Jackson's. *What is he up to now?* you wonder. You don't wait to find out. You firmly close and lock your trailer door then head into a quick shower followed by a peaceful, dream-filled sleep.

The next day on the set is not your best. Buffy doesn't say more than "look up," and "close your eyes," as she perfects your hair and makeup.

You think she's a little rougher with the brushes than she needs to be, but it could be just your imagination.

Every time the director yells, "Cut!" you glance around to see whether Colm is anywhere in sight. Your disappointment mounts as the hours pass and he fails to make an appearance. Maybe he'll surprise you with a visit to your trailer later you tell yourself as the day ends.

On your way back to the trailer, one of the crew members jogs up to you and hands you a magazine, "Jeffries wanted me to bring this to you," he says. "Told me to tell you good job keeping the rumor mill humming." You glance down at the cover, which features a *Tropical Tango* publicity close-up and the headline, *WE* EXCLUSIVE: HAS **ANNA** FOUND LOVE ON SET? *WE WEEKLY* GETS UP-CLOSE AND PERSONAL WITH THE SULTRY STAR!

You try to distract yourself from thoughts of Colm by leafing through the magazine. As usual, the article contains vague information, quotes from "sources on set," linking you to Jackson (which annoys you slightly) and to "a hot new mystery man" (which is closer to the truth). There's not a solid fact in the story and you dismiss it quickly and pick up the script you were planning to spend the evening reading. The night grows later and later, and before you know it, you're sound asleep. It's past midnight when you awaken. You rise groggily, try to put thoughts of Colm's continued absence out of your mind, lock the trailer door, and tuck in for the night.

The next day brings more of the same. When the sun begins to set and shooting wraps, you still haven't seen hide nor hair of Mr. Tall, Dark, and Scottish. This time you decide to go look for him.

You're starting to feel frustrated. Was it your imagination, or did he genuinely seem interested in you the other night? Is he playing some kind of game? At this point, you really don't know, but you're determined to find out.

You wrap yourself in a thick white robe and slide on a pair of flip-flops, then head out the door still in full hair and makeup. You make two laps around the back lot and cannot find Colm anywhere. Over at craft services, stuffing slices of yellow cheese into his mouth, stands the scrawny photographer who arrived with Colm.

"Hey," you say as you approach him, "have you seen Colm?"

"Over dere," he responds through a mouthful of cheese, and cocks his head toward the trailer behind you.

"Thanks," you tell him. As you walk around the backside of the trailer, you glimpse a figure hunched on a low folding chair sitting in the long shadow cast by the huge vehicle.

"Colm?" you ask.

He glances up coolly.

"What are you doing over here?"

He lifts a clipboard filled with notes. "Thought it would be obvious. Working."

"Why are you back here? Are you hiding?"

Colm roughly throws the clipboard onto his lap. "Just helping myself to some shade. Not ones for the glaring sun, we Scots."

You laugh and walk closer to him. "You should have told me. You could have used my trailer. Lord knows it sits empty all day."

Once again Colm seems to appraise you with an odd detachment. "Quite all right. I wouldn't want to intrude."

You can't believe what you're hearing. What happened to the man who was so warm and intimate just the other day?

"Colm," you ask him, "what is going on? You're acting really strange. Did I do something to upset you?"

He draws in a long breath and blows it out just as slowly. "Anna, I appreciate your concern but I'm a grown lad. Really. And I shouldn't have put you or myself in this position." He pauses as if to say something else then decides against it. "I expect I made more of our evening together than I should've. What was I to expect? Here you are on a movie set with a handsome American actor. These things happen."

You cross our arms defensively and take a step back, feeling sheer puzzlement. "What things happen, exactly?"

"Anna, there's no reason for a charade. It's quite understandable. It's to be expected you'd want to charm the media. And that you'd fall for your costar. A little clichéd, maybe, but who am I to judge?"

Every word Colm says cuts like a shard of jagged glass. You shake your head to clear your thoughts. "Colm, there's nothing—I don't know what you heard . . ." But you have a sneaking suspicion you do know what he's heard and where he's heard it. You can scarcely believe it, yet you wouldn't put it past that manipulative jerk.

"Colm, I swear to you, there is nothing, and I mean nothing, going on between me and anyone else on this set."

You see a look of uncertainty flicker over Colm's face for a moment then the cold resolve sets in again. "Anna," he says with resignation, "you do not owe me a thing." He drops his eyes back to his clipboard.

What on earth would Jackson have told him that is causing Colm to pull back so suddenly and completely? You have no idea, but you intend to find out.

With a frustrated frown you tell Colm, "I'll be back," and you march off across the set.

You bang hard enough on Jackson's door to make your fist throb. After the first set of knocks he doesn't answer, so you knock again, even harder this time, rage flowing through your veins. You almost hit him in the face when he finally flings open the door.

"Whoa, whoa, whoa, Anna." Jackson's slow smile and smug amusement makes you even angrier.

You shove through the door and slam it behind you as Jackson leans casually against the doorframe. For the first time you notice his hair is wet and tousled and he's wearing nothing more than a thin, white bath towel wrapped low around his hips.

He gives you a slow once-over and clicks his tongue approvingly. "Well, don't we make a pair?" he drawls with a slow smile. "You in your robe and I in my towel."

You, however, are not in the mood. "Don't be a jackass!"

He raises an eyebrow. "No," he corrects, "it's Jackson, I think you must have misunderstood."

"Don't try to be cute. You know what you did. Why would you do that? Are you really so insecure that you have to fabricate a relationship between us?"

"Ahhh," he says slowly, "so you talked to Scotty."

So he knows, you think, *and he even acknowledges it.* "Why? Can you just answer that?"

"You know," he says, "Anna, I'm not exactly making anything up." He takes a bold step toward you. "Just predicting the future."

Moving even closer, he grabs the belt of your robe, pulling you toward him. "You can't deny there's something between us."

You pretend fascination and lean in to him, taking a breath and summoning your acting skills. "You know, Jackson, you're right, there is something between us. It's too big to deny. Huge, really." Then, with a dramatic shove you push your way free. "It's your ego! There's no way I could ever get past it!"

You turn to march out the door, and as you open it, you hear Jackson from behind you. "Hey, Anna, one more thing."

"What?" you ask, not bothering to turn around. For a long moment, he says nothing, so you ask again, more annoyed than ever, "What?"

You turn to see him sauntering toward the back of the trailer, and as he does, he casually drops his towel, leaving his bare buttocks exposed. You feel yourself blushing as you can't help but stare. His rear end is tight, perfectly chiseled, and strong, twitching as he walks away. You know the image will be burned into your brain for nights to come, "Ugh!" you yell out as you hurl yourself down the stairs, not bothering to close the door behind you.

Before you take a step further, time seems to slow and you feel an odd sense of helplessness. You have the presence of mind to think this must be like what it's like to watch a car accident occur, vertiginous and disorienting but oddly focused and precise at the same time.

Buffy rounds the corner of the trailer and takes in the scene at a glance—you in your bathrobe, Jackson's retreating, bare backside, your face still flushed from the heated exchange.

She stops in her tracks, and the look of pure disgust on her face is one you'll never forget.

Before turning on her heels she mutters, "You two deserve each other."

You feel like you've been sucker-punched and can't even get a word out as you watch your friend walk away. *Could this day get any worse?* you wonder.

As it turns out, it can. Walking back to your trailer, you hear a commotion on the back lot behind you. Before you can process what is happening, several crew members run in the direction from which you just came. You wander slowly in their wake, in a dazed state of shock, dreading what you are about to see.

You shove into the shouting and cheering crowd and you cannot believe your eyes.

Colm and Jackson are going at it like a couple of teenage boys, fists flying. You can see Jackson's landed at least one good shot. There's a slash of red under one of Colm's eyes, but he's seething like a tiger about to take down his prey.

Jackson swings and misses, Colm ducking to just barely avoid a right hook, and then he smoothly rounds on Jackson, delivering a solid upper cut to the gut, coupled with a right cross landing squarely on Jackson's nose. There's a sickening crunch as Jackson drops like a rock, one arm wrapped around his midsection as the other hand flies to his streaming nose. You feel the bile rise in your throat as blood begins to seep through his fingers.

Jackson manages to rise to a seated position while security pushes roughly through the crowd to pull Colm away. Jackson's hands still cover his bloodied face and as Colm is led away you can hear Jackson screaming, "He broke my nose! He broke my nose!"

As you hurry to catch up with Colm, you notice a few people glancing inquiringly in your direction. At this point you really don't care what people think. You just want to be sure Colm is okay.

The door to the security trailer slams shut a second before you get there. You climb the stairs and knock timidly. A burly guard opens the door a crack and you glimpse Colm sitting on a stool with his hands wire-tied behind his back. He looks utterly miserable.

"Colm," you begin, pushing open the door, "are you all right? What happened?"

The big security guards steps rudely between the two of you, "I'm sorry ma'am. This is a private matter. We're going to have to ask you to leave."

You manage to plead, "Colm, come see me later, please?" before the door is shut firmly in your face.

You return to your trailer and try to distract yourself by reading through more of the script as you wait for word from Colm. Unable to concentrate, your mind keeps wandering back to the fight and the moments before it, to the bloody cut below Colm's eye, to the surge of blood from Jackson's nose, to the look of disgust on Buffy's face.

You shut the script in frustration. You haven't processed a single word. Finally, as you are about to give up and resign yourself to what you're sure will be a sleepless night, there's a knock at the door.

An exhausted and banged-up version of the handsome man you've been thinking about all afternoon stands on the little stairway. He doesn't quite make eye contact. You usher him quickly inside and fill a Ziploc with ice for his swollen eye, now turning an alarming shade of purple.

The musky smell of sweat emanates from Colm and you feel a sudden wash of attraction, despite the circumstances. "Tilt your head back," you instruct, placing a finger gently under his chin and the ice gingerly on his eye.

He clenches his teeth just slightly, and you can tell he's trying hard to hide the pain he is feeling.

You let a few moments pass, then ask, "So, what exactly happened out there?"

Colm squints at you with his one open eye and grins. "I kicked his arse is what happened."

You try to hide your amusement. "You know what I mean."

He sighs and leans his head back even farther. "Only so much of that cocky bastard can be tolerated. Someone had to take him down a wee notch."

"Well, you certainly turned out to be the man to do it."

"Hmph," he agrees in a satisfied way.

"And what happened with security?"

"Well, that's the tougher part. Mr. Movie Star may or may not press charges. I may or may not have broken his perfect nose. Chibbed him good, I did."

"Mmmm . . . I think his pride is probably hurt worse than his nose."

He clears his throat then sighs. "And I've been ordered to leave the set."

This news hits you like a sledgehammer. You can't stand the thought of seeing him go, especially with so much uncertainly lingering between you.

"Colm?"

"Hmm?"

"You do realize that there is nothing between me and Jackson, don't you?"

"You know, Anna, I do believe you," he pauses for a moment. "I believed you when you told me, I just—and then, when you told me he was lying, and I could see the determination in your face, it just made me so angry. I don't know that I've ever been so angry in my life, if I'm honest."

He stops for a moment, and you give him time to continue. He winces as you lift the bag of ice from his eye to take a look. It doesn't look much better.

"You know," he continues, "ever since I've been in the States it's amazed me that there are people able to get away with almost anything. It's been under my skin and I just blew up. Even you celebrities are just people. No offense."

"None taken," you reply with a laugh.

Once again you're struck by how instantly comfortable Colm makes you feel. You don't need to be anything other than yourself around him, and he doesn't consider you anything other than a regular person. It's a feeling that's new to you.

Although you're not one to verbalize your true emotions, so used to hiding behind the mask of whatever character you portray, you know you risk losing this man and this feeling if you don't say something to him now.

For a moment you are paralyzed, trying to find the right words to say, yet you're totally overwhelmed by the deep physical attraction you feel. You just hope Colm feels the same.

You slip your hand behind his neck and begin rubbing gently. Colm sighs with pleasure.

"You're still all tensed up," you tell him.

"Mmmhmm," he replies.

"Here," you say, "let me work some of those knots out."

You set the bag of ice on the table, take his hand firmly, and lead him back to your room. The lights are off and the ambient glow from the tiny windows submerges you into a murky dimness. Feeling your way, you guide him to your bed. You kneel beside him and begin a slow and gentle back rub.

Slipping your fingers into the thick hair at the base of his neck, you work your way down to his broad shoulders, kneading away the tension. Colm lies totally still, only moaning appreciatively every so often.

As your fingers work their magic, you feel your courage resurface.

"So . . ." you begin. "I was thinking . . ."

"Were ye now?" Colm teases, his voice muffled by the pillow.

You take a deep breath and force yourself to continue. "I was thinking that it's a shame you have to leave, just when we were getting to know each other."

Colm replies, "Mmph," which could mean anything, leaving you unsure of what to say next.

You continue on, "Anyway, this is going to sound stupid, but I have to say it."

He waits for you to go on as your fingers continue to work.

"Okay, here it is. Colm, I really like you."

"Mmmmhmmm?"

"And, I really don't want you to go."

"Doesn't appear you or I have much say in that, given the recent developments."

You wait for Colm to say something more as you continue the rhythm of your massaging fingers. He feels heavy and totally sedate beneath your hands.

"So, that's what I wanted to say," you finish. You're glad Colm can't see the blush you know is turning your face a bright red. Have you said too much? Colm remains totally silent.

You pause in mid-massage, desperate to find a way to be sure this man knows how you feel. You certainly do not feel one iota closer to knowing how he feels about you—and the silence isn't helping.

You work up your courage again and continue to massage, your hands pressing hard as they move down his spine.

"Where will you go? I mean, are they going to *deport* you?"

Colm snorts a short laugh, "I've no idea, Anna. Likely depends on how far your friend—er, Jackson—takes it. Just hope his nose looks better in the morning."

"So," you press on, "you'll go back to LA, and then wait to find out what happens?"

"I suppose. Hadn't really got that far." He pauses and turns his head slightly before continuing. "But I can assure you, Anna, I will find you."

Total relief and pleasure washes over you at his words. But he continues, "You know how you say we hardly know each other?"

"Uh huh."

"But in an odd way, Anna, I feel I've known you all my life. And I want to spend much more of my life getting to know you."

A surge of warmth flows through you at the promise in those words. You can't think of a way to tell him how he's made you feel—even though you've only met—how completely right this seems. You don't want to break the spell and you let the silence sit as you savor the moment.

Working your fingers down his back, you stop to massage each tense muscle. His lower back is firm and tapered, and you straddle his waist to work in circles just above his belt line. Once his back feels sufficiently relaxed you move to his arms, enjoying the definition of his strong biceps, his sinewy forearms. You take each finger and firmly squeeze the tension from each one. Now that your eyes have adjusted to the dim light, you notice how delicious his slightly calloused palms look, and you can't help but lean down to plant a kiss lightly in each one.

Colm begins to turn over slowly. "Anna, that was—"

You silence him with your lips, pressing yourself against the length of his body in an urgent kiss. You bask in the delicious taste of him, kissing his cheeks, his chin, lingering on his neck, breathing in his spicy scent. You move up again to kiss his beautiful eyelids.

"Ow!" he yells.

"Sorry!" You'd completely forgotten about Colm's swollen eye. "I'm so sorry! Are you okay?"

Colm sits up with a low laugh. "I'm fine, Anna." He takes your face between his large, rough hands and kisses you slowly, then leans back onto his elbows. "Just relax and let me have a look at you."

A slow smile spreads across his face as his eyes move from your face down to your neck. You can feel the heat of his gaze as it travels down, lingers at the swell of your breasts, then continues to your waist and hips.

When he speaks, Colm's voice is huskier. "Anna, you are truly perfect."

This makes you smile, and you lean in to kiss him, pressing your palm gently against the rough stubble on his cheek.

He reaches up one hand behind your neck and pulls you to him. He skims your top over your head in one smooth motion and deftly flips you onto your back, then hovers over you for one more moment before lowering his mouth to your stomach. His tickling kisses are the perfect complement to the delicious abrasiveness of his scruff as he works his way lower. You are momentarily disappointed when he moves up again, but then he reaches around to remove your bra and sends you into ecstasy as he uses his mouth on one sensitive nipple and his fingers on the other.

You reach down, intending to slide your hand into his waistband, but he intercepts you, interlaces his fingers with yours, and moves down once again. Using his free hand, he undoes your shorts and slides them down over your feet. He takes a minute to look at you once again, then runs his hand down the curve of your hipbones and lets his fingers play along the lacy edge of your thong. Then he hooks a finger under the elastic and pulls them free as well. He runs his hand gently over your clit and bends to kiss it lightly. He looks up, gauges your expression, then returns to kiss more hungrily.

Your insides clench at every touch of his lips and tongue, and you gasp as he reaches up to pinch and caress your nipple. You find you're ready much too soon, and gently tug at his shoulder. He looks up for a moment but then smiles before resuming.

You feel yourself getting closer again and have no choice but to give into the moment. Colm senses your readiness and pulls his hand from yours, thrusting his thumb deep as he brings you closer with his tongue. He finds a sensitive spot and the sensation is too much to bear. You arch into him and come with a groan. "Oh, Colm," you sigh, as waves of pleasure wash over you. You shiver as he flicks his tongue over your sensitive skin one last time, then slowly kisses his way up to your lips.

His jeans strain against his bulge. You smile and reach for him again. You trail one finger lightly up the hard ridge and Colm breathes in sharply, but as before, he stops you. He looks into your eyes. "Let me just hold you," he says.

He pulls you to his side, wrapping one arm under you. The fingers of one hand trail lightly across your hip, while the others gently strokes your hair. You kiss him once then rest your head on his muscular chest, resisting the urge to reach lower. You listen to his heartbeat and feel yourself begin to surrender to sleep. You've never in your life felt so safe and so at peace.

Much too soon, Colm draws in a deep breath and sits up. "Anna, I'm exhausted. I should go."

"Please," you say, "let me—"

He interrupts you with another lingering kiss. "I'm sorry for the day I've put you through, Anna, but glad I could leave you with a bit of pleasure."

You bite your lower lip in frustration.

"Please, Colm," you say, "just stay."

"How I wish I could, Anna. You've no idea."

Despite those words, Colm rises from the bed, stretches his back, and saunters slowly toward the door. You walk with him toward the door, a million thoughts running through your mind. He turns to face you, and you can't hide the disappointment you feel.

Colm bends down to lean his forehead against yours. "Anna, remember what I said." He kisses you lightly one last time on the bridge of your nose and with that, he is gone, leaving you feeling like an empty vessel.

The days on set trudge forward at the speed of molasses. The thickly applied makeup cloys in the hundred-degree heat and the hot costumes stick and chafe, making you want to rip them off. You haven't slept well since Colm left, and there are mornings you can barely bring yourself to get out of bed.

Jackson's nose is covered with such a thick layer of tape and gauze. You can't tell how bad the damage really is. He's sidelined to recover for a few days and the shooting schedule is adjusted accordingly, so at least you get to avoid that confrontation.

Buffy, on the other hand, has moved from vitriolic hostility to a disaffected flatness that is even more disturbing. Ever the professional, she comes in to do her job but no more. You can't figure out what you can say that will heal the wound of misunderstanding that now seems to run so deep.

As shooting wraps, all you can think about is returning home to find Colm. He hasn't so much as sent a text since leaving the set. Even though you've been listening for crew gossip about Jackson's plans to sue, you don't hear a word.

The last day of shooting breaks cloudy and cool and you hope and pray the few beach reshoots can be wrapped despite the overcast sky. You sit in your trailer waiting for Buffy to arrive, leaf back through the script you've finally finished reading, and try to shake the cloud your experience here has cast over everything else in your life.

An hour later, your annoyance at Buffy's lateness turns to genuine worry. Buffy's never missed a day of work since you met her. The knock on your door summoning you to the set will come any moment, so you decide you'd better go looking for her.

You wander the back lot and ask the few straggling crew members still hanging around craft services or making their calls to other trailers whether they've seen Buffy. No one has. You go to the set to look for her but she's nowhere to be seen.

Jackson's trailer is the last resort. You know you have no choice but to go see whether she's there. The last thing you want to do is to interrupt the two of them together but you don't know what else to do.

Jackson's answers the door after you've knocked only twice. "Anna," he drawls with his usual lopsided smirk, "to what do I owe this pleasure?"

"I'm trying to find Buffy. Is she here?"

"Haven't seen her," he says smoothly. "I thought she spent the night with you."

"With me? Why would she be with me?"

"Well, she does share your trailer."

You shake your head in frustration. "Jackson, she hasn't spent more than an hour in my trailer since you and she started—whatever it is you started. She's been staying here, hasn't she?"

Jackson gives a casual shrug, "Well, she's spent some time here, sure, but it's not like we've been shacking up or anything."

"Well, she's certainly spent a lot more time with you than she has with me lately." You glance around Jackson's trailer and notice he hasn't actually asked you to come in. There are no signs of anything out of the ordinary, but still, something just doesn't feel right. Maybe it's just this gloomy day, but you can't shake the feeling.

Jackson's nose, you now notice, is unbandaged. Other than a little redness and a bit of a blue tinge below his eyes, it looks totally fine.

"You certainly made a speedy recovery."

"No thanks to your boyfriend," Jackson shoots back with an angry sneer.

You decide to press further, not about to let him off the hook.

"When was the last time you saw Buffy anyway?"

Jackson laughs and folds his arms over his chest, "What is this? CSI St. Thomas? When was the last time *you* saw Buffy, Anna? I don't have time to play detective."

"Seriously, Jackson, can't you just answer me? I'm worried about her."

Jackson rolls his eyes. "She's not responding to your beck and call for once in her life and now you're worried about her? Maybe she had something to do, Anna. Maybe she just didn't feel like working today. I know this will come as a shock, but the whole world does not revolve around you, sweetheart."

Again, you have the feeling that Jackson is using his hostility to cover something. He certainly hasn't answered anything you asked directly.

"Jackson, I'm going to ask you again, and I hope you answer me this time. When was the last time you saw her?"

"All right, all right, cool your jets, Anna." He pauses and looks down at the ground for just a moment too long. "Last time Buffy was here was the morning before last. She left to do your makeup and I haven't seen her since. You guys have been fighting. Everybody knows that. Give her a minute and she'll be back. She's pissed at you, Anna, but she's not stupid. She doesn't want to lose her job."

Once again something doesn't ring true in Jackson's tone, though you can't quite put your finger on it.

Walking back to your trailer, it finally dawns on you: his reference to everyone knowing you and Buffy had been fighting. A seed of uneasiness plants itself in your stomach.

Throughout the day you become increasingly worried. In Buffy's absence, you're forced to share Jackson's makeup artist, a busty bleached-blonde who doesn't have half of Buffy's skill, but at least she gets you through the shoot and doesn't make any attempt at conversation.

After day two with still no sign of Buffy, you decide to approach Jeff Jeffries to voice your concern—or part of your concern, anyway.

Jeffries half-listens to you as he watches dailies on a little screen in his trailer, a double-wide decked out beyond belief. He runs a chubby hand over his balding head and finally breaks away from the screen to give you his attention.

"Look, Anna," he begins, "I know she's your friend and you're worried about her. God knows we're all worried about her. She's costing us time and money here. Jackson's girl is good, but I'm having to pay her double and it's taking you twice as long in the makeup chair." He clears his throat and heaves a foot onto the ottoman in front of his oversized leather chair. "But look, she's probably taken up with some local, and between the Jackson thing—don't think I don't know about that—and the problems with you, she needed a little break. Why do women do these things? I don't know." He pauses again, grunts, and brings his other foot heavily up to rest beside the other. "One thing I do know," he tells you before returning his full attention to his video screen, "is when she does show up, she's fired."

"Nice," you mutter, knowing you'll find no help here, and head for the door, making a mental note not to work with Jeffries again any time soon.

Security proves to be equally useless. A hassled-looking officer takes a written report and promises to ask for the help of local authorities, but when you check back in the next day they almost laugh when you ask how much progress has been made. The same uniformed genius who shoved you out the door the day of the Colm and Jackson incident says he's still waiting for a return call. "We're on island time," he offers by way of explanation.

The rest of the cast celebrates the final day of shooting but you're in no mood to join them. You seethe watching Jackson joke and flirt, seemingly completely unbothered by Buffy's disappearance.

Finally, you make the heart-breaking call to Buffy's mother, Rose, to ask whether she's heard from Buffy. When she tells you she hasn't, a tearful conversation follows wherein you tell Rose about what happened between you two and about your suspicions toward Jackson.

Rose takes the next flight she can and meets you on the island. You vow to stay with her until you find Buffy, and in the meantime, to take the story to as many media outlets as possible. The crew and cast finally depart and you're surprised but unsurprised at the same time, by the total lack of concern for your friend.

You continue to have the nagging feeling that if only you'd persisted in trying to reach her, to prove to her that there really was nothing going on between you and Jackson, to just keep being her friend no matter what, that none of this would have happened.

The studio contract requires you to travel for a three-week press junket for *Tropical Tango*, and your next project starts meetings immediately after the press tour wraps. The two weeks you and Rose have spent looking feels like two days, and you still have so much searching to do.

You've promised to stay and look for Buffy for as long as it takes, but you never thought it would take this long. Local authorities are finally helping, but with frustrating, island-laid-back sluggishness. You're painfully aware that each day that passes means a greater chance you may never see Buffy again.

If you stay to keep searching and forego the press junket, you'll lose a substantial percentage of your *Tropical Tango* fee and possibly even future work when word gets around you haven't honored your contract. Although you know Rose is leaning on you in her daughter's absence, you're not sure what more there is you can do other than be there for her. You've turned over every rock you can think of and still have not even the slightest lead. The police are telling you they are working overtime looking for her and to leave it in their hands. You have your doubts, but your professional obligations are pulling at you. A steady stream of phone calls, e-mails, and texts from your agent, Jeffries, and finally from the studio urge you to honor your obligations.

Rose is more than understanding of your dilemma and encourages you to do what you feel is right. "Go, Anna," she urges you. "You've done as much as you possibly can. I can take it from here." You can tell part of her wants you to stay, but you know she'll never say so.

The pressure and sleepless nights wreak havoc on your mind. You're almost paralyzed with indecision. You try to call Colm but the call goes directly to voice mail. You leave a message you feel certain he'll never get.

Finally, your agent calls to say you have three days to report to the New York set of your next project or you'll be replaced. Still, you feel that if you have just a few more days to look, maybe you'll turn over a rock you haven't yet. At the same time, if you're being completely honest, you have to admit that your hope is beginning to fade. You just don't know what to do.

To stay on the island and continue your search for Buffy, turn to page 116.
To leave the island and report to NYC, keep reading.

Absolutely ridden with guilt, you say a tearful goodbye to Buffy's mother and board a plane headed for New York. The chill that greets you when you arrive on the set is palpable and the wintry cold of the city hits you like a slap in the face.

Worse still are the glossy headlines announcing—ANNA CHAMBLISS MISSING IN ACTION!—along with speculations of an island affair or the insinuations of more sordid reasons for your "unexplained absence" and the question, IS ANNA HEADED FOR REHAB? Astoundingly, there are no mentions of Buffy's disappearance.

A mere mention of Jackson's name in connection with the story on the *Hello Show* brings the threat of a libel suit by Jackson's attorney, so you surrender that angle. Though you still suspect him, you know nothing can be proven until Buffy—or her body—is found, so you concentrate on lighting a fire under the island police to step up their search effort. Like the media, their interest seems to wane too quickly. You're well aware that the last thing they want is a negative smear on their most lucrative industry: tourism. Everyone around you seems to want to forget, to smooth it over as quickly as possible, as though Buffy never even existed.

Colm's interest in you follows a similar pattern, and you know you have no one to blame but yourself. He calls you as soon as he listens to your message, then for a few weeks he calls you daily, pleading for a return call. You text him that you'll call when you can, but in an odd way you don't want to allow yourself any pleasure until Buffy's been found. Eventually, the calls every day become two or three a week, then once a week, and the tone of his messages becomes more and more glum. His final communication, a simple text saying, *Hi, A, pls call when u can* goes unanswered, and it's with an odd sense of pleasurable masochism you realize you likely will never hear from him again.

The box office on your new film doesn't do well. You're distracted throughout the shoot and rush off set as soon as the day is over. You know it isn't your best effort, and strangely you don't really care. You continue to dog every newspaper, magazine, television, and radio station until the producers turn you away as soon as you approach. Those that agree to an interview preface it with a caveat that the "disappearance" story is not to be mentioned.

You have yet to sign on to your next project and notice the scripts you receive are dwindling. You find yourself with more free time than ever before, but feel sluggish and ineffective.

One day there's a knock at your door. It's Buffy's mom, Rose, thanking you for your many efforts on Buffy's behalf. She looks years older than when you last saw her, new lines are etched into her face. She reaches out to take your hands and looks in to your eyes. She thanks you for all you have done to keep Buffy's memory alive, but also begs you to let it rest. "It's too painful," she tells you, "seeing a new headline every day."

"Well, it's hardly every day now," you begin to protest. "I can barely get an interview anymore. It's ridiculous. You and I both know they're just trying to gloss it over."

She gives your hands a squeeze and looks up at you, her eyes pleading with yours, "Let it rest, honey. Let her rest. No matter what, we'll always have her here." She places a bone-thin hand lightly over your heart. "You know that, don't you?"

A fresh wellspring of emotion bubbles to the surface, and you burst into tears you didn't know you had left. Buffy's mother holds you as you cry, and though you feel you should be the one comforting her, you are immensely grateful for her embrace.

The family holds a small memorial for Buffy, a celebration of her life, and you attend the intimate gathering feeling like the outsider you are. For a while you correspond with Buffy's mom, but that too soon fades as you find less and less to say to one another. Oddly, she seems to be moving on, and you are somewhat resentful that you find yourself still so consumed with grief and longing for your friend.

You find a new agent, focus on your career, and the work begins to pick up again. You suddenly find acting to be a wonderful escape and you dive into every role with a new sense of urgency. Being on set takes you away from your guilt and frustration and gives you a much-needed break from reality. Although you do nothing other than work, you love what you do and are rewarded handsomely for it. It's only occasionally, after a particularly difficult day, that you stare at your shelf of glimmering awards and wonder whether they can ever take the place of the friendship you've lost. When those feelings surface, you find they are nothing that a full glass of red wine and a new script won't cure.

Occasionally, you hear some news about Jackson. At first you follow his trajectory rabidly and with a growing sense of disdain, but his star rises and falls equally swiftly. Now he gets just one or two supporting roles a year. You secretly savor the fact that he's not aging well, while you look every bit as young as you always have.

Of course it helps that your current fling, a successful Hollywood plastic surgeon, gives you a nip and tuck whenever you feel like a little tightening up is in order. Oren is a tall, beautiful man with a head of thick, curly black hair and he's fifteen years your junior.

You met during a consultation for Botox, which led to a passionate encounter right in his office, with you reclined in his examining chair and him fully dressed with his lab coat and fly unbuttoned as he groped at your breasts and thrust like a teenager, coming to an end much too soon. You visited him again the following week for your first injection of Botox, which miraculously smoothed your newly emerging crow's feet, and a second injection of Oren, which miraculously soothed your neglected libido. This time, he hiked up your skirt, hastily moved your thong aside, and bent you over the examining table, reaching around to squeeze a breast in each hand as he worked.

The next visit you decided to take charge. You wore an even shorter skirt with nothing underneath, and, sitting Oren down on the seat usually occupied by a waiting patient, you climbed onto his lap and unzipped his fly, wrapping your legs around the back of the chair to provide just the angle you need to find your climax as Oren thrust inside you. You found it thrilling that someone could walk in on you at any moment, and loved it that Oren wore his lab coat, its length just right to cover any evidence of your activities as he shook your hand, feigning professionalism, and guided you out of the office. You thoroughly enjoyed scheduling a follow-up, and the delicious anticipation of your next visit.

Now, your relationship has progressed outside of Oren's office, and the two of you find increasingly adventurous spots to fuel your newfound addiction to your illicit encounters—restrooms stalls in expensive restaurants, a walk-in closet at a dinner party hosted by one of Oren's colleagues, even a chaise lounge on a fully visible hotel balcony. His creativity is contagious, although you have to admit your favorite trysts are still those during which he keeps his lab coat on, which proves even more fun when there's nothing else under it.

One day, you happen to be watching the news when a headline at the bottom the screen catches your eye. Its shocking simplicity knocks the breath from your lungs: JACKSON MICHAELS FOUND DEAD AT 39. You increase the volume and listen raptly as the reporter unfolds the sordid scene. Michaels was apparently staying in a seedy motel and found hanging from a cord in the closet, with another cord wrapped around his genitalia. "Was it some sort of sex game gone awry? Authorities have yet to give an official cause of death," the doe-eyed anchor reports innocently.

Sex game or suicide, you couldn't care less. At last, you feel a welcome sense of closure. You sip your wine, lean back into the cushy pillows of your sofa, reach a hand out to stroke Oren's thigh, and think,

Karma's a bitch, before turning off the television and turning all of your attention to the man ready and waiting beside you.

THE END
To take Anna on a new Bedventure, go back and choose a new path.

From page 112...

You know in your heart that you would never be able to forgive yourself if you left, that you have to continue your search for your friend. You commit yourself anew to finding Buffy. That same day, like an answer to at least one of your prayers, there's a message from Colm. You play it over and over, savoring his melodic voice. "Anna," he tells you, "I've done nothing but think of you since I boarded that plane. I cannot wait a minute longer to hear your voice. Please call me back as soon as you can."

You call him that night, after another day of dead-end searching. Just the sound of his voice does wonders. Holed up in your hotel room, you allow yourself an hour with him on the phone. Colm's support is a salve to your injured soul. "I do believe you're doing the right thing, staying to look for her," he assures you. "You shouldn't even be giving your work a thought now, Anna. It'll be right there waiting for you when you've finished your work there."

You thank him through your tears and before hanging up you promise to call him with an update as soon as you can.

It's been three weeks since shooting wrapped and there's still no sign of Buffy. You've scoured the island, taken photos of Buffy to every restaurant, bar, and island shop, even spent days combing beaches full of tourists in hopes that someone will recognize her.

You pass a little island newsstand one morning and see your own face staring back at your below the headline, *WE WEEKLY* EXCLUSIVE! **ANNA CHAMBLISS** A NO-SHOW ON THE SET OF HER NEW ROMCOM! WAS SHE FIRED? *WE* GOES INSIDE THE RUMORS.

You don't bother to stop to read the rest. You are fully focused on finding your friend, and could not care less what the tabloids say.

Rose spends her days searching as well. She calls and visits local hospitals, medical facilities, even the coroner's office, asking the dreadful question, "Has a Jane Doe has been brought in?" She turns up nothing.

Day after grueling day passes, each more emotionally exhausting than the one before, and you become more and more certain the reason you find no clues on the island is that every clue you might have found left on the flight back to LA with Jackson.

You share your thoughts with Colm one evening, and to your surprise, he doesn't object. He seems to have suspected the same thing all along. However, he's not quite as optimistic you'll get anywhere accusing Jackson and has a better—if more pessimistic—sense about how the justice system works, especially when there are multiple jurisdictions involved.

"Anna," he tells you in a gentle lilt, "I know you're frustrated. You've been a wonderful friend to her and ye continue to be. But until someone turns up some evidence . . ." His voice drops and he hesitantly adds, "or a body . . ."

You can't even bear that thought and you end the conversation quickly, more determined than ever to find some small scrap of evidence, anything at all.

As the days pass, fewer and fewer people are willing to listen when you approach with Buffy's photo. The glossy print of Buffy's smiling face has become soft and rippled from being carried everywhere you go.

Even tourists who recognize you begin quickly backing away when their request for an autograph turns into your request for them to help in your search for your missing friend. But how else can you let people know how urgent it is to keep searching? You know you can be a little passionate in your pleas, but you also know it only takes one lead.

As the weeks turn to months you get fewer and fewer calls from your agent and fewer and fewer scripts sent to you. You hardly remember to eat and lie in bed for a few sleepless hours every night. The lack of your hair stylist, the dark circles under your eyes, and the jutting bones in your arms and chest make you look much older than your years.

Your communication with Colm becomes briefer and less frequent, too. Although he calls you daily, sometimes you pick up, other times you don't. Guilt kicks in every time you feel a pang of pleasure at the sound of his voice on your voice mail, but most times you can't bring yourself to answer when he calls. You don't want to give him the impression he might have a chance until you finally have some answers. Even though there's a little sense of loss each time you send his call to voice mail, you push the feeling away, and distract yourself with the business of finding Buffy.

You decide to give the island authorities one more shot. The local police station is housed in an inappropriately flamingo-pink stucco building. You practically have to force your way in to talk to the "chief."

He listens to you with a serious expression on his face, nodding mechanically as you once again review all of the details of Buffy's disappearance and beg for his help.

When you finish, he leans slowly forward, resting his forearms on his desk, looks you in the eyes, and asks you, in a slow island lilt, "Do you think we haven't been looking? De you believe we don' do our jobs?"

You realize you've gone down the wrong path with this man and you instantly regret it.

"We've been looking, Miss Anna Chambliss. We've been turnin' over every rock and every stone on this island." He pauses to let this sink in. "You think we want some tourist finding her? That we don't."

He heaves a heavy sigh and lifts a cloth to wipe his shining brow. As he continues, his tone turns gentler.

"We know you been looking too, Miss Anna. We know what's going on in our island. But let me ask you this." He reaches out a warm hand and grasps your bone-thin palm in a way that feels some-how fatherly. You meet his gaze and listen. "We been looking, you been looking, everybody been looking for months now. You think it's possible there's nothing to be found? Sometimes people go miss-ing 'cause they don' wanna be found."

You leave the station utterly disappointed. You know, you are certain, there's something to be found. People don't just disappear into thin air. But, in the dark hours of the night, when circling thoughts keep you from sleep, you can't help but think that people do just dis-appear—maybe not into thin air, but into water, or under sand and dirt, or into worse places.

Your call to the Los Angeles police is another cold slap in the face. Not only do they tell you they're preparing to close the case, they also inform you that as far as they are concerned Jackson Michaels is no longer a person of interest. "Mr. Michaels has provided sufficient evidence to clear his name," explains the officer, his tone formal and dismissive. "Unless you are the next of kin there's no further information I can provide." He cuts off your protest with a single sentence before ending the call. "Miss Chambliss, you may want to familiarize yourself with the expression, 'No victim, no crime.'"

Then, on a rare rainy island day, Rose asks that you visit her in the little hotel room she calls home.

"Of course," you tell her, hoping she's found a sliver of evidence that will fuel your search.

She sits you down on the tiny, wicker bench that serves as the only seating in the room and takes both of your hands in hers. "Anna, honey," she begins, as her eyes begin to fill with tears.

"What is it?" You feel the panic rising in your throat, sure that you're about to hear the worst. But what she tells you is almost just as bad. She's given up.

"Anna, I will never, ever be able to thank you enough for everything you've sacrificed to be with me and to help me try to find her." She pauses for a moment, apparently unable to even utter her daughter's name. "You've done more than even a sister would. I think you've done more than I have."

"No," you interrupt her, "I haven't done nearly enough."

She raises her hand to stop you. "You've been a saint, Anna." She sighs and grasps your hands more tightly in hers. "This isn't an easy decision, and it's one I'm still struggling with, but I have to go back to my life, Anna. I'm going to leave the island."

Unable to believe what you're hearing, you begin to object. You need Rose here for so many reasons. As she speaks, you realize she's been your support as much as you've been hers.

Rose places her hand gently over yours, "I want to thank you, Anna, for everything you've done . . ." She trails off and a single tear tracks slowly down her cheek. "But Anna," she says, her shimmering eyes, the same big, blue eyes she gave to her daughter, locked fiercely to yours, "I know in my heart she isn't here anymore." She swipes at her eyes then drops her hands into her lap, and you notice her nails are ragged, her skin almost transparently thin. "And I know in my soul she isn't coming back."

Your heart swells with love and pity, but at the same time, the daughter, the little girl in you, simply can't fathom how a mother could leave without knowing, without finding her child.

So many words spring to your lips, some angry, some cold, some empathetic and strong, but you hold them inside and embrace Rose instead, wrapping yourself in her arms as you cry together.

You pull the last tissue from the little box on the dresser and blot at your tears, willing them to stop. "When do you think you'll leave?" you ask. You're shocked by her answer.

"My flight is tomorrow, Anna. I know it's soon, but I also know that if I don't do this now I might never go. And I have to go. It seems selfish, I know, but I have to, Anna. Please understand."

You take a breath and answer her with all the empathy you can muster. "I do understand. And I will stay here and keep looking. I'm not giving up, for her and for you."

Rose looks at you again, and you can see she has something more to tell you.

"Anna, this last part is the hardest. I can't live your life for you, but I do hope you'll consider what I'm going to ask." She draws herself up to address you. "I want you to come home with me." She silences you with her words as you begin to object. "Anna, this is not good for you, either. Look at you: You're bone-thin. You've completely stopped working. You're giving your whole life over to this. You need to get your life back, honey." She looks at her hands and continues, "You're like a daughter to me, you know that—" She stops to clear her throat. "If you won't do it for you, do it for me. Please get off of this godforsaken island and come home."

You say nothing as you consider the prospect of packing up your things, boarding an airplane, leaving Buffy behind . . . it sends a cold shiver down your spine.

Rose immediately senses your reluctance. "Just think about it tonight. Please. You're not leaving her, Anna. She'll always be with us."

Walking back to your room, you don't bother with an umbrella despite the wind and rain. Somehow the soaking darkness seems fitting. You know you have a very long night ahead of you.

You barely sleep that night, reexamining the search so far. As you rise and pull the heavy curtains, the glaring sun stings your eyes and you know your decision has been made. You tell Rose you have a few loose ends to tie up on the island but promise you'll follow her back to California within the week. There are a few places you want to revisit and you have a few more questions for the police. Did they thoroughly question every member of the film crew? If so, what new answers might they have? And you just remembered the photographer who was on set for just a couple of days—maybe he'll know something. It's like a nagging itch you can't quite scratch.

On the careening taxi ride to the airport, you chat idly with Rose, avoiding the topic of Buffy. The cab driver plays toneless steel drum music, and Rose fills you in on the plans she has to reconnect with her little circle of friends when she returns home. You fight the surge of irritation you feel. You know she has every right to reclaim her life and Buffy is her daughter after all, but still. Looking through the dusty taxi windows, you're warmed by the sight of locals throwing open their brightly colored shops and restaurants and greeting tourists with friendly smiles. The sun is just beginning to heat the air and the palms sway softly in the breeze. For a moment you feel more at home than you have any place else in your life. The thought of leaving the island brings on a clenching anxiety you pretend not to feel.

The rusty taxi kicks up a cloud of sandy dust, and you wipe away a salty stream of sweat from your brow as you tip the driver and pull Rose's little suitcase from the back seat. It takes your eyes a moment to adjust as you step from the bright-white sun into the shade of the open-air terminal. Head down, you walk briskly to the counter to deposit Rose's suitcase and stand by her side while she checks in. Suddenly, you feel the solid weight of a hand on your shoulder. You spin around and stand blinking in surprise.

"What are you doing here?" you manage to stammer.

Colm widens those magnificent eyes and lets out a hearty laugh. "Well, isn't that a fine how do you do?" All at once, you feel the weight of the world lift. Even the sky seems bluer and the breeze a bit cooler. You find yourself smiling and realize how unfamiliar it feels. How funny that you didn't even realize how much you missed this man.

Then you remember Rose standing beside you, and the smile quickly drains from your face. You feel suddenly guilty that you should be experiencing even a modicum of happiness in the face of so much loss. Rose looks down at her hands and at first you think she is crying. Then she looks up with a guilty grin and takes your hands in hers. "I'm so glad to finally see you smiling!" she says, squeezing your fingers.

Then she does something amazing. She goes to Colm and gives him a long, firm hug. Taking his face in her hands she leans close and whispers, "Thank you for coming."

You realize what she's done, this woman who has lost so much, putting herself aside to give you back something you had lost, too. She takes one of your hands and joins it to one of Colm's. "Now, I have a plane to catch. Get out of here, you two!"

You begin to protest. "Rose, let me—"

She cuts you off mid-sentence. "Honey, you've done more than enough." She folds you into one last, long embrace then walks purposefully down the little corridor toward her waiting flight.

Watching her go, you feel a sense of sadness mixed with a gratitude so strong it almost hurts. You take a breath and turn to Colm.

"I can't believe you're here."

He looks down at your face and with one finger lifts your chin. "I'm just pleased you're smiling. I wasn't certain you would be. But I wouldn't have it any other way." Then he frowns a little and a cloud washes over his eyes. "It's time you and I had a talk."

On the taxi ride back to your hotel you tell Colm everything you've been holding back for the past months. He listens as you divulge your suspicions, list your frustrations, and he dries your tears of anger and pain. "I was just so surprised she left like that, with so little warning." You can't help but share your shock at Rose's departure. "But, Colm, now that you're here, I won't have to do it alone. Thank you so much for coming to help me find her."

Colm takes a moment then exhales a long, slow breath. He looks up into your eyes. "Anna," he tells you, "I didn't come to help you look. I came to take you home."

You feel a punch to your gut and pull away from him. "Home? Colm, this is my home now, at least until I find Buffy. I know she's here. I can feel that she is. I'm going to find her."

Reaching out to take your hand, Colm calmly tries to reason with you. "I know you want nothing more than to find her, or find what happened to her at least, but, Anna, it's been three months. Three months. That is a long while. And I know she was your friend, but would she want you to give up your life for her? I know I didn't know her well, but I don't think she would have, Anna."

You feel a quick surge of anger and jerk your hand away from his. "You don't know her, you're right. And I'll ask you to kindly refrain from referring to her in the past tense. She's my friend; she's not some kind of lost cause. And if you think I'm giving up just because you decide to waltz back in to my life, you don't know me, either."

Colm closes his eyes and rubs the bridge of his nose. "Anna, I didn't mean . . ."

"It doesn't matter what you meant or didn't mean. All that matters is finding Buffy. You can either help me or you can go."

The words sound cold even to you, but you know this is exactly the resolve you need to keep on course. You've had to draw on your strength many times in your career, and to depend only on yourself, and you'll do it a hundred times more if you have to.

Colm looks at you as if trying to work out a puzzle. Finally, he shakes his head and spreads his hands. "Fine, Anna"—his voice is stern and even—"I will help you. But my return flight leaves in three days. My hope is that you'll be sitting next to me on that airplane."

You soften and slide back toward him, your mood considerably brightened. "That doesn't give us much time to find her, but if we double our efforts then maybe we'll all be leaving here together!"

Files and legal pads littered with sticky notes sit in a precarious stack on your utilitarian hotel room desk. Leafing through the pad on top, you fill Colm in on the latest. "So, we've looked pretty much everywhere, but there are these tiny out islands we haven't been able to get to yet. It's a long-shot, but there's a chance."

You reflexively drop the rumpled pad of paper as you feel Colm's hands on your shoulders. You can't believe how quickly his touch overwhelms you, how much you've missed his warm, strong hands on your skin. He dips his head to kiss your earlobe as he whispers, "We'll get to all that, Anna, but for now I want to spend some time on you."

He guides you to the bed, eases you face down onto the bedspread, and uses those magical hands to ease every tense muscle in your body. He begins with your neck and shoulders, his fingers providing just the right amount of pressure. The pleasure of his touch clashes with your intense sense of guilt at wasting even a moment of the time the two of you could be searching for your friend. As his hands work their way down your back, pausing to massage your buttocks before moving to your thighs, you can't help but remember the last few times you and Colm were this close. It was always Colm who pulled away much too soon. So much of you wants to give into this man as he trails his fingers lightly up the insoles of your feet, over your calves, and teasingly back up your inner thighs with just the whisper of a touch. You've never wanted something so much in your life.

Colm puts a hand on your shoulder and gently turns you over to face him then, straddling your legs, he cups the back of your head and leans in to kiss you. As his tongue dances with yours, you once again see a starburst before your closed eyelids and feel a rush of pure emotion toward this magnificent man. You allow yourself a few heavenly moments to bask in Colm's embrace before summoning every bit of willpower to gently pull away. You turn your head to the side and slow your breathing, forcing yourself to picture Buffy standing before you, her eyes beseeching you not to let her go.

"Colm, I'm sorry," you tell him. You feel a tear trickle slowly from the corner of your eye.

"There's nothing to be sorry for, Anna, nothing at all." Colm turns your head back to face him and is every bit the perfect gentleman as he takes your chin between his fingers and kisses you, lingering for just a moment. He wipes the tear from your cheek then follows the path of his finger with a kiss.

Something about the tenderness of his touch breaks through the hard resolve you've built up like a wall around your emotions. Your heartbeat quickens as you kiss him, a kiss that he returns in full. You are so grateful for everything this wonderful man has brought into your life and for his incredible patience and understanding. But it's time to show him how you feel, how deeply you appreciate him. Slowly, slowly, you work your way down from his mouth, kissing every inch of him as you go, over the rise of his Adam's apple, down the length of his neck, across his shoulders, over his muscled chest and arms. He tastes just like he smells, spicy and masculine. You work your way lower, over his taut and muscled stomach then you cautiously move your hand gently even lower. You find him firm and more than ready, large and warm through his thin boxer shorts.

He groans appreciatively as you kiss him gently on the insides of each thigh then work your way higher, easing him out of his boxers.

Colm's breathing becomes ragged and as you move to take him

into your mouth, he gasps and sits up a tiny bit. "Anna, you don't have to,"

"Shh," you interrupt him, as you take as much of him as you can between your lips, swirling your tongue around him. Soon he's sitting up again, and breathing much more quickly. His voice is vastly deeper when he speaks. "Anna, it's not fair for you to have all the fun."

You laugh as he takes you by the waist and deftly flips you onto your back, pressing your head back into the softness of the pillow with a deep kiss. Now it's Colm's turn to explore every inch of you. As he lingers on every sensitive spot on your body, you feel any residual reluctance completely drain away. He takes his time on each breast, gently suckling each nipple before returning to your neck and lips with more kisses. Dipping his head lower, he traces a line from your belly button with the tip of his tongue, pausing at the top of your panties. "These'll have to go," he says with a gleam in his eye as he skims them over your legs and feet. He groans again as he moves his hand between your legs and feels that you're ready for him.

You can't wait to feel him. Suddenly it seems you've been waiting all your life. But, true to form, he keeps you waiting a moment longer, and burrows his face into your most sensitive area. Now it's you who can't help moaning as Colm's tongue explores you, bringing you just to the point of climax. You don't want to end this way, though, and you lift his face with your hands and pull him up to meet you. "I'm ready, Colm."

"That ye are, my Anna, that ye most certainly are," he agrees with satisfaction as he lifts his body over yours then enters you, gently at first, then more powerfully as you rock together. This time neither of you pulls away and you meet each other as waves and waves of fulfilled longing and desire wash over you both. "I love you, Anna," Colm whispers into your ear as the waves begin to subside, "I've never loved anything or anyone more."

You're surprised to find your response comes completely naturally. "I love you, Colm. So much."

He shifts himself to lie facing your back, cradling you in a full-body embrace, his knees behind your knees, his arm draped over yours, fingers entwined with your own. You feel the urgency of him begin to fade as his breathing slows, and the last thing you remember before falling asleep is his breath on your neck and his low voice promising, "I'm here with ye now. Just rest, Anna, just rest."

You awaken with a renewed sense of purpose, feeling more refreshed than you've felt in months. Glimmers of the night before wash over you as your eyes adjust to see Colm sitting in the little chair beside the window, leafing through your stack of notes. He has a legal pad in his lap and he's making some notes of his own. You're so relieved to see he means business.

He glances up and notices you've awakened. "Good mornin', sleuth. Seems you've been up to a fair amount of detective work."

You stretch and throw the covers back then rise to rest your elbows on Colm's chair as you glance over his shoulder.

"I have. But like I said, everything's been a dead end. So far." You breathe a sigh, ruffling the tiny hairs on the back of Colm's neck.

Colm shudders and reaches back to grab your hand, pulling it around to plant a soft kiss in the middle of your palm. You feel a shiver race down your spine. "Hey"—you laugh, pulling your hand away—"you're giving me goose bumps."

Colm laughs a husky response. "What is it they say about turnabout?"

You feel yourself melting into the warmth of Colm, his voice, his touch. Once again you can't believe how quickly you can be distracted. You snap yourself out of it and firmly pull away. Clearing your throat and heading to the bathroom you announce, "I'm hitting the shower. We have work to do."

The two of you spend the next twelve hours in a tiny runabout hopping from scraggly out island to scraggly out island. Tiny and rocky, they take only a short time to cover from end to end. By the time the sun begins to set, you are sand blasted, sun burned, and exhausted. Poor Colm's nose is bright red. Despite liberal reapplications of sun block coupled with a baseball cap, his fair skin looks charred and ready to blister and peel.

You retire exhausted to the hotel room and fall into bed, with just enough energy to snuggle, Colm's long limbs wrapped around yours, but too tired to do any more.

The next day brings more of the same and though you try to hide your frustration, you find yourself short-tempered and snappish. The prospect of your suddenly foreshortened stay on the island is causing you unbelievable stress, as is the constant searching, the continued dead ends, and the knowledge that in one short day Colm will be leaving, with or without you. When he first arrived you thought maybe he would be the answer, the knight in shining armor who would help you rescue Buffy, and that the three of you would leave the island together, living happily ever after.

You rise the next morning to the telltale ping of rain on the roof and find a rare island tempest outside. The palm trees bend in the brisk wind and the rain comes down in steady, slanting sheets. You look out at the water and see whitecaps on the surface, impossible conditions for travel to the last few islands you haven't yet been able to reach.

Colm takes in the look of disappointment on your face. "It may clear yet. The forecast calls for the rain to end by midday."

You sigh with frustration. "It's not enough time. We have six more islands to search. It will take a whole day . . ."

You sink down onto the bed. "Why? Why does it have to rain today? Today of all days?" You slam your fist into a pillow. You were so hoping that today would bring an answer, definitive one way or another. You would either find Buffy and leave with Colm or you would finish your search of the islands and know for sure that you'd explored every possible avenue.

Colm suggests you go through the notes one more time while you wait for the squall to pass. The exercise results in more frustration, a mass of dead ends with no viable leads.

"I know there must be something I've overlooked, but I really cannot see what it could be," you tell Colm as you straighten the pile of papers and rise one more time to look out the window in hopes the rain has lightened. To your dismay, the sky is still a solid grey.

"Anna, you've been very thorough. I've never seen anythin' like it." He pauses, thinking. "You've tracked every lead within your control. There's just one brick wall you've hit over and over and it appears impassable. It's a hard thing, but when a man has somethin' to hide there are times there's no way to the truth."

"I know, Colm, I get that, but I just keep thinking if I can't find her, at least maybe I can find some little scrap of evidence, something that leads to another piece of the puzzle that leads to another until we finally find out . . . but so far there's not even that first little scrap." You shake your head at the thought of how much time you've spent on this and how little your efforts have rendered.

"It is such a hard thing. I know it has to be, Anna. But you have done everythin', everythin' you possibly could do." He stands and takes you by the shoulders. "I propose the followin': You and I to-gether pay a visit to the constable and inform him of our departure, but require his promise that he continues to keep the case open and alive, and that he contacts you immediately when the slightest hint of evidence is found. You're only a plane ride away." He pauses to let it sink in. "Deal?"

You close your eyes and press your palms to your eyelids, shak-ing your head as you answer against your better judgment.

"I guess so, Colm. I'll be honest that I'm not at all certain I'm doing the right thing. But I guess so."

Colm lifts you to your feet and kisses you tenderly. "Ye are, Anna. Ye are doin' entirely the right thing."

You return from the police station more rattled and uncertain than before. The officer there seems irritated but grudgingly agrees to take your phone calls and to keep you informed after you leave. "Yes, Miss Anna, yes, Miss Anna," he says repeatedly. You think you can hear him breathe a sigh of relief as you turn and walk out of the sta-tion.

Colm keeps his arm firmly around your waist as he propels you toward the waiting taxi. You can't help but look once more over your shoulder before you shut the taxi door.

Back at the hotel, you brush the dust from your suitcase and pack slowly and listlessly, glancing out the window over and over. You find yourself playing little games in your own mind, tempting fate to make a decision for you. *If the sun comes out*, you think, *it's a sign I'm supposed to stay*. Or, *If I hear thunder, it's a sign I'm supposed to go*. Of course, nothing changes and the sky remains the same re-lentless steel grey it's been all day long.

At last the few final items are packed. You scour the room, making sure you're leaving nothing behind. The most recent pile of notes, at the moment your most valuable possession by far, goes into your carry-on bag.

You zip your suitcase and look around the room one last time. It's fitting somehow, you think, that the rain should be falling as you take your leave, as if the island is mourning the loss of Buffy.

Colm picks up your suitcase and together you walk out the door. The very moment you step outside, a ray of light slices through the clouds, blinding you both. You shield your eyes, look up at the sky, and are instantly dazzled by the sun shooting from behind a huge, grey cloud. A glance toward the beach confirms that the water has calmed, the translucent blue surface rippling gently. You don't know what it means, but you feel the sudden change is sending you a message.

"Ready?" asks Colm, sensing your hesitation.

"Colm, I'm not sure . . ."

You look up at the sky again. You're unable to move, watching the clouds break apart, the blue island sky overtaking the grey.

"Anna. We really don't have a lot of time, the flight—"

"I know, Colm. I know what time the flight is. I'm just not sure I'm supposed to be on it."

Colm seems to crumple physically. "Not supposed to be on it? Anna, what does that mean? You've packed, you've made your decision." He gently cups your elbow and nudges you forward. "Please walk with me."

Colm begins to take a few steps but you find yourself rooted to your spot. You feel utterly and completely torn. You take a moment to look at Colm, who you know very possibly could be your future and who genuinely seems to care about you more than anyone else before him has, and you feel a sense of something slipping through your fingers. But looking back at the coastline of the tiny island you've come to think of as both a puzzle and a home, you feel Buffy slipping away, too. What should you do?

To move on and leave the island with Colm, turn to page 138.
To say goodbye to Colm, perhaps forever, and continue your search for Buffy, keep reading.

"Colm," you call from where you are standing. He turns to you, a look of pleading overtaking his handsome features. You look down at the sandy walkway and know this is where you are meant to be. You harness your resolve and look him in the eye. "I'm so sorry. But I have to stay."

Colm makes one last, futile effort. "Anna, please think this through."

"I have. Over and over again. I have tried with every fiber of my being to convince myself I should leave. But now that I'm actually facing it, I know more strongly than I've ever known anything in my life that I simply can't. I won't give up. I hope you can understand."

Colm runs his fingers through his thick black hair and shakes his head. "I can't say that I understand. You've done everythin', Anna, looked absolutely everywhere." He shakes his head again and sighs, a deep wrinkle creasing his brow. "But I can't convince ye of that. Ye have to know it yourself. And I won't stand in the way of what ye feel ye need to do."

Gently, he walks toward you, placing your bag at your feet. He takes you into his arms and holds you for a long moment, then kisses the top of your head and whispers, "If ye change your mind, I'll be waitin'."

As he walks away, you angrily fight the tears that fill your eyes. You know you may very well never see this man again, that you've made a decision that might change the course of your life. But it's your decision, and you know in your heart it's the right one. You turn and walk back to your little room, dark now compared to the dazzling sun outside, unpack your stacks of research, and refocus yourself.

As the months pass, the ache of Colm's leaving subsides. You find yourself spending more hours alone in your room. Eventually, you purchase a little piece of property on the island complete with a run-down, miniature house, and you begin to devote some of your efforts toward making it a home. Every plant you add to the garden grows at an unbelievable speed, and soon your little house is secluded by a veritable jungle garden. Even though the lush greenery blocks some of the light in the house, you find you are often relieved to return to the dim coolness of your private sanctuary.

Months turn into years, and the time seems to fly. You barely check your e-mail anymore, and the only TV you ever see is at the little diner you frequent for most of your meals. You intentionally keep yourself away from newspapers and magazines, and instead consume novels you never before had time to read.

You know you've gained some weight but take long walks on the beaches to help stay fit. You don't own a scale or a full-length mirror and are perfectly happy this way. In any case, the shapeless, flowing tropical dresses you wear make you feel elegant and comfortable.

One day, as you return from your morning ritual, a breakfast of pancakes, toast, eggs, and bacon, the glossy cover of a magazine resting on the little island market newsstand catches your eye. Normally you're able to sail right past the display without a second glance, but this cover makes you do a double take. The silhouette is oddly familiar, though you can't place it at first. Moving closer, you make out the slightly blurry blue dress, the shot taken from behind the bending figure. You pull the reading glasses you've only recently been forced to acquire down onto your nose, peer at the photo, and then notice the headline:

EXCLUSIVE PHOTOS OF THE RECLUSIVE ANNA CHAMBLISS: INSIDE HER HIDEAWAY!

Your heart pounds as the feeling of violation begins to set in. You grab the glossy rag from its flimsy metal rack and quickly pay the shopkeeper, grateful that he's disinterested enough not to notice it's you on the cover.

The run back to your villa leaves you winded. You plunk down heavily into your armchair and quickly leaf through the magazine's inky pages. You're relieved to see there's not much substance to the story, but disheartened to see that it hits a little too close to home.

Another unflattering and blurry shot of you bending over your garden hogs the page opposite the thin column of text. The photo has obviously been altered. There's no way your backside is that wide. Inset is a trade photo of you before, in full glam mode. The caption reads, "An unrecognizable Anna Chambliss in her island hideaway."

As you skim the ugly words, a numbness sets in.

Little has been known about the whereabouts of one-time headliner Anna Chambliss since her disappearance from the Hollywood scene almost ten years ago. Now, she's been discovered living a hermit-like existence in a tiny hut on the island on which she filmed her final project. A rustic hut, overgrown with vines and weeds, has served as a hideaway for the reclusive star, whose weight has ballooned over the past decade. Recent photos of the actress reveal her fuller figure and her once-famous tresses now streaked with grey. "No one here really knows who she is," says an island local. "She keeps to herself." A Hollywood source tells WE, "Anna went a little crazy after she lost her best friend years ago. She shut the world off and clearly prefers her privacy." What will be next for Anna now that she's been rediscovered? Only time will tell.

You toss the magazine into the nearest garbage can. You know you've gained some weight, but it's certainly not as bad as that silly magazine makes it look. Standing in front of the bathroom mirror, you take a good, hard look at yourself. It's true, you can only see your reflection from the waist up, but still, you aren't blind. You know you're no longer a size two, but you're also not a size XL either. In fact, most of the island shops' size Large dresses fit you just fine. And you can't help that you've been blessed with the ample bust that makes that size a necessity.

Your eyes move higher and you turn your head slowly from side to side, running your fingers through the unruly mass of your hair, wild from the island's perpetual humidity. There may be a few silver strands here and there, but certainly not the "grey-streaked tresses" the tabloid describes. Satisfied that it's not as bad as all that, you curl up in your comfy corner chair with your latest murder mystery and soon fall asleep.

When you awaken, the angle of the sun tells you it is at least late afternoon. You slip on your flip-flops and saunter out to the garden. A sharp yell makes you whip your head around, "Anna! Anna! Over here!"

A sound you haven't heard in years sends your stomach into a plummet as the click and snap of camera shutters surrounds you. "Get off my property!" you yell, before ducking back inside and slamming your door. Your heart hammers as you pull the blinds and lock the shutters to keep the prying eyes outside.

You jump at every noise that night and arise bleary-eyed the next morning. You open the shutter of your front window just a crack to peer outside and are relieved to see no signs of prying eyes. Just in case, you make a quick trip to the bathroom and unearth an ancient foundation, mascara, and lipstick. You apply just a little and then run a brush through your hair. Unable to tame it, you decide to tie it into a messy ponytail. It will give them less to work with, you think, if you're a bit more presentable.

As you leave for breakfast, you turn onto the little crushed-shell walkway and are pleased to find no paparazzi lurking. You make it all the way to the diner and take your usual seat on the covered terrace, enjoying the smell of sizzling breakfast food while a light breeze sweeps across your face. You thank the waitress as she brings you your plate, heaped with fluffy scrambled eggs, stacked with pancakes, and piled with crisp bacon. You salt and pepper the eggs, give the pancakes a healthy dousing of syrup, and begin to eat. As you do, something catches your eye from the corner of the patio. Are the palm leaves moving more than makes sense in the light breeze, or is it your imagination? No, you're certain the breeze isn't that strong . . . Then you spot an ugly telephoto lens protruding from the foliage and wielded by a cowardly paparazzo. "Hey!" you shout, advancing on the cameraman. "Hey! Get out of here!"

The waitress reappears and backs you up, "Git, you slitherin' snake!" she shouts. The cameraman is gone as quickly as he appeared. You sit back down to your breakfast, grateful for the help of the waitress, but find your appetite has disappeared.

Almost a week to the day later, a new photo appears on the front of *WE*, and this time it's even worse than before. An image of you leaning in to devour what looks like an enormous plate of food dominates the cover, while a smaller photo in a box below shows you in attack mode, wielding your fork as you advance on the photographer. The headline reads ANNA CHAMBLISS' CRAZED RAMPAGE! WHAT SENT THE RECLUSE INTO A RAGE?

You don't even bother to read the article. Instead, you head for the local hardware store to purchase NO TRESPASSING signs, which you post in front of your house. You spend the rest of the day in a state of agitation and worry.

The next few days only get worse. One photographer turns into three and then five. You realize the sensational photos must be worth a lot for these parasites to travel all this way. You begin to order your meals in and you leave the house only when you have to. A prisoner in your own home, you now truly feel like the recluse they've made you out to be.

One day a week later, you have no choice but to leave the house for a few essentials. You decide to make the trip into town at night and only after you've washed and brushed your hair, applied your makeup, and put on your prettiest dress, plus your largest pair of sunglasses. You hope for the best and think perhaps you've made it when about halfway into town you're accosted by incessant flashing.

You're momentarily blinded and stumble onto the sharp shells of the little path. You brush the fragments from your knees, hold onto your pride, and continue gamely to the store. The flashes follow you all the way, no doubt documenting your every purchase. Back at your house, you finally lose the cameraman, who is wise enough to stop at the edge of your yard.

Your heart pounding, you drop the little bag of groceries, sink to the floor, and cry. You've worked so hard to set up the perfect shelter, to remove yourself from the negativity of Hollywood and the media, only to have it find you and ruin everything. You know in your heart you'll have to do something drastic to make them leave you alone, but short of ending your own life or ending one of theirs, you don't know how to do it—and neither seems like a particularly good option. *Maybe it is time for a change*, you think, and try to figure out what that change should be.

One morning the next week, there's a knock on the door that interrupts your breakfast. You put down your coffee cup and warily approach the front door. Without opening it you shout, "Who's there?"

A deep, male voice rings from the other side of the doorway. "Anna, I'm not a reporter. I'm here on business. I have a proposition for you that I think you'll find interesting. If you'll give me fifteen minutes of your time I'll explain it all. Have you heard of a television show called *Sashaying with Celebs*?"

Five weeks and one signed contract later, you find yourself being buffed and prepped for your debut on *SwC*. Your spray-tanned body is stuffed forcibly into the sturdy foundation garment for your embarrassingly skimpy, tassel-and-glitter-covered costume. The makeup team applies a second set of false eyelashes, carefully dotting the glue along your eyelids. You step gingerly into your costume and sit carefully (the only way you can sit without losing the circulation in the lower half of your body) and allow one stocking-covered foot then another to be strapped into a shiny, silken dance shoe.

Though everything feels like it's chafing and too tight, you can't help but gasp a little when you catch your reflection in the mirror. Your hair has been colored, cut, and styled to its former fullness with the help of glossy amber extensions. Your skin looks perfect, and the spray-tan has even added some definition to the upper arms you were so worried about exposing. You give a little twirl and squeal when your hunky but very homosexual dance partner, Alexei, sidles up to you and slips his muscular arm around your waist. "Magnificent!" he growls, apprising your newly glammed look.

The few minutes on the flashing ballroom stage feel like seconds and before you know it the crowd is on its feet in applause. "What a comeback!" declares the notoriously hard-nosed British judge from behind the bench. You score solid 7s and are pronounced the contestant with the most potential. You go to bed that night feeling light and joyful for the first time in ages.

The grueling weeks of practice and rehearsal are worth it. The weight falls off and your costumes get smaller and more revealing. Before you know it, the costume designers are even cutting out the midsection of one gown to bare your newly taut tummy.

You make it to the semifinals and then move on to the very last show, this small accomplishment making you happier than you can remember ever being. Agents approach you with memoir proposals, sitcom pilot scripts, and even a supporting movie role. Your head is spinning with the opportunities that lay before you, and only in the very darkest hours of the night do you feel the guilt creep in for the friend you lost and for the life you left behind in your tiny island abode.

The final show looms large. You'll have to perform three dances and you're praying you remember each step you've rehearsed so many times. Your stomach feels like it's filled with the world's largest and most ferocious butterflies. As you enter the glittery little holding room to sit beside your competitors, excitement overwhelms every other emotion. Alexei steps gracefully to your side and plants a tender kiss on your lacquered cheek. "We got this," he whispers into your ear. You return his sentiment with a huge smile and feel an overwhelming sadness at the thought that this is it, the last night of all this brilliance.

As usual, the show goes by in a blur. You shiver with nerves backstage as the judges tabulate the results to decide who the winner of the coveted bronzed top hat trophy will be.

As you nervously pick at the edges of your solidly lacquered nail gels, a voice interrupts your thoughts. "Uh, excuse me, Ms. Chambliss."

Something about the voice sends you into an even greater state of anxiety and your heart feels as though it's about to freeze in your chest. You know you should turn around to face the speaker but for some reason you seem to be completely paralyzed.

Alexei squeezes your shoulder, breaking your trance. "Anna, someone's here to see you."

Slowly, you turn your head in the direction of the voice. He looks almost as you remember. The same rugged features, the same perpetual five o'clock shadow, the same piercing grey eyes, the same shock of dark hair falling over his forehead. Maybe a few more lines . . . but when he speaks, the same gorgeous brogue sends a chill through you to your toes.

"Hello, Anna. Would you have time for an interview?"

"How did you—" you begin. In answer, he holds up the laminated media pass hanging from the long lanyard around his neck.

Much later, as you dust off the glitter and confetti clinging to your hair and set your newly acquired bronzed top hat trophy on the vanity table in your nicely appointed hotel room, you feel as if everything has come full circle, or almost.

Colm sits on the vanity bench, looking a bit like a bull in a china shop, but it's the only place to sit in the little room, aside from the bed.

"Congratulations," he tells you, "you sashayed like a pro."

You laugh, feeling the years apart slipping away. He rises from the delicate bench and takes your hand in his. "Would ye sashay a bit with me?"

He begins to spin you around the room then pulls you in more closely, so closely that you feel the delicious scratchiness of his stubble against your cheek. You remain like that for a wonderful moment, feeling the years of icy boundaries begin to melt in his arms.

Chills run through you again, this time ending not quite so low as your toes, when he whispers gruffly into your ear, "We have to do something about all this makeup."

He pulls you into the bathroom and turns on the shower. Steam begins to roll in gorgeous clouds as he slowly undresses you. For a moment you are frozen with self-consciousness. You know the Anna he will be seeing is not the Anna he remembers. Nervously, you turn your back and allow him to lower the zipper of your dress. You try not to think about what his reaction will be when he sees what lies underneath. Even though you've lost quite a bit of the weight you gained during your years on the island, you're nowhere close to the size you once were, and you know your age will show.

Colm reads your hesitation and gives you your time, then slowly turns you to face him. He gently knocks the straps from your shoulders and lets the dress fall to the floor. His eyes run up and down your body and you feel more naked than you've ever felt in your life. You can't seem to meet his gaze when his eyes return to your face, but he takes a finger under your chin and lifts your eyes to meet his.

"Anna," he tells you, his voice husky with desire, "you've never looked more beautiful."

As you shower together, he uses a soft cloth to gently wipe the makeup and tears from your face and holds you until you finish crying. Then he slathers the loofah with soap and works it in delicious circles all over your body, concentrating on your breasts, your belly, your buttocks, and thighs. He kisses you as the warm water runs over you both, and your heart thaws completely in the warmth of Colm's embrace. Finally, you allow yourself to look at him. His body is beautiful; his arms elegantly muscled, his legs and backside firm, only his belly shows just the slightest softness.

You gaze lower and take in the length of his cock. He gleams slick in the water from the shower, and you reach to take him into your hand as he moves the loofah lower, running it smoothly up each thigh then finding the most sensitive spot between your legs and rubbing the slightly abrasive sponge gently there. As he works, you discover the benefit of the sheath of his foreskin, using it to bring him to the point of pleasure. When neither of you can wait another moment, Colm turns off the water and wraps you in a soft towel, drying every inch of you and stopping to kiss you every few seconds as he does. He guides you to the bed and, kissing you hungrily, uses his fingers to bring you back to the edge of desire. When he is sure you are ready, he shifts his body to pause above yours for a moment and looks down between you. For a moment you're sure he will pull away, but instead he thrusts to fill you with every inch of him. As you climax together, waves of pleasure crash over and over you and you melt completely into this man you have loved from the first moment you met. Later, he holds you close under the soft, warm covers of your bed, and everything feels right again.

"There's so much to tell you . . ." you begin as you lay in his arms. But he silences you with a gentle kiss and holds you tightly to him.

"Just rest now, Anna. I'm not going anywhere. And we have all the time in the world."

THE END

**To take Anna on a new Bedventure, go back and choose
a new path.**

From page 129 . . .

You feel the anxiety that has become such part of your existence in this place begin to drain away as you make the decision to leave the island. Slowly, you extend your hand and allow Colm to take it. Firmly but gently, he walks you to the waiting taxi. You look back only once before closing the door, whispering one last goodbye to Buffy.

Your re-entry into the world of LA is bumpier than you expected. Tabloids and paparazzi hound you relentlessly, trying to flush out the details of your hiatus. "Anna!" they shout. "How was rehab?" Rumors of plastic surgery, engagement, and even a hidden wedding swirl. The only piece of information the tabloids get right is that your agent dropped you unceremoniously upon your return. There are many moments you consider booking the next flight back to your island hideaway.

But then you come home to Colm, who wraps his arms tightly around you and tilts your face up to his, declaring you a "wee, bonny lass," an expression which never fails to bring a smile to your lips and warmth to your heart. At least Colm has some control over what is printed in *WE*, and your flattering coverage in that popular magazine seems to kill some of the rumors and improve your public image. Offers from reality show talent scouts come pouring in and then finally a slow trickle of scripts begins to follow.

Colm is careful to take his time with you and is the consummate gentleman in every aspect of your relationship. You take long hikes together every evening, enjoying the simple intimacy of holding hands, and each night you lie in the cocoon of Colm's embrace, feeling safer and more complete than you ever imagined you could. When you wake in the morning, you feel a surge of grateful joy to find him beside you, and turn to him and take his face between your hands, the delicious roughness of his cheeks slightly abrading your palms.

Colm's presence beside you is a healing salve. Although you continue making regular calls to the island authorities, you find you have much less control at this distance and get far briefer responses. Eventually your calls and inquiries become fewer and farther between.

One morning, as you sit on the little balcony, finishing your coffee, the doorbell rings. Colm answers and slides open the screen door with a serious expression on his face. "It's Rose," he whispers. He reads the look of concern and confusion on your face and shrugs his shoulders.

You slide past him and greet Rose, who is standing in the entryway, fingers tugging nervously at her beaded necklace. Gathering her into a hug, you notice how thin and frail she feels. She looks like she hasn't slept in days. Your heart drops. You don't even want to imagine what she is here to say.

"Do you have a minute to talk?" she asks.

"Of course," you tell her. You'd do anything for this woman. You lead her into the living room and sit beside her on the sofa. Colm leans in, pokes his head around the wall, and excuses himself politely. "I'm just off on a quick errand. Can I bring you something to drink, either of you?"

"No, thank you, dear," Rose tells him,

"I'm good, thanks," you reply, your voice a little strangled. He gives you a small grin of encouragement before he leaves.

"Anna," Rose begins, "I've been doing a lot of thinking. It's been almost a year."

"I know," you tell her, feeling the old emotions wash over you, bringing a sudden spring of tears to your eyes.

"Which means almost two since you last saw her," Rose pauses for a moment before continuing. "I know how much you love her, Anna, and I know how hard this has been on all of us." She takes a breath then bravely soldiers on, "Anna, I need to tell you something. I can't go on . . ." Her voice breaks and she takes a moment to compose herself. "I need to tell you the truth."

You say nothing, giving Rose the time she needs. She breathes out a slow, controlled breath and meets your eyes.

"Anna, please believe me when I tell you this—I didn't know either, not until right before I left, and then I had to protect her. Please try to understand."

"Rose, what are you saying?"

"I'm sorry, Anna, I'm trying to explain—it's just . . . She doesn't know I'm here and I don't know how much to say. But I feel like I need to tell you everything. It's not fair, what we've put you through."

Suddenly your head is spinning, your heart racing. Did you really hear what you think you heard? You know it can't be right, but still, you want so much to believe it, to hold onto those words. *She doesn't know I'm here.* You control your breathing and do your best to hide the shock you feel. You want Rose to continue. You squeeze your trembling hands together then take Rose's hands in yours. "Go on," you tell her.

"That day I came to you, on the island. It was only the night before that the call came in. She sounded so panicked, Anna, I could barely follow what she was saying. She begged me, made me promise I wouldn't breathe a word to anyone. She was so afraid of what he might do. She wouldn't even tell me where she was at first. She'd just lost trust in everything, everyone. But she needed me, Anna. So I had to leave, to go to her. And I couldn't tell you, I just couldn't. I'm so sorry, Anna. It's eaten at me every day since I left you. The one solace I had was that I'd already arranged for Colm to come—please believe me when I tell you this—I had planned that long before I ever knew, and you were beginning to lose yourself in that search. When she called, and I knew she was safe, and I knew Colm was coming to help lift you out of that awful place, it just seemed like things were finally righting themselves, like our prayers were being answered. It all happened so quickly."

She pauses for a moment, then continues, "She's all I have in the world, Anna. And then when she told me the truth—what she had been through, and that she was expecting, I had no choice but to protect her. She wanted so much to keep the baby, Anna, and she was convinced he would come after her. We just couldn't risk anyone knowing."

A dizzying mix of emotions begins to emerge as Rose finally speaks the words you have been waiting for so long to hear. "But she's alive, Anna. It's time you know. She's alive."

You laugh giddily and let the pointless sense of betrayal fall away as tears of joy and relief wash down your cheeks. "She's alive! Oh my God, I thought you were here to tell me—it doesn't matter what I thought!" You grab Rose by the shoulders and embrace her again. "Where is she? I have to see her."

"It's not that simple," Rose says, straightening up and moving slightly away from you on the sofa. "She would be furious if she knew I was here, Anna. She has a lot more at stake now than just her own safety. There's the baby to think about, too."

"Is she here in LA? Is she okay? Is the baby a boy or a girl? How old is he—or she? Please, I want to know everything."

"I know you do, Anna, and the time will come. But for now, just know that Buffy is safe. I'm going to work on her. It's changed her, what she's been through, and she's just beginning to feel safe again. I can't take that from her. But I also couldn't let you grieve any longer."

You know you have no choice but to accept this small gift you've been given, however incomplete it feels. "Thank you, Rose. Thank you for telling me. Even if I never get to see her again, at least I know she's safe. And that's so much more than I was expecting. But I hope she'll forgive me. I hope she knows how much I miss her."

Visibly relieved, Rose rises and takes your hands again. "Thank you, Anna, for understanding. I was hoping you would. I knew you would. You are a wonderful friend and a beautiful person. I'm going to work on her, I promise."

With that, Rose picks up her purse and walks out the door. You feel as though the weight of the world has been lifted from your shoulders. At the same time, you feel incredibly exhausted. You curl up on the sofa, unsure whether to laugh or cry, so you do both as you wait for Colm to return.

He does moments later, and you realize he must have been just outside waiting for Rose to leave. He takes one look at your face and gathers you into an enormous hug. "I'm so sorry, Anna," he says.

You look up at him with what must look like an insane smile. "She's alive, Colm. I don't know whether I'll ever see her again, but she's alive!"

His baffled "Mmmph?" followed by "Well then, that's brilliant!" has you laughing hysterically.

"I know, it is brilliant!" you agree, and you settle beside him on the sofa to tell him the little bit you know. The next few weeks seem endless as you wait for word you know may never come from Rose. Your emotions swing wildly and you find yourself bursting into tears at odd moments. Colm is there through it all, supporting you when you need it and giving you space when you don't.

"You're in a bit of shock, Anna. It's to be expected with news like this." He is truly the perfect match for you, calming you when you need it most. You realize how lucky you are.

You do your best to distract yourself with work. A handful of offers present themselves—commercials, scripts for TV movies or trite sitcoms, even an artsy indie film. You read carefully through everything that comes your way, but nothing seems right. At last, a script arrives that looks promising. It's a pilot for a sitcom about an aspiring actress living with a male roommate and his young son. It's witty, sarcastic, and right up your alley. You read a little to Colm, who laughs in all the right places.

"This could be something," he says with a glint in his eye.

"It is intriguing," you agree, "but what if it gets picked up? We'd be committed to living in New York for who knows how long."

"One step at a time," Colm tells you. "Step one, sounds like you need a good agent."

"Hmmm . . . I do. An agent and a manager." Your eyes meet his and you can see the idea already fully formed. "You'd want to do that?"

"Might as well get paid for it," he laughs, ducking the pillow you throw at his head.

Colm begins spending less and less time at *WE* and more and more time reaching out to the many contacts he's built up over his years working as a Hollywood journalist. He arranges for flattering photos to signal your impending comeback to be printed in only a few of the top national entertainment magazines.

He comes into the kitchen one morning as you're rinsing the last sip of coffee from your morning mug. "Guess what?" he asks, looking every bit the cat that ate the canary. "The phone's started ringin'."

You look up at him quizzically. "What does that mean?"

"It means," he tells you, drawing you into his arms in a huge bear hug, "that people are startin' to call lookin' for ye—'stead of the other way round."

You laugh at the sudden increase in his brogue, always heightened when his mood is, too.

"In fact, I'm here to tell ye I've two, count 'em, two, film scripts on the way right now. You may just have your pick of a project."

You're so excited you can hardly stand it, and you jump up and down like a little girl. The thought of a TV series is exciting but film is where your heart is. "Thank you, thank you!" you squeal, kissing Colm on his scruffy cheek.

As promised, two scripts arrive by courier within a day. Both are fun and full of promise. Then, two days later, a third script arrives. It's about an actress trying to come back after some hard knocks. It's as if it was written for you and the mix of hilarious bits with touching undertones pulls at your heart. You read it in one sitting.

Your heart skips with excitement as you march into Colm's office. "This is it," you tell him. "I have a really good feeling about this one." "Brilliant," he says, with warmth in his eyes. "It's yours then." He picks up the phone to set the wheels into motion.

Day one of shooting feels like falling back into the rhythm of a dance you know in your soul. The chemistry of the cast is electric and you love every moment. You are thrilled and relieved when the critics do, too.

Everything is falling into place, and you know you wouldn't have any of it without Colm by your side.

Your first hiatus, you surprise him with a trip back to Scotland to visit his family. You've arranged for a hotel near his childhood village, not wanting to step on anyone's toes, and a little nervous at the thought of meeting his family. Still, you know it is time.

Colm beams as you walk arm in arm down the long airport terminal corridor. You can feel him physically relax as he enters his homeland. You pass a newsstand and spot a glossy tabloid with an inevitable Anna Chambliss headline: ANNA CHAMBLISS FINDS HER KNIGHT IN SHINING ARMOR! IS AN ENGAGEMENT IN THE WORKS? WE HAS THE ANSWERS!

Colm squeezes your hand as you pass by. "The media—they never do give up, do they?" He laughs ironically.

In the taxi to the hotel, Colm takes your hand. "You're freezing!" you tell him, pulling your hand back and tucking it between the layers of your thick wool scarf.

"I'm nervous, Anna." He pauses before continuing, "There's something I haven't quite told you."

A pit of dread forms in your stomach as you wait to hear what is coming next.

"It's just"—Colm is tongue-tied again and clears his throat before he goes on—"it's just I haven't quite told you exactly everything about my growin' up. I was thinking it'd be better if I show you."

He gives the taxi driver what might be an address but sounds more like a name. You can't tell completely because the two have fallen into an almost indecipherable brogue.

"Mmph" is the driver's only response, as he takes a sharp turn onto a tiny, winding, graveled roadway.

Colm's hand clamps more tightly to yours as you ride up the bumpy drive. A canopy of majestic, emerald trees with knobby, ancient-looking trunks gives way to more manicured shrubs on either side of an ornamental iron gate. You cross through the gate and into a circle with an age-worn, non-functional fountain in its center. Beyond the circle sits another pair of overgrown ornamental shrubs, and beyond that, the most magnificently dilapidated stone castle you've ever seen.

"We won't be more'n a few moments," Colm tells the driver.

The loose stone drive leads to a wide, chipped, and worn stairway. You can see the path centuries of footsteps have left on each stone tread, concave and darkened toward their centers. You look at Colm inquisitively, trying to gauge what is going on. He tucks your hand firmly into the crook of his arm and guides you up the enormous stairway.

Before he opens the door, he turns you to face him. "Anna," he begins nervously, "I'm sorry I didn't tell you all this before. It's a lot to swallow. I know that. I'm just asking you to keep an open mind."

The massive entry door yawns open with an enormous creak as Colm leads you into a dimly lit but breathtaking grand hallway. The soaring ceilings are lost in shadows and the light slants in toward the floor at odd angles through dust-covered windows. There's stone as far as the eye can see, worn smooth with age and dotted with ancient rugs, themselves worn threadbare in places, and pieces of what must be furniture covered with heavy, dust-laden tarps. It looks haunted, bewildering, and altogether magnificent.

"What?" you begin, your eyes adjusting to the dim light.

Your voice echoes wildly through the empty rooms as you reach out to touch the cool, grey stone of the walls.

Colm turns to face you again, sweeping his eyes around the huge hall. "It's ours, Anna, if you want it."

"What? How?" is all you can manage.

"I'll explain everything to you, I promise. It's a lot to care for, I know. It's been more'n my family could do for the past hundred years, as you can see. But I think we could make something of it. Anna, what do you say?"

"What do I say?" you stammer. "I don't even understand what is going on right now."

"The castle's been in the family for centuries, Anna. But it takes a load of work—a whole staff to keep it running, in fact. It's not something my family were able to do. I was telling you the truth about my growin' up. That part, anyway. This was never home to us. But I've always dreamt that someday I could come back here and bring her back to how she used to be. She could be glorious, Anna."

And in his eyes you see his vision. For a moment, you picture the windows hung with rich draperies, the cold, stone hall warmed with firelight, the floors covered with fine rugs, and the furniture uncovered, gleaming and resplendent, its wood reflecting the glowing flames.

"Yes, Colm," you tell him with a smile, suddenly realizing that restoring Colm's ancient family castle would be an amazing adventure. "I think it could."

Your visit to Colm's childhood home is charming. His mother and father are kind and gracious hosts. Colm's mother is sturdy and maternal, embracing you in a cloud of warmth that smells of something earthy and sweet. Her dark locks are tamed back into a low bun shot through with tendrils of silvery grey, a few errant curls escaping to frame her lovely face. His father is wiry and weatherworn, but just as warm as she, his sparkling eyes ringed with wrinkles unmistakably left by years of happiness. They want to know all about you, although clearly there's quite a bit Colm has told them already, and they ask you question after question in their lovely, lilting brogues throughout the hearty meal.

After the dinner plates are cleared, Colm guides you by the hand to the little hidden garden in back of the cottage. Your head is fuzzy with the red wine you've drunk and your body is humming with the warmth of good company and a rich meal. In the center of the overgrown lawn, a small fire dances in an iron cauldron, and lit candles perch on the uneven stones scattered artfully about, lending a magical quality to the chilly night.

Colm brings you to a low stone bench, wrapping a thick flannel blanket around your shoulders. He sits beside you, rubbing his hands together over and over in front of the little blaze. He seems very nervous, and your heart quickens its pace, reacting instinctively to his sudden change in mood.

All at once, he drops to one knee and the breath catches in your chest. He plunges his hand deep into his pocket and brings out a sparkling, gorgeous, perfect solitaire.

"Anna," he begins, and tears leap instantly to your eyes, "the moment we bumped heads all those years ago, I knew. Don't know whether it was a concussion from which I've never recovered, but from that day I have been head-over-heels for you. If a concussion it be, I don't ever care to be clear-headed. You've brought everything good into my life, and I hope to return the favor."

You're laughing even as a tear tracks its way down your cheek. The laugh begins somewhere small and quiet then grows louder and more joyful as Colm speaks.

"We've been through some shite, you and I, but there's no one else in the world I'd want to go through it with, the happy times and the hard times."

Colm looks down at the ring in his hand, the diamond sparkling like some magic charm, reflecting the many colors of the firelight. Then he looks up at you, a glow of pure happiness in his eyes.

"Would you do me the great honor, Ms. Anna Chambliss, love of my life, of becoming my bride?"

You leap to your feet, pulling Colm to his, feeling like a little girl on Christmas. You fall into his arms answering over and over again, "Yes, yes, yes!"

You wed in the great hall of the majestic castle, which has just begun to show a glimmer of its former glory. A team of world-famous decorators, experts in historic restoration, and fabulous advisers have begun their work. Between their efforts and the significant elbow grease you and Colm and have put in, the hall has been thoroughly scrubbed of its dust and cobwebs and ornamented with hundreds of candles, elegant sconces, and thousands of flowers dripping from every available corner and crevice. The service is intimate and simple, and as you walk down the long, candlelit aisle toward your waiting groom, the intricate lace of your heavy train trailing behind you, you are filled with the absolute rightness of the promise you are about to fulfill and the wonderful anticipation of the life you are about to begin. You're trembling a little as you meet Colm at the altar, but when he takes your hands in his, the warmth of his touch and the love in his eyes steadies you.

As you turn to face the small crowd assembled in the rough-hewn pews that line the altar, Colm leans down to whisper in your ear, "I've a small surprise for you, my lovely bride." He guides you to the last row and pauses to watch you take in the wedding guests you weren't expecting.

Tears begin to stream down your cheeks, blurring your vision as you take in the face you thought you might never see again. She's a little thinner than you remember and seems a little taller somehow, but the ginger curls are the same, as are the great, blue eyes brimming over with joy and love. In her arms is her spitting image, a beautiful, round-cheeked toddler with her mother's full head of curls and huge, sparkling eyes. There's nothing you can see of her father in the child and that, too, is a relief.

"I can't believe you're here!" you tell her. Then you glimpse Rose sitting just on the other side of her daughter. "Thank you, both," you manage, and then take the hand of your new husband and squeeze it with immense gratitude. "This makes everything just—perfect!"

Buffy laughs and reaches an arm out to grab you into her soft embrace. "Grace," she tells the little girl, "this is your Aunt Annie."

"Princess!" says the toddler, pointing at your gown.

"Well, yes, she can be a bit of a diva," laughs Buffy, and from that moment on, it's like nothing has changed. Colm graciously shares your "honeymoon" with Buffy and Grace, and you spend long days in the castle and countryside catching up on all you have missed.

Buffy reluctantly opens up about how difficult and frightening it has been living in virtual hiding, how alone she has felt, how she's barely wanted to step out of her mother's house for fear of being discovered. The few times she has ventured out, it's been in full makeup and a dark wig. She can't bear the thought of raising Grace in fear, but she doesn't know what choice she has. At least the little girl has Rose to take her out of the house. Maybe, she says, one day it will all resolve itself. "That last night with him, he swore if I ever left him he would find me. I knew I had to go, that if I waited any longer I would be risking everything, and I'm so sorry I couldn't tell you. He is evil, Anna, and he's relentless. But you knew that."

"You did the right thing," you tell your friend, and you mean it.

Four glorious weeks pass too quickly. You feel whole once again, more complete and happier than you ever thought possible. The four of you have become a family, little Gracie a ray of pure sunshine. You wish you could stay here, all of you together forever, but the happy news that the sitcom pilot you shot before you left for Scotland been picked up has you due back in New York next week. You know they could probably find a replacement, and after all you really did want to stick to films. Still, the sitcom seems like such a perfect fit, and TV has become almost as well received and as well done as film lately. And you have an idea.

Once Buffy and Grace have gone to bed for the evening, you find Colm sitting in his cozy study, pouring over the plans for the castle grounds. You wrap your arms around his strong shoulders, breathing in his wooly, spicy scent. "Colm, what would you think about asking Buffy to stay? She doesn't really have a home anymore and she feels like she has to hide all the time back in the States. I know it's a little selfish, but that way we would get to be with her when we're here, too. Who knows if she would even go for it, but I was thinking she might."

Colm turns and kisses you gently on the bridge of your nose. "That's an idea, indeed. Would be good to have someone here, keeping track of the cottage," he winks. "Making sure the crew isn't slacking off. I wouldn't mind it a bit. Let's ask her. Together."

Buffy is thrilled to be asked but hesitant at first. Her home is in LA, but the thought of real freedom, the possibility of a life free from constant fear, wins her over at last. It's a better outcome than you could have dreamed. You'll be back in three months once shooting wraps and until then, you're only a phone call or computer screen away.

You and Colm take an apartment in New York City where you stay during filming. Colm spends his days fielding requests for meetings and appearances and filtering through the seemingly endless stream of scripts, but finds his passion in the woodworking his father taught him. He creates a beautiful dining table, complete with splendidly detailed bench seating, and immediately begins work on another piece.

You and Colm travel regularly to the castle to join Buffy, Gracie, and the crew in your pet project, restoring the crumbling old manse to its former majesty. With a property this old, there's always a new issue. You begin to realize it's a project that will never be complete, which in a way you love.

Before your first anniversary, you decide to open the grand hall and its adjacent rooms to the public. Colm's mother, a warm and generous host as well as an impressive history buff, happily leads tours of the cavernous rooms, while his father, a natural entertainer, makes an occasional kilted appearance. The reedy bellow of his bagpipes announces his entrance and startles his guests, giving him a chuckle as he marches through the hall. Buffy keeps the operation running smoothly, little Gracie running free, her voice ringing joyfully through the echoing halls. You laugh when you hear her speak with a little bit of a brogue, and Buffy rolls her eyes. "Can't be helped," she explains with a giggle. "She's around it all day. Soon I won't be able to understand her, either."

For your first anniversary, Colm surprises you with a completely refurbished bedchamber, walls draped in rich tapestries, floors warmed with elegant rugs, and the defunct fireplace restored with a cheerily roaring fire blazing in the grate. Best of all is the magnificent centerpiece of the room, a monstrous four-poster bed Colm has crafted by hand, complete with a silken canopy, rich velvet bedsheets, a heavy, silk coverlet, and an abundance of feather pillows covered in the most amazing silken shams. You leap onto the bed, pulling Colm down.

"It's gorgeous," you tell him mischievously, "but it is a little stiff." You kiss him like it's your first day together. "Let's break this in."

You quickly strip off Colm's sweater and run your hands over his muscled chest, then reach down between you and plunge your fingers into the soft hair below his waistband. He is ready, smooth and hard against your hand as you stroke him.

"These," you say, unzipping his jeans and hastily pushing them down around his ankles, "have got to go."

You free him from his boxers, and take him hungrily into your mouth, raking your fingernails gently down his stomach. Then you roughly push him onto his back, quickly pull off your jeans, and straddle him as you lean in for a kiss.

"Anna, what has gotten into you?" He laughs, then runs his hands under your sweater and skims it over your head while you press yourself to him, his cock stiff and hot against you. He sits up and reaches around to your bra, unfastening it. You're ready, now. You take him into you and dig your fingers into his chest as you rock, and as he reaches up to take your nipple into his mouth, you come together, your ecstasy echoing off of the stone walls of your bedchamber.

You lie together in the decadent bedding until your breathing slows, but then quickly smooth your hair and pull Colm up with you. "Come on," you say, planting a quick kiss on his lips, "I have a surprise for you, too." You pull on your jeans and warm wool sweaters then lead him out toward the castle's back lawn and cover his eyes before opening the massive wooden door. "Okay," you tell him, "you can open them now." Colm opens his eyes and with a joyous chuckle he takes in the brand-new garden you've helped Buffy design long-distance and had planted and pruned. The low shrubs lead to taller sculpted topiaries, forming a simple and traditional labyrinth, and at its center sits a babbling fountain with a low stone bench on each side. Carved discreetly in a ring at the base of the fountain is the scripted inscription COLM AND ANNA.

You walk the serpentine paths hand-in-hand and sit on the low stone bench side-by-side. The sun slants through the high clouds and warms you as you lean your head on Colm's firm shoulder. Colm tilts your head up and kisses you thoroughly. He ends the kiss with a beautiful smile. "Anna, thank you for this."

You feel that nothing could ever be as perfect as this moment and can hardly believe this incredible man is thanking you, when he's given you everything—unconditional love, a life you could have only dreamed of, even a castle for heaven's sake. You squeeze his hand and kiss him again then look him squarely in the eye.

"Colm," you tell him, "I have one more surprise." You place his hand on your still-flat belly, not yet showing even the slightest sign of the life growing inside, yet filled with the promise of everything yet to be. Colm begins to laugh again, an infectious, magical sound that fills the garden. You laugh along with him, tears of joy and promise springing to your eyes as Colm wraps you in his warm embrace, your tiny prince or princess locked safely between you.

And you all live happily ever after.

THE END

To take Anna on a new Bedventure, go back and choose a new path.

From page 2 . . .

The ride to the set seems interminable. Bodhi, your driver, tries to engage in small talk but gives up, and after a few minutes of silence you raise the tinted partition window. Now, staring at the dark pane of glass, you can see your life with Hampton playing before you.

Remembering your first meeting with Hampton is like trying to recall a dream. Brief images come to mind as you think back to that fateful day. There you were, an up-and-coming movie star, beginning to command higher and higher paychecks and even headlining projects. You were reluctant when Hampton's manager called your manager to request a meeting. Naturally, you thought it was about a script and you were thrilled and a little nervous at the prospect of meeting movie legend Hampton Rhodes. Not that he was really old, but he started his career at the tender (and very sexy) age of eighteen with a muscle-baring, scene-stealing bit part in the classic chick flick, *Treacherous Ventures*. Hampton proved the most consistently successful male box office draw for almost two decades and you, along with every other red-blooded female thirteen years or older, had a crush on the handsome leading man.

The timing couldn't have been worse. Your publicist warned it wasn't a good time for you to be seen having dinner with a man more than once, much less to begin dating in earnest, so you were more than hesitant when Hampton revealed he wasn't interested in talking about a project, but that he was interested in *you.* He had seen some of your work and he was "taken" by your talent. He was so persistent and charming, so full of charisma, you felt like you were being drawn into some kind of magnetic field you couldn't escape.

You're so lost in your thoughts you don't even notice that the car has sailed past security and come to a halt on the back lot. Bodhi raps on the partition, making you jump. Your ears ring with the sound of your pounding heart as you step onto the bustling movie set. You can feel the heels of your stilettos sink slightly into the dirt as you lean down to ask Bodhi to wait for you.

The first thing you see is the back of a canvas director's chair filled by the unmistakably coiffed Justin Blathers, Hampton's manager. You'd recognize the back of Justin's starched and sprayed head anywhere. The sight makes you instantly uncomfortable. You never feel at ease around Justin. Something about him is a little too perfect, his body too hairless, his fingernails a little too clean, too trimmed, too shiny.

The set appears to be business as usual. Some of the crew mill around with an air of impatience and self-importance while others sit slumped in their chairs, scrolling through their e-mails, all waiting for the next scene to be called, the light to suddenly change to the ideal brightness, or the actors' hair and makeup to be re-perfected for the next shot.

"You know this is how he works," Justin whines into his phone as you approach. "He'll be out when he's ready, then he'll do it in one take."

Typical, you think. *Hampton's still in his trailer keeping the whole crew waiting.* You quickly change direction and set off across the back lot toward Hampton's trailer, which glimmers like a bloated, beached whale in the distance.

Suddenly you hear Justin's too-cultured voice, with its edge of studied British accent, trilling ever closer behind you.

"Excuse me! Miss Chambliss—Anna? Anna!" He grabs you by the shoulder in an attempt to stop your progress. "Is there something I can help you with?"

You look at him coldly. "No, Justin, thank you. I'm just here to pay my fiancé a quick visit." You brush past him, but Justin continues to trail you like an annoying puppy, barking at your heels.

"Really, Anna, I think Hampton needs his privacy right now. He's preparing for his scene and as you can see, everyone is waiting for him."

Everyone, you notice, except Nigella. She's nowhere to be seen. But you can easily summon her snakelike features—the sharp, pointed nose, the vermilion lips, the sleek black hair that hangs almost to her waist, the perfect, sinewy body . . . you narrow your eyes and walk more quickly, steeling yourself.

Justin assails you again just before you reach the trailer door. He grabs at the sleeve of your jacket, knocking you off-balance. You pull back against him and step out of one of your shoes, its heel stuck in one of the step's metal slats. You can hear sounds coming from inside the trailer and you feel a gentle rocking as you balance yourself on your single-shoed foot.

Justin's voice rises higher in warning, though you can't make out his words. You hear a loud sigh from inside the trailer and then, unbelievably, a laugh, followed by what sounds like a groan. You wrap your fingers around the cold handle of the trailer door but before you can twist the handle you are startled by a sharp bang from behind you. You turn to see a woman walking down the steps of her own trailer, her dark hair set in perfect waves. She looks up once to glance in your direction and you swear you see a tiny smirk on her face— Nigella! But if Nigella's not in there with Hampton, who is?

You turn slowly back toward the trailer door, take a deep breath, and walk into a scene that will play horribly over and over in your mind thousands of times in the weeks to come.

Your eyes take a moment to adjust to the dim light. The first thing you see is the back of Hampton's head, the coarse, jet black hair you know the feel, even the scent of, so intimately. The rest is a blur of glistening limbs and rhythmically moving body parts, underscored by the sharp smell of sweat and sex. You feel suddenly dizzy and force yourself to focus. Your eyes lock onto a single bead of sweat that rolls slowly down Hampton's lower back and disappears between his thrusting buttocks. His hands dig deeply into the waist of someone he's holding urgently against him.

But who?

You begin to see black spots in front of your eyes, and as your knees give way, you scramble to keep your balance, a difficult task with one leg three inches higher than the other thanks to the shoe you left outside the door. The noise of your clumsy stagger into the wall behind you finally gives you away.

Hampton spins to face you and with a look of horror pushes roughly back from the person he's so obviously abandoned you for. You look right past Hampton into the sheepishly grinning face of the crew member you know only as "Patrick," one of the director's many assistants.

Bile from your empty stomach rises sickeningly to your throat as you stumble back out of the trailer, leaving the door swinging open. You run unevenly across the dusty back lot, pushing past the few crew members who have stopped to stare. Everyone else seems to have assembled around the edges of the set, huddled together and whispering to one another, waiting to watch the main event to unfold.

Did everyone know? And if everyone knew, why didn't you? You catch a glimpse of Nigella peering closely at you as she leans her head to whisper something to Justin, and once again you see a tiny smile on her painted red lips.

Some of the crew members have their smartphones trained on you and you know this ugly scene is moments from going viral. Feeling like a trapped animal, your only instinct is to run and never stop. You force yourself to think. You are an actress, after all, perfectly capable of hiding your emotions and presenting a happy face to the world, even if you are falling apart inside.

What you need to do is put on a brave face, climb back into the waiting car, and send a quick text to your publicist. He'll know how to spin the story so that this all ends up helping your career. Despite what might be posted online, no one aside from you, Hampton, Patrick, and Justin know the whole truth, and none of them will want the story to leak. But you are so angry, so incensed that Hampton Rhodes would use you, lie to you, and then cheat on you—with a man no less!—that you cannot think clearly.

One call to the press would out Hampton for the cheat he really is. There were always rumors, speculations surrounding almost every actor in the business. But you never believed they were true. Now you wonder. Was your whole relationship some kind of publicity campaign designed to advance Hampton's career, with no regard to yours?

You know you have a choice to make—one that will seriously impact Hampton's career, your career, and both of your public images. You can go on and act as though nothing serious happened, quietly break up with Hampton, and let the press spin it however they please as you decline to comment. But maybe the best idea is to deal with Hampton directly, and to deal with this now. You turn on your bare heel and head back toward the trailer. No matter what happens, you're not leaving without the other half of your sixteen-hundred-dollar Manolos.

To retrieve your shoe, return to your car, and let fate take its course, turn to page 4.
To confront Hampton, keep reading.

Outrage and indignation bubble inside you and before you know it, you're on your way back across the set.

Try as you might, the shoe is securely wedged into the trailer step's metal slat. You wiggle and pull, trying to minimize the damage to the silk-covered heel. Suddenly you are aware of a shadow over you and look up to see Hampton, wrapped in a shaggy brown robe you've never seen before, smirking down at you.

"Need a hand with that?" he has the gall to ask, and from behind you, you hear the low, silky voice of Hampton's costar.

"Let me," Nigella offers as she smiles and reaches for your shoe.

Trapped between the two of them, you feel both helpless and enraged. You shove Nigella's perfectly manicured hand away from your shoe but she grabs for it again.

Then, from the dim interior of the trailer, you see Patrick's impish face peek out over Hampton's shoulder. The shamed and at the same time triumphant look he gives you, empowers you with strength you didn't know you had, and you push Nigella sharply back, take the shoe firmly in your grip, and pull . . .

Looking back later, you'll never be able to remember the exact details of what happens next. In the moment, you are aware of Hampton flailing wildly, his hand over his right eye as he falls back into Patrick's arms. Nigella shoves you roughly aside as she runs up the trailer steps. Your last memory before everything fades to black is Hampton's howl spiraling higher and higher like a siren in the night.

The next image you recall clearly is a glaringly white, sterile room and the incessantly beeping equipment at your bedside. An uncomfortably cool liquid drips into your hand through a tubed catheter.

The moment your eyelids flutter open, your driver, Bodhi, looking rumpled and sleep-deprived, and your assistant, Buffy, her hair sticking wildly up at the back of her head, jump to their feet and gently approach your bedside. You're suddenly freezing and pull the thin bedsheet up to your chin. You note that the door to the room is closed and the privacy curtain almost completely drawn around you.

"Jeez, Anna," Buffy says. "You scared me to death."

Bohdi rounds the other side of the bed and takes your fingers in his warm, rough hand, so large and comforting. You suddenly feel small and safe with these two concerned friends at your side.

You smile and Bodhi gives your hand a little squeeze. "There's my Anna," he says in a low whisper.

Is it your imagination or do you see the glaze of tears in his eyes?

Buffy clears her throat. "It'll all be fine," she tells you, locking her eyes reassuringly with yours.

Something seems to be blocking the words you're trying to force from your throat. "What?" is all you can manage to ask. You feel tears trickle down your cheek.

Bodhi leans in and with a single, gentle gesture, wipes the tears away. "Anna, you're going to be fine."

Suddenly, vague images of what happened jump sharply into your conscious mind.

"What about Hampton?" You search both of their faces for an answer. "Is he okay?"

"Anna, you—" Buffy's answer is cut short by a brief rap at the door.

Suddenly your doctor is at the foot of your bed, clipboard in hand. "Good to see you're back with us," he says in a hearty, too-loud voice. "Your blood results are in. Your iron's a little low, but you are definitely not pregnant."

You grimace slightly. "I could have told you that."

The doctor glances down at his notes. "My prescription is for rest and hydration. I'm also going to give you an iron supplement and something to help you sleep. Only take it if you need it. I want to get the rest of those fluids into you and then you're free to go. You should be out of here by this afternoon. I trust one of you will take her home?"

"I will," both Buffy and Bodhi volunteer.

Four hours later—although it feels more like twelve—you are waiting to be officially discharged. For some reason they've brought you a wheelchair, even though you feel perfectly fine. "Hospital policy," the nurse explains. As you sit waiting, a shadow darkens the threshold. You look up to find Hampton standing in the doorway.

Clothed only in a hospital gown, he looks frailer than you've ever seen him. The bandage wrapped around his head and covering his right eye adds to the impression.

For one crazy moment you expect him to apologize—maybe for cheating on you, for lying to you, for so many things—but instead he grabs the handles of your wheelchair, pushes you roughly to the corner of the room and sits down firmly on the vinyl-clad bench beneath the window, inches from your face. He looks directly at you with his single uncovered eye. His words are curt and clearly rehearsed.

"Here is what is going to happen," he instructs. "I will release a statement to the press. You will neither agree nor disagree with any of it. Your only response is to be 'no comment.' You will never speak a word of what went on between us. Don't worry—I'll make it look like I called off the engagement. And this"—Hampton gestures dismissively toward his bandaged eye—"will not be mentioned. You will agree not to be seen publicly with another man for a period of six months. In exchange I will refrain from suing you for everything you might be worth and effectively ending your career." He pauses, letting his words sink in. "Agreed?"

You tear your eyes from his bandaged face and look down into your hands. You feel smaller and sadder than you ever have in your entire life. "Hampton," you begin, "I am so sorry about your eye . . ."

"Save it, Anna." The coldness in his words sends shivers through your body. He turns on his heels and exits into the stark, white light of the hospital hallway.

It's midnight, ten years later. You're buzzed from the giddy high of the applause still ringing in your ears during the opening-night standing ovation you've just received as the headliner of a new Broadway play, *Regrets*. Such a pithy title, you think: *Regrets*. Though really, you don't have any. Your career is better than ever and you have your choice of projects as well as leading men. With so much success and endless accolades, you are rarely alone, very rich, and very happy.

You slide into the back of a yellow cab and direct the driver to head to a trendy NYC bar above which, in a private room, the rest of the cast and your closest friends wait to celebrate your Broadway debut. You smile to yourself as you anticipate the night ahead, filled with flowing champagne and maybe a little fun with your current fling. You don't really care what the reviews say tomorrow. You've always been your own worst critic anyway.

Before the cab can pull away, your latest leading man and fellow cast member, the extremely good-looking and slightly younger Birkin Kramer, slides into the cab beside you and tosses the latest issue of *WE Weekly* in your direction. The glossy cover features a photo of Hampton with his picture-perfect family trailing through a crowded LA airport. There's Nigella in oversized sunglasses and skinny jeans, carrying her single biological child on her hip while three adopted kids cling to her thighs as the cameras flash around them.

You have to hand it to Hampton, he knows how to keep the PR machine well oiled, and you certainly don't feel an ounce of sympathy for Nigella. She knew exactly what she was getting into. As you study the photo, you notice only one of Hampton's eyes meets the camera directly. His signature smile reveals a row of flawless whitened teeth and provides a perfect distraction. You wonder whether anyone else notices the extra glint in his right eye. The prosthetic is really very good. If you didn't know the truth, you would probably never even notice it.

You should thank him one day. Without his help you might never have grown the thick skin that has allowed you to make tough, sometimes painful decisions and to proceed forward without second thoughts into a career filled with successes.

The car heads downtown and Birkin stretches his muscled dancer's arm behind you.

"Hmmm . . ." you purr as you settle into his embrace, tossing the magazine lightly into his lap. "What a beautiful family."

Birkin lifts the magazine to catch the light off the street outside and studies the cover, never looking in your direction as he asks, "What really happened between the two of you anyway?"

You smile to yourself as you gently ease the magazine from his grasp, run your fingers through his hair, and repeat the response you've given so many times before. "It's a long story."

And one you'll never tell.

THE END

To take Anna on a new Bedventure, go back and choose a new path.

From page 60...

It's been almost half a century since you walked out of Bodhi's life. After all of this time, the gossip magazines still follow you regularly, but not for your movies or romances anymore. As you lay in your hospital bed at Cedars-Sinai Medical Center you are surrounded by beeping machines and imprisoned by the tangle of wires and tubes that feed you, hydrate you, and medicate you. The days and nights drift by in a blur as you fade constantly in and out of consciousness.

You find your mind wandering with increasing frequency back to that last day with Bodhi in Kauai. If you had stayed, how different your life might have been. You can't help but wonder if every small decision you make in some way determines the outcome of your fate. Would a different choice that morning have kept this disease that has laid waste to your energy, your career, your health, and your beauty at bay?

You've made so many attempts in this last year to find Bodhi but finally lost the will to keep trying. If you had found him you would have explained. You'd had to make a difficult choice in that early morning moment, and you decided to choose yourself and your career. The years that followed were a whirlwind. Your brief absence from Hollywood actually managed to increase your fame and your press coverage. Your return catapulted you into more dramatic roles, increasing your longevity far past that of the usual starlet.

So much has happened, a heady but slightly fuzzy blur of premiers, press, awards, and work, always the work. Looking back now you don't really regret any of it ... but still you wonder ...

You slip into another dreamless, morphine-induced sleep, and later, much later, perhaps hours, perhaps days, you surface slowly to a feeling of warmth. You blink your eyes to clear the haze and find yourself gazing into a familiar set of topaz eyes. The browned skin around them is more lined than you remember, but the strength in the hands gripping yours is the same.

Your throat is so dry and you can't seem to find enough air, but you manage a whisper. "Bodhi. Where have you been?"

He leans in, his graying hair brushing gently against your cheek as he tenderly plants a lingering kiss on your forehead and climbs gingerly into the little bed beside you, gathering you in his solid embrace and gently pulling up the paper-thin sheet to cover you both. "Anna," he tells you, as everything fades to black, "I've been with you all along."

THE END
To take Anna on a new Bedventure, go back and choose a new path.

From page 55...

You dial the number and interrupt Trudy as she answers the call. "I need to talk to Jeff Jeffries." Yes, you tell Trudy, you are aware he is awaiting your arrival, and yes, it is extremely important that you speak with him now.

As you hold for Jeff to come on the line, you know you're overstepping just slightly. Jeff Jeffries's reputation as a brilliant director, responsible for some of the most successful rom-coms in recent history, belies the short, balding, glasses-wearing man behind the legend. He also has a reputation as a master manipulator, but you're not about to be manipulated. You hear your heart beating in your own ears as you prepare for battle.

Finally, you hear the click on the other line. You know you have to be the one to speak first. "Jeff," you begin. "I'm sitting here on the tarmac unsure about what to do. First I'm told some unknown actor is stepping in for the costar your studio promised me, then your secretary treats me like a recalcitrant child. I'm trying to keep an open mind, but I have to tell you I'm starting to feel like I need to cut my losses. I don't think you'll disagree that without my name on your film it's going nowhere. But I have to be honest: I don't know that I can work with this Jackson character. I've already had more than one unpleasant run-in with him here in LA. In fact, if you knew the details, I think you'd cut him loose in a heartbeat, and I can only imagine what it will be like on a closed set. So, before I tell my pilot to bring me to you, I need to know what you're planning to do to make this an endurable experience for me. I'm going to require a private meeting with you to discuss the situation when I arrive."

There's a long pause while you wait for Jeffries's response. At last, you hear a low sound coming from the other end of the line. Incredibly, it sounds like laughter, a nasal sniggering someone is trying to keep in check.

You can't believe what you are hearing. Is Jeffries actually laughing at you? "Hello?" you say into the phone.

"I'm sorry, I just didn't know I was making your life so miserable."

You cannot believe your ears as you register the unmistakable drawl on the other end of the line.

"What can I do besides laugh? Darlin', you are truly adorable when you are angry."

You are so enraged you can hardly control your voice. "Is that Jackson?" you ask incredulously, though you know the answer.

"Anna, I thought maybe I could save Jeffries some time by talking to you myself and pleading my case, but clearly your mind is made up about me. I would tell you I'd summon Jeffries to the phone, but I don't think he can help. It sounds like you need to talk to a professional."

"Excuse me," you reply as calmly as you can manage. "I do not need to talk to anyone but my manager. Enjoy your time filming a flop." You are about to hit end on your phone when you hear Jackson again.

"Whoa, whoa, whoa. Anna, wait!"

Your fingers itch to end the call, but you roll your eyes and hold the phone to your ear, saying nothing.

"Anna?" Jackson asks.

After a long silence you respond, "I'm here."

"Anna, look, please come to the set. Everyone is waiting on you and upset that you aren't here yet. There's some crappy intern getting ready to sit in for you and I don't think she actually knows how to read, so we really need you here right now. And it's not that Jeffries didn't want to talk to you. I just thought I could give the guy a hand and maybe make things up to you. I know I came on a little strong the other night, but I didn't mean to ruffle your feathers. I was hoping we could still be friends. I guess I overestimated."

Here he goes with the pathetic apology again, you think to yourself. Still, you can picture the table read, and you do wish you were there reading your own lines and fleshing out your character. You'd be wrapped in the Caribbean warmth, sipping a coffee, smiling as you picture the finished film. Then you think about the end of the day, returning to your trailer and knowing Jackson is prowling about somewhere on the set. . . . But still, you'll have Buffy there to run interference if there's a problem. There will be plenty of people around, and once the shoot wraps you'll never have to deal with Jackson again. You plan to stipulate a few conditions when you do talk with Jeffries, one being that your post-shoot press junkets will be solo.

"Jackson, I appreciate you trying, but I do have some issues I'm going to need to resolve. Those are between Jeff and my manager." You don't want to give him the satisfaction of imagining he has gotten even a millimeter under your skin. "It really has nothing to do with you."

"Alrighty then," replies Jackson. "Don't say I didn't try."

He's quiet and for a moment you think the conversation is over, on your terms at last, but it's not to be.

"Oh, and Anna," he tells you, "I should probably tell you, as a friend, that Jeffries talked with your manager right before you called. I happened to overhear most of the conversation, I think. Jeffries is well aware of your dissatisfaction with—the circumstances."

"And?" you ask him.

"And, the conversation was pretty brief. It sounded like your manager had a lot to say, but it was kind of funny. Jeffries didn't say much."

You're getting more and more uneasy and incredibly irritated as Jackson strings you along. Finally you take the bait. "So, what did he say, Jackson?"

"She's under contract." Then he hangs up.

You close your eyes, breathe, open them, and decisively hit the end button on your phone, then shut it down completely. You look up at the hovering flight attendant who is obviously pretending not to eavesdrop. "Alright," you tell him, "let's go."

He turns as if to move toward the cockpit but stops himself and arches one droll eyebrow. "You are quite certain this time?"

You don't bother to answer as you insert your headphones and lean back into the seat, hoping you'll at least be able to sleep.

Turn to page 72.

From page 90 . . .

The thought of betraying your best friend is too much to bear. You fight every urge in your body and pull forcibly away from Jackson. With your back to him, you begin to make your way to shore.

"Hey, just a minute," Jackson shouts. "Where are you going?"

You turn to look him in the eye, "Jackson, you know we can't do this."

"Can't what, cupcake? Nothing's happening here."

Suddenly he is at your side, and his hand is back on your arm, his face close to yours. You try to pull away, but his grip is firm. "Jackson, just stop."

"Well, darlin', I don't see how that's fair. You got me all worked up here. I told you I'm not one to give up so easy."

You feel a rising panic as Jackson pulls you back out into the water and you realize you have no control over what is going to happen next.

He turns you roughly and twists your arm behind your back, just hard enough to be uncomfortable. You resist the urge to cry out, calculating your next move. He presses himself against you from behind, and you feel his urgency beneath the slick skin of his wet swim trunks.

He's talking into your ear, his voice taking on an unmistakable gruffness. "This doesn't have to be a fight, Anna. This was going to happen one way or the other all along. I know you can feel it too. No reason to deny it. All fighting's gonna get us is tired."

His free arm has moved up to your bikini top and he's gripping your breast, hard. Again you resist the urge to make a sound. Something in you knows it would only make things worse. You stand perfectly still as Jackson works with his hand, still twisting your other arm. Your feet are free, though, and you try the only thing you can think of, bringing your right foot up to connect with his groin. He somehow anticipates your action and brings his knee up protectively, blocking your blow.

"Well, you little spitfire," he drawls into your neck, "if you like it rough, that's okay by me."

He wraps his leg around yours and now you are completely pinned in the water up to your neck. Sheer panic begins to rise as you realize you have no way of escape, and if things go really wrong there's only the water to catch you.

Jackson's hand moves quickly down, skimming your hipbone and then in one swift move unties the strings on your bikini bottom. He has the piece off in two seconds and is grinding hungrily against you. You feel him reach down again and realize he's pulled his swimsuit out of the way. You can feel him stiff against your bare backside. He twists your face roughly to his, bending your neck at an excruciating angle, and kisses you hard and long, plunging his tongue into your mouth. You know you can't fight, there's no way you'll be able to overpower him, and you're vaguely aware that your mind is going where your body cannot in an effort to protect your sanity. Funny, you've read about this kind of thing happening, you just never thought it would happen to you.

You feel like you're viewing the scene from afar, almost like watching a movie, when you notice a shape moving toward you from the shore. Buffy wades into the water, moving slowly but surely toward Jackson. She approaches like a dangerous animal, calculating every step.

At the same moment, Jackson notices her too. He eases his grip on your arm but keeps his leg wrapped around yours under the water and too deep for Buffy to see. He actually manages to smile at Buffy, a look of sheer hunger in his eyes.

"Come to join in?" He asks through gritted teeth. "Three's more fun."

Then everything seems to happen at once. Jackson lunges for Buffy, you fall from his grip, and Buffy leaps toward Jackson, a gleaming object hanging from her hand. It collides with Jackson's skull with an audible thump as Buffy swings her arm down in a powerful arc. The gold liquid slides down Jackson's face and into the water followed seconds later by a deep red liquid. For a moment, time stands still. Jackson is stunned, unmoving, watching the growing ring of crimson in the setting sun. His eyes clear for a second and he looks almost as if he's going to cry. "Buffy, I didn't . . ." he manages before falling headfirst into the blood-tinged water.

"Oh my God, oh my God," you can hear yourself repeating over and over again. Buffy, on the other hand, is silent, her eyes cast down at the huge, broken bottle dangling limply from her hand.

"Buffy!" you cry. "Help me!" as you tug desperately at Jackson's shoulder, trying to turn him over in the water. You manage to maneuver him face up and almost wish you hadn't. His eyes stare unseeing at the sky and you think you glimpse bone through the deep, bloody gash on Jackson's forehead. Bile rises to your throat but you fight it back. You don't know whether he is dead or alive, but you know you need to get him back to shore. Looping your arms under his, you begin a long, backwards slog toward the sand, pulling what feels like dead weight.

Buffy stands still, watching, zombie-like. The heavy glass bottle hangs from her hand, reflecting the sunset above and the bloodied water below.

By the time you manage to drag Jackson to shore, you are huffing and puffing like you've just run five miles. You fall to your knees in the grainy sand beside his lifeless form and begin to administer the rudimentary CPR you learned on a movie set. You breathe and compress, breathe and compress, concentrating on nothing but trying to bring him back. You know the chances are slim, but you keep trying, hoping against hope that Jackson will suddenly sputter back to life.

After what seems like an eternity, you feel the light touch of a hand on your shoulder, and look up to see Buffy standing beside you. Her voice is flat and toneless. "It's over," she says.

She pulls you from Jackson's side and straddles him, staring down into his dilated, unseeing eyes. Without warning, she bends in one motion and slaps him hard across his slack face. Then she begins to cry, huge, heaving sobs wracking her body as she grabs Jackson by his ankles and pulls him back into the water. You watch wordlessly as her tiny frame, all sodden hair and bedraggled clothing, hauls the large figure farther out to sea.

You know you can't let this go on any further. You wade into the sea beside her and place your hand gently on her forearm. She looks at you with tear-filled eyes and all she says is "Please?"

To insist that you and Buffy bring Jackson's body back with you, turn to page 167.
To grant Buffy her wish, keep reading.

The line between right and wrong seems suddenly blurred. You could return with Jackson's body, but you have no idea how the justice system works on this tiny island. You need to protect Buffy, to be there for her at last. It doesn't escape you that you may avoid a scandal yourself, too. Is it right that Buffy's life—and yours—should be ruined by a single action committed in a moment of self-defense? Is it wrong to protect your friend? What's done cannot be undone, one way or the other.

You step back onto the beach and gaze out into the fading hues of the sunset as you watch your friend, your confidant, your sister, carry Jackson's body into the water. It's as though you've left reality. Maybe, you think, you are in a dream. Maybe you'll wake up sunburned and relieved, and all of this will seem silly and far away. Maybe you won't remember this at all.

These thoughts float through your mind as you watch Buffy bend down to place a single kiss in the middle of Jackson's cheek. Then, she pushes his floating body, suspended in the salty sea, ever so slightly. He floats out slowly until the dark and the water swallow him up and he is no more.

Buffy makes it almost to shore but then falls to the ground a few steps short of the beach, splashing into the salty foam. You go to her and the two of you sit at the shoreline, holding each other and sobbing as darkness falls. You know you will never reveal what happened here, and that you and Buffy will be bound by this vow of silence for the rest of your lives.

It's funny how through time and repetition, a lie can become the truth in the mind of the teller. After a few months you believe it yourself when you tell the story of watching Jackson disappear into the deep water with his snorkeling gear. How after a few minutes you realized he hadn't surfaced, and how you and Buffy spent hours in the little runabout searching in widening rings until it became too dark to continue. How you returned to the main island begging for help. How nothing was ever found.

The mystery surrounding Jackson Michaels's disappearance only amps up your star power, and your name and photo become inexorably intertwined with the retelling of his story. The tabloids cast you as Jackson's grieving love interest. Michaels becomes a Hollywood legend in the ilk of the ill-fated, up-and-coming movie star. His family sells the rights to his tale, which becomes an hour-long *WE True Hollywood Special*.

The years pass and you find yourself on many other movie sets, and in many exotic locations with Buffy by your side. Your refusal to take any project set on a Caribbean island is understandable.

The trauma of that fateful day proves too much for Buffy. Her bleeding begins shortly after Jackson's death. She convinces herself that perhaps there never was a baby, after all. In any case, that glimmer of life was not to be.

You realize as time goes by you've made a solid trade: Buffy's freedom for your own. You date casually from time to time and become fondly known as Hollywood's eternal bachelorette, famous for flings with your costars and infamous for your unceremonious breakups as soon as the shoot wraps. You visit plenty of "new Hollywood" bungalows but you are always in control and never bring a man into your domain. You are painfully aware you'll never be able to really let anyone know you completely. There will only ever be one person who knows all of your secrets.

Eventually, Buffy moves into your beachfront home and silly rumors circulate. None of it hurts your PR, though, and you really don't care what people think. As long as you are working, you are happy, and so far the work is steady and consistent. One day the offers may begin to dwindle, but you don't think about that or anything else too deeply. For now, you've found an acceptable life.

In all your years together, you and Buffy never so much as refer to that day on the island. Sometimes you think perhaps she's blocked it from her conscious memory. But other times you catch her sitting out on the balcony at sunset, sipping a glass of wine and staring out into the sea, perhaps wondering what other secrets the vast ocean holds, and dreaming about what might have been.

THE END
To take Anna on a new Bedventure, go back and choose a new path.

From page 165 . . .

It takes every ounce of courage for you to make the decision that you do, but you know you have to do the right thing, for you and for Buffy.

"Buffy," you say, "I'm sorry. I can't."

Buffy drops the big bottle of Jim Beam into the water and watches as it slowly drifts off into the distance. Wordlessly, she pulls the little boat so that it floats by Jackson's feet and together you haul his life-less form into the bottom of the boat then wrench the anchor from the sand.

Buffy never meets your gaze as you gather up your things from the beach and toss them onto the runabout's wooden seat. She gives the motor's cord a hard, determined pull and the engine roars to life. Slowly, in the darkness, she guides you back to a course you would never have predicted your life would take.

The next few months seem interminable. Through endless, ex-hausting hours of interrogation, you tell your stories truthfully. You cannot understand why it's not a clear-cut case of self-defense. The prosecution wants a murder charge and now Jackson's family is making noises about a civil suit. Every morning you wake up to the fresh nightmare of this awful saga. You can't escape the scandal of it. Every tabloid magazine runs a similar headline: JACKSON MICHAELS MURDERED ON TANGO SHOOT. WAS ANNA INVOLVED? INSIDE THE COURT-ROOM!

Thanks to the efforts of celebrity attorney Rich Glockman, you and Buffy remain on house arrest. Your trial date looms in the dis-tance and Buffy's belly swells with each passing day.

The trial takes less than two weeks. It's televised on *Justice TV* and you watch the grueling recaps every night, glued to the television like an ordinary civilian, desperate to read between the lines of the com-mentator's summaries. During the long days in court, you furtively glance at the jury to try to figure out what they are thinking, but their expressions are uniformly emotionless and bored, their faces unread-able.

It's finally your turn to take the stand. The prosecution's questions are startlingly simple and swift. You feel both relieved and slightly disappointed that you aren't given a chance to tell your side of the story. Then you realize the strategy must be to isolate Buffy, to rob her of any sense that you assist or support her. If she acted alone, her punishment will be much more severe.

Buffy's testimony is heart wrenching. The attorney for the prose-cution, a balding man who stands less than five-foot-five, peppers poor Buffy with a relentless line of rapid-fire questions delivered in a smarmy, nasal voice. Buffy speaks in a quiet monotone, answering as succinctly as possible, as you're sure Rich has advised her to do.

"Ms. Templeton, what was your relationship with the deceased?"

"We were seeing each other."

"How did you meet?"

Buffy clears her throat and answers, "We met while I was at work."

For a brief moment, Buffy's eyes flicker to meet yours, instantly bringing you back to that moment in the makeup room, a moment that now seems like eons ago. Why didn't you try harder to talk her out of dating Jackson? Your gut told you all you needed to know about him. You have tremendous guilt coupled with fear for your friend. Oddly, you feel no sense of trepidation for your own well-being.

The hours of questioning progress along the same path with tedious repetition. The same questions are often posed in multiple ways. Only once does Buffy show any emotion, in response to the attorney's most personal question. "Ms. Templeton, please characterize your relationship with the deceased. Clearly it was intimate." He gestures toward her burgeoning belly. "How often did you and Mr. Michaels engage in activities of a sexual nature?"

"That is none of your business!" she spits through clenched teeth. Rich stands at the same moment to object. Before the judge can make a decision about whether to let the line of questioning continue, the prosecution surprisingly withdraws the question and announces it will rest. You breathe a sigh of relief, but realize it's the defense's turn to question Buffy, who has now clearly been pushed too far.

Rich allows Buffy to sit silently for a moment. She stares at her hands, which rest gently on her belly, and only looks up when he asks, "Buffy, can you tells us exactly what happened the day of Mr. Michaels's death?"

Buffy locks eyes with her attorney, looks straight at the jury, lets out a long breath and begins to tell the story. "We all decided to go for a boat ride . . ."

She speaks stoically at first, her words calm and evenly paced, but as she continues, you can see her begin to break. Her enormous eyes first grow glassy then fill with tears and spill over. You cry silently with her, and as she speaks you dab your eyes with your well-worn tissue.

Buffy ends her testimony, telling the jury how heartbroken she is that her unborn baby will never get to know her real father. For the first time the jury shows some emotion; some are sniffling, some swiping at their eyes. You can't help but wonder whether their tears are the result of sympathy for Buffy, now left alone, for the fatherless child, or for the man who will never get to know his baby. You alone know that Buffy's tears are completely genuine.

At last, the attorneys give their closing statements. You adjourn to the Spartan hotel room and wait.

The jury takes less than a day to deliberate. You shake like a leaf as you approach the courthouse. Buffy, too, is a nervous wreck as you wait for the jury to announce their findings. She paces wildly back and forth in the hall outside the courtroom doors and drums her fingers incessantly on her huge belly.

The doors open and a hush falls over the darkly paneled courtroom. You make your way to the defense table and sit breathlessly to await your fate. Rich squeezes Buffy's hand as she faces the judge.

The moments that follow are a blur. The next thing you know Buffy is in hysterics as she's handcuffed roughly and led from the courtroom. You reach for her, but suddenly Rich is at your side, his hand firmly on your shoulder, forcing you to sit helplessly as you watch Buffy being ushered away.

The case becomes a scandal, the unfinished movie is never completed, and you fall into a deep depression, spending more and more hours alone in your bed. Buffy is sentenced to twenty years in prison for second-degree murder. Rich vows to appeal, but the process can take years, and the fight seems to have gone out of Buffy.

You cannot bear to leave the house except to visit the prison. When you're not with Buffy, you sleep for hours, unable to find the strength to do anything else.

One night, you get a call. The baby has arrived, a little girl. Buffy is inconsolable. "I only got to hold her for a second! They didn't even really let me see her!" she wails. "They took her away from me! They took her away!"

You contact Social Services and begin the adoption process. You never even consider anything else.

You keep a quiet life these days. Little Jackie takes up most of your time. The paparazzi slow their stalking and some days you can even go to the park unmolested. You visit Buffy once a month, and Jackie's smiles and laughter brighten your and Buffy's lives.

With good behavior, Buffy will be released before Jackie's out of high school. You'll keep her safe until then. For now, you write your memoir and bide your time.

Your agent calls one afternoon while Jackie is at school. "Remember me?" she jokes. Apparently Jeffries has called to say that the studio wants to try to finish the long-shelved *Tropical Tango*, to be re-shot with the newest up-and-comer, in the same location, and in 3D. The never-completed film has taken on a cultish air of mystery. Jeffries wants you to headline. "Think of the buzz," says your agent. "It'll put you right back in the spotlight. America loves a comeback, and Hollywood has a blessedly short memory."

You laugh for a moment before you answer. It's a temptation, but only for a split second.

"Hollywood may have a short memory, but I don't."

You hang up the phone and grab your purse and keys. It's time to pick Jackie up from school.

THE END
**To take Anna on a new Bedventure, go back and choose
a new path.**